Between Land And Sea

A Little Mermaid Retelling

Paul Mouchet

Paul Mouchet Publishing

CONTENTS

To my wife, who believes in me, even when I struggle to believe in myself. Without her support and infinite patience, I would have never realized my dream of becoming an author.

And, to my big sister Louise, thank you for helping me bring my stories to life.

CHAPTER 1

DRAVEN

The sight of Calypso, with her flowing red hair and luminescent green tail, swimming into my dreary, stark office, made my heart skip a beat. A school of lantern fish swarmed the mermaid, eliciting a giggle from her as their light reflected off the delicate scales covering her body. She seemed to glimmer as she circled me, and a simple smile from her was enough to make my pulse race. This young beauty was a gift from the gods, and I cherished her deeply. I never would have imagined such an amazing creature could love me back. Not in a million lifetimes. Yet, here she was, the only person I ever dreamt of, coming to spend time with me. I was the luckiest merman to have swum these pristine seas.

Despite having been together for over four cycles, the thought of asking her to marry me sent a chill up my spine. Fear of her rejection churned my stomach. I was thankful for the seawater that surrounded me, carrying off the slimy film of nervous sweat that was leaking from every pore. What if she didn't think I was worthy of her and refused to give me her hand in marriage?

"Hello, my love," Calypso said as she playfully pushed me away from my parchment-covered desk. She sat on its polished stone top, sending my work scattering across the floor. "Why is my big, handsome merman working so hard, so early in the day?" She slid from the desk and onto my lap, twisting strands of my long, black hair around her finger. "Why don't you and your burly muscles come with me for a swim? Pele has barely risen and we can watch him ascend into the morning sky together."

I wanted to scold her for messing up the presentation I had worked on all night for the royal council. I was beyond exhausted and the notion of gathering up the parchments and properly reordering them weighed heavily on me. It seemed as though she either didn't understand or didn't care about my responsibilities to the merkingdom.

As crown prince, I needed to be dependable and show my father that I was worthy of ruling the Gaelinora Sea while he was away doing whatever he did when he wasn't home. It had been over three cycles since he last visited our kingdom. In that time, I had come of age, but my mother, the queen, refused to bestow upon me the royal scepter, the symbol of rulership, until she was satisfied that I was mature enough to wield its powerful magic.

The entire world, all my fears, all my concerns, melted away when the love of my life wrapped her arms around my neck and kissed me. Her passion flowed into me, stealing my breath, making my chest swell like a rising tide. I knew, in that moment, that we were meant to be together.

Truth was, I loathed politics. But as the crown prince of the merkingdom, it was my responsibility to solve the problems that plagued our underwater realm. But the never-ending parade of petty grievances and inconsequential disputes left me feeling drained. The petitioners would come to me with their complaints, making it sound as if the fate of our kingdom hung in the balance, when in reality, it was all much ado about nothing. What did it matter if someone's pet urchin nibbled on a neighbor's prized kelp bed, or if someone planted fast-growing coral too close to their properly line? I longed for adventure and intrigue. I wanted to do something that made me feel good about myself and my actions.

There was one aspect of politics that I found intriguing — the shadowy world of espionage and secrets. Despite the adamant warnings of my mother's royal advisor, Beithir, I had continued to investigate rumors that had been circulating about the leader of a human town that bordered our eastern shores. Lord Vayne, as he was called, had been spreading vicious lies about merfolk, accusing us of luring ships to their doom with our enchanting songs, only to feast upon the sailors who fell into our waters.

If it wasn't for the danger the lord's words could cause, the absurdity of his claims would have been laughable. The thing was, we wanted nothing more than to coexist peacefully with the humans, and we had saved countless sailors from the treacherous waters surrounding our kingdom. I yearned to speak with the people of his town, to show them that we were no threat to them. But first, I would have to find a way to uncover the truth about Lord Vayne's nefarious intentions.

If I could repair the merkingdom's relationship with the land dwellers, I would not only impress my parents but also prove to them I was capable of running this domain.

"Where's your mind at?" Calypso asked, tucking away a stray strand of my hair. "Are you fretting about those dull humans again? Do you still hope to convince them that we aren't the terrible monsters they believe us to be?"

She had successfully guessed the source of my preoccupation, but, unlike Calypso, I didn't think humans were dull and I knew that they couldn't be ignored. They had many good qualities, things that we merfolk could learn from, but they could also be dangerous and deadly. A million different thoughts raced through my head, threatening to drag me away from this moment.

Was I truly so obsessed with my mission that I couldn't see what was right in front of me?

I had the most beautiful mermaid in the entire kingdom vying for my attention, and yet I remained fixated on the contents of the scattered parchments strewn across the floor of my office. I had known about the human problem for many moons, and it could certainly wait a few days. It wasn't going anywhere, but Lord Vayne's hate-filled words consumed my every waking moment.

"Well," she said, running her fingers through my overly long locks. I hated my hair being like this, but Calypso made it clear that she loved the way it flowed over my shoulders. My mother, on the other hand, loathed its length. For reasons she refused to share, the queen never approved of my relationship with her. Beithir seemed to dislike the mermaid just as much, but I suspected it was because of her association with Arion. The feud between the royal advisor and the high mage had been raging on forever, but I had never learned the reason behind it.

"Are you even listening to me?" Calypso yanked my hair hard enough to drag me out of my ruminations. I flashed her a sheepish grin, hoping to mollify her with a bit of charm. The darkening of her green eyes suggested that now was not the time to be cute.

"I'm sorry. I swear on my father's name, you have my full and undivided attention." Based on the scowl on her face, it was best I kept it that way if I didn't want her to yank my hair out in thick hanks.

"I asked you if you're going to tell me what you've been keeping secret for the past moon?" Calypso's anger had already drained away, replaced with her infectious look of curiosity. "Rumors around the palace suggest that you'll shock the entire kingdom when you reveal it."

My sheepish grin broadened uncontrollably. I did have something planned, and I was hoping it would be a surprise for Calypso as well. Tonight, I would ask her to marry me. As much as this public announcement wracked me with fear, I was mostly nervous about my mother's reaction. A sour taste filled my mouth at the thought of how she might behave at the ceremony.

"It won't be much longer," I said, cupping Calypso's exquisitely soft cheeks in my hands. I brushed my thumb across her skin while I lost myself in her radiance. "I do you hope you'll be excited when I share it with you. I'd hate for it to go badly in front of my mother, Beithir, and the rest of the court."

Calypso nuzzled her cheek against my hand, her expression bright with playful curiosity. "Is it the sort of thing that might have future ramifications?" she asked, her gaze fixed firmly on me. Barnacles and bubbles. I loved the way her eyes sparkled. I waggled my eyebrows and shrugged. A smile twisted her mouth as she moved her face closer to mine. "Might it be of particular interest to a girl who will soon be coming of age?"

Screaming starfish. Did she already know? Was she trying to force me to ask her right here, right now? I tried not to let my excitement show, but as she puckered her perfectly kissable lips and widened her eyes, I knew she was reading me like an open book.

"I think we should change the subject," I said, wiggling my way out of her embrace. "You'll find out soon enough, and I don't want to discuss it right now."

"How's Arion going to react to this announcement?" she asked, clutching onto my arm, refusing to let the subject go. "Is this something he will approve of?"

Gaia, save me. I hadn't even considered the high mage's reaction. Arion and Calypso were very close, and they often shared secret time together. I suspected he was giving her private lessons in the magical arts, despite being forbidden from doing so. According to rumors, Arion had tried to curse his previous apprentice. As punishment, King Triton had turned him into a giant red crab and forbade him from ever taking on another private pupil. The king had permitted the disgraced merman to continue on as headmaster of the Academy of Arcana, but his teachings were limited to lore and basic mer-magic. But then again, my love played by her own rules, and she was extremely difficult to refuse once she set her mind to something.

I swear, it was as though she had cast a spell on me, the way she could make my stomach flip when she swam into a room or took my breath away with a single touch. Despite our never having been *intimate*, the mere thought of her made my blood boil with desire.

Gaia save us all if she learned to use actual magic. This mermaid would be utterly devastating.

I was doomed.

"Come," I said, taking her hand, trying to coax her out the door. She followed willingly, wrapping her arm around mine, letting me lead her away.

We swam quietly together through the palace halls before exiting into the open sea. Pele's rays shone down from the heavens, lighting our world in wondrous shades of blues and greens. Small fishes swam in large groups, their bright scales reflecting the morning light.

"Where are you taking me?" Calypso asked. Pele's brilliance paled at the warmth of her loving smile. "You wouldn't be taking me to Lover's Grotto, would you?"

My fin turned pink at Calypso's question. The grotto was a place young mermaids visited when they were looking for some amorous activities. As much as I would have enjoyed her company there, today was the day I had planned on proposing. It just seemed inappropriate to me.

"No," I said, desperately hoping my face wasn't reddening too badly. "I had thought we could visit the coral gardens."

"Really?" Calypso squealed with delight. "You're taking me to where we had our first date?"

I nodded brightly, thrilled that she remembered. "I thought it would be nice for us to spend some quality time together. We've both been so busy lately."

Calypso squeezed my arm again. "Just me, and you, and the warm western currents to keep us company. Have I told you lately how much I love you?" The mermaid's eyebrows shot up as she pursed her lips.

"You have, but I will never tire of hearing it." I wrapped my arms around her, my nose pressed up against hers. "And I will love you back with all my heart, from this moment, until my last moment before becoming one with the sea."

"I will never let you become sea foam," Calypso said, placing her hand over my heart. "Our connection transcends life and death. I will be with you for all eternity. I will be your anchor on this plane. When the time comes, we will travel to the Beyond hand-in-hand, together forever."

CHAPTER 2

CALYPSO

After a wonderful morning exploring the magnificent coral beds of the sea's western shallows with Draven, he left me to deal with some *important matters of state*. His awkwardness suggested it was all a ruse and that he needed time to prepare for tonight's ceremony.

I swam into the private chambers that were set up for me at the palace. It didn't matter how long I'd lived here; the beauty of my room always took my breath away. It was richly decorated with precious pearls and gleaming shells of every color. Sunlight filtered through the water, casting ethereal patterns on the smooth walls and polished floors. The ceiling was high, adorned with intricate patterns of coral and gemstones, woven together in a mesmerizing dance of colors and shapes.

In one corner of the room, a bed of shimmering seaweed awaited its occupant, its softness beckoning to be lain upon. Nearby, a small table held a delicate shell containing a sweet-smelling perfume, and a tray of fresh oysters harvested from the ocean floor that very morning. The vanity that filled the far wall was a work of art in itself, adorned with fine jewels and trinkets from all corners of the sea.

I spun around in slow circles, wondering what I had done to deserve such a wonderful life. There was a gentle knock on my door and, with a contented sigh, I threw it wide open.

"Get in here," I said, dragging Luna into my room. The little mermaid was my best friend and Prince Draven's younger sister. She was only a few moons younger than me, but she was more carefree and wild-spirited than anyone I had ever met. The princess was forever getting into trouble, and she loved dragging me into the mix.

But since Arion had taken me on as his secret apprentice, I didn't get to be with her as much as I'd have liked. A problem she never let me forget.

"I don't have time for you today," Luna said in a snooty tone, rolling her eyes and crossing her arms over her chest. Her sea-foam green hair swirled about her head in dramatic fashion, a trick she learned from her mother. While all mermaids had some inherent magical abilities, most of the merkingdom's population was *mundane*. About the only magic they ever used was singing to the fishes to make them easier to catch. I had no issue singing for my dinner, but we merfolk were so much more than that. Despite the dire consequences of being caught, Arion promised to help me unlock my potential. Considering my lack of experience casting spells, he said he had never before seen anyone who radiated such intense power.

Draven certainly didn't notice. He was too busy trying to be a good prince and make his mother and father proud of him.

"I'm sorry," I said. I really was. I missed the adventures we went on together, like raiding the sirens' shrimp gardens. "You know how it is."

"No," Luna replied, much too quickly. Fire flashed in her eyes. "I don't know how it is because you're keeping secrets from me." I wanted to object, but the princess knew me too well. "And if you can't trust me enough to say what's been occupying your time day and night, besides my brother…"

I hated the accusatory tone in her voice. It cut through me like fire coral. And she was right, which made it all the worse. We had never kept secrets from each other before. We shared everything.

"I'm getting private magic lessons from Arion. He's taken me on as his apprentice." The words spilled out before I could stop them. I instantly clamped my hands over my mouth, my eyes wide.

Luna's eyes also went wide, and like a mirror, she, too, clamped her hands over her mouth. Her look of shock and surprise quickly morphed into giddy joy. "I knew it!" She swam in front of me, pressing her face uncomfortably close to my own, her relief readily apparent. "I knew you weren't cheating on Draven. Mother said you were. She said you were sneaking about with another merman."

My head snapped back at the notion. "Why would anyone think I'm cheating on him? I love your brother. With all my heart. Even if he's been preoccupied with trying to prove himself to the queen so that she'll give him your father's stupid scepter. Why would he want to rule the Gaelinora? It's going to be an endless supply of tedium."

Luna rolled her eyes. Hard. "I tried to tell her, but her royal advisor is constantly whispering in her ear. Sometimes I think the two of them are enjoying a little extracurricular *politicking* of their own."

"Luna!" I screeched out, my head snapping to the door of my room. "You can't say things like that. Even if you are the princess, to speak of the queen in such a way… you just can't!"

Once again, she rolled her eyes and waved me off as though the notion was commonplace. "It's not like the king is ever around anymore. The great and powerful Triton is likely off with one of his wives in some other ocean or sea or deep-water lake. You think Draven spends too much time playing ruler? It's all my father ever does. It's been forever since he's come home."

"Still," I said, shaking my head adamantly. "You can't say those sorts of things, not to anyone, including me. You shouldn't even think it."

"It's nice to see you worrying about nothing again." Luna smiled and swam around me in a tight circle, her shimmering blue tail fin brushing over my head. "It's been forever since you scolded me for being me. I've missed that."

"After tonight," I said, a mischievous grin pulling at the corners of my mouth, "maybe I'll be able to go adventuring with you more often, like we used to."

"Pfft." Luna waved me off. "After my brother proposes, you'll be so tied up in red kelp that you likely won't have time for me or Arion."

My heart leapt into my throat. I would have gasped at Luna's words, but I was too busy worrying that I was about to blow up like a puffer fish. I had hoped that's what tonight's surprise would be, but up until this moment, it had felt like the wishful thinking of a love-struck teen. It didn't seem to matter how hard I pressed Draven, he refused to confirm his wish to marry me. My belly fluttered as though a thousand tiny fish were trying to find their way out of me.

"He's going to propose tonight? At the party? Tonight? Are you sure?"

My friend's head bobbed rapidly, sending her hair into a tizzy. "Surely you had to know that. Draven's been planning it for weeks now. It's going to make mother's head pop. She has been telling my dear brother that it's a bad idea and he needs to wait."

My lower lip thrust forward and my brow furrowed. "Why is proposing to me a bad idea? What did I ever do to her? Draven and I have been together for over four cycles."

"Forget my mother," Luna said. "After my brother proposes, and you accept, it will be a done deal and she'll have to learn to live with it."

"Are you sure it's tonight?" Whatever hurt I had been feeling disappeared, chased off by the dozens of eels that were writhing in my stomach. The party was about to start. The image of me being up on the royal dais with so many eyes fixated on me set my heart racing. I shot Luna a pleading glance. If I was going to be thrust into the public eye for a wedding proposal, I needed to look better than this.

Giving me a broad smile, Luna's eyebrows perked up. "Oh, it's tonight. I'm sure of it. Merfolk and other dignitaries have been arriving at the palace for the past three days. For something that was supposed to be a secret, it seems the entire sea has been invited to attend. We need to get busy and fix your hair and makeup." She eyed me up and down, from seashells to tail fin, and blew out a long stream of bubbles. "The rest of you is ridiculously perfect. Is it okay to tell you how envious I am of your beauty? Because I am. A lot."

"Please," I said. My face was burning so badly I feared my fins were turning pink. "I only look this good because I'm swimming close to you." I flashed a sly grin.

Luna started off by nodding her agreement. When she caught onto my barb, her face contorted with outrage. A moment later, she was laughing so hard I feared she was going to burst a scale. Of all the things I loved about my friend, her willingness to laugh was very high on the list.

CHAPTER 3

DRAVEN

As I entered the Seashell Hall, hundreds of voices echoed through the cavernous space. The walls of the throne room were lined with shimmering pearls and intricate coral carvings, and the water was thick with the salty scent of the sea.

I swam slowly up the center aisle as trumpets blared and drums beat out a complex rhythm. I acknowledged the guests as I passed by, dignitaries and common folk alike. The assembled masses were all dressed in their finest attire, their tails shimmering in the light of the glowing orbs that hung from the inlaid gold ceiling. The merfolk were arranged in neat rows, each one vying to get a glimpse of the proceedings that were to take place at the front of the public hall.

The throne itself was a marvel to behold, made of solid gold and encrusted with precious jewels. It stood at the far end of the room, flanked by a pair of imposing mermen guards. My mother, Queen Morwynneth, sat upon it, the king's royal scepter in hand. Her wavy sea-foam green hair flowed down over her shoulders, almost to her lap. Robes of the finest silks draped over her slender, regal form while a thin circlet rested gently atop her graceful head.

As I made my way through the crowds, I watched as Beithir swam over to the queen, appearing from behind a wall of kelp curtains that separated the hall's public area from the palace's private rooms beyond. He held his serpent-head staff close to his lithe body, its ruby eyes seeming to stare at me as he moved.

My mother scowled at me, shaking her head, as I took my place at her right hand. Her advisor refused to even bother acknowledging my presence. I blew out a deep breath in an attempt to calm myself, a futile gesture considering who was making her way up the main aisle.

I struggled to keep my jaw from dropping as the mermaid drew near. The grand hall was packed to the point of bursting, and every pair of eyes were firmly locked on my bride-to-be. With how much my mother objected to what I was doing, her desire to invite so many to the ceremony was utterly baffling. Throughout our meeting with the royal jeweler to craft a suitable engagement ring, she never stopped nattering at me. She was like a cleaner fish, picking at every aspect of Calypso, pointing out in minute detail why she was an unsuitable partner. She went on to say, to insist really, that, as prince of the realm, and the soon-to-be ruler, I needed to focus on my duties to the merkingdom and 'if that red-headed trollop can't learn to accept that you have responsibilities beyond keeping her happy, then she can stuff herself into a giant clam shell.'

Mothers!

"Hi," Calypso said as she slipped her arm around mine. "You look lost in thought. Is everything alright?"

I swallowed hard, desperately trying to quell my annoyance with my mother. "Yes, of course. I was mesmerized by your beauty and I became swept away by the currents of my love for you." My overly colorful words made Calypso blush and giggle, but the way her eyebrows shot up, I knew she was just being polite. She wasn't taking the bait. Not even a nibble.

"Big crowd tonight," she said, her gaze sweeping over the sea of faces staring up at us. "I can't wait to find out why everyone's here." Her eyes were much too wide. As she turned back to face me, her hazel-greens threatened to drag me under, forever lost in their swirling whirlpools of beauty. My stomach twisted. What if she refused my proposal and humiliated me in front of the entire kingdom?

"I can guarantee you'll be more than surprised," the queen said far too sharply. "Of that, I have no doubt."

Calypso shot me an exasperated look and patted my arm, completely ignoring my mother's barbed tongue. "It's okay, my love. I'm sure everything will go swimmingly."

This was yet another reason why I loved this mermaid so much. She would never leave me squirming on the end of a hook. I was so caught up in my ruminations, I barely even noticed my sister swimming up the aisle with Arion, her hand resting lightly on the headmaster's large red pincer.

I stole a glance at my mother, who looked like she had just eaten a bad shrimp, while Beithir's lips curled into a wide grin, his eyes gleaming with a sense of fulfillment that could not be contained. There were days I wanted to slap the air of superiority right off that arrogant merman's disgusting face. I couldn't wait to rule this realm. My first order of business would be to fire the advisor's scaly fins and permanently banish him from the kingdom.

"Swim straight," my mother said to Luna as she took her place at her left hand. "You're slouching." There was an odd timber to the queen's voice, like she was on edge. I gave my sister a questioning look and received one back in kind. Obviously, I hadn't imagined it.

"What's with all the soldiers?" Luna whispered, motioning with her chin behind me. I glanced over my shoulder, shocked to see two dozen royal guards dressed in full arms and armor. They weren't wearing the traditional ceremonial uniforms, which were purely ornamental and offered no practical military advantage.

When I turned back to reply to my sister, the twist in my gut suddenly worsened. There was at least an additional regiment of guards swimming up the main aisle, and a dozen more taking up positions on each side of the throne room.

"Mother?" I shot her a look of confusion, unable to fathom why she had brought her entire guard to this public event. When she refused to acknowledge my question, an overwhelming dread washed over me. I had no clue what was happening, but fully armored guards had no place at a royal proposal ceremony.

"Let us begin," my mother intoned, her crystal-clear voice echoing off the shell-encrusted walls of the great hall. She swam to the front of the dais, her chin held high as she waited for the people to settle down. "First, I'd like to welcome our esteemed visitors from the southern reaches of our kingdom. Your presence here is noteworthy and appreciated. I also wish to acknowledge the entire royal court, including my trusted advisor, Beithir, who will be standing in for my perpetually absent husband, King Triton."

The way she referred to my father got my blood up. He was the god of the seas, with duties and responsibilities beyond our fathoming, and here she was, disparaging him with her backhanded insults during this public ceremony. Bile rose in my throat as Beithir swam up beside my mother, resting his hand on her bare shoulder, his scales brushing up against hers.

"My dear people," the advisor said, his voice much louder and more commanding than I'd ever heard. If I didn't know any better,

I'd swear he was magically enhancing it to sound more important than he actually was. Beithir had once petitioned the queen to be in charge of the Academy of Arcana, but my father refused to give him the post. Instead, King Triton placed that honor upon Arion, starting a lifelong feud between the two mermen. Shortly after my father had left the kingdom, my mother appointed Beithir to be her royal confidant. While the position lacked the prestige of being the magical headmaster, it firmly placed him in a position of power over Arion, which he relentlessly used to make the headmaster's life as unbearable as possible.

"Loyal citizens," Beithir continued, surveying the crowd with a sneer, his gaze flicking disdainfully over each and every attendee. "I am honored to be standing before you this day, at Queen Morwynneth's side, while we pass Triton's holy scepter on to her son, Prince Draven, naming him as Guardian of the Realm."

The queen turned to me, a wry smile on her face. She held out my father's scepter to me and inclined her head slightly. It was an overly ornate head and a jewel-encrusted handle. Despite my father's flair for dramatics, this ostentatious symbol of power definitely leaned towards being garish.

I gasped at the news as excitement coursed through me. Never could I have imagined today would go this way. Not only was this going to be my proposal ceremony, but my mother was also naming me ruler of the merkingdom. My jubilation suddenly soured as I realized that I wasn't ready to accept this honor. I had no speech prepared and would have preferred my father being here to celebrate this moment with me.

"Mother?" I shot her a questioning look, but she didn't meet my eyes. Instead, she turned to the crowd while her entourage of guards moved up behind her. My heart sank. This was not going as I had expected. Something was afoot. Why had she invited her guard onto the dais? What was going on? I tried to read her expression, but her face was inscrutable.

I slowly swam forward, unsure of what I was supposed to do. Calypso stayed close, squeezing my arm tightly.

"Congratulations," she said. I glanced down at her. She appeared as surprised as I was at the news. There was also a hint of disappointment etched into her eyes. Clearly, this was not the ceremony she was hoping for, but she was trying hard to not let her disappointment show. "You're going to be the best ruler this kingdom has ever seen."

She said all the right words, but I didn't hear the complete truth in them. I doubted she was lying to me, but she wasn't being one hundred percent honest, either. While my eyes were locked onto Calypso's, my mother had moved to intercept us before we reached the front of the dais. She glared at me with an intensity that could have scared eels. Slowly, she peeled away her contemptuous stare before focusing her withering disdain on my love.

"Get away from my son, witch." The words were like venom. Calypso instantly recoiled. She released my arm and put some distance between us. "Seize Headmaster Arion and his apprentice as well," my mother bellowed, pointing a crooked finger at her. The guards who had been at the front of the dais immediately converged on Calypso, grabbing her roughly by the arms. With spears drawn and at the ready, the guards at the back of the dais moved forward, pressing their silvered tips against Arion's shell, threatening to skewer him if he made any sudden moves.

Without ceremony, the queen thrust King Triton's scepter into my hand. It felt heavy, like a burden I wasn't prepared to bear. My mother's words echoed in my head, taunting me. "You're the new

Guardian of the Realm. Now, do your job." The magic in the royal relic swept through me, driving me to heed her commands.

Why had my mother called her a witch? Why was she ordering her guards to take the mermaid I loved and the academy's headmaster into custody? I wanted to say something. Anything. This was wrong, so very, very wrong. My mind reeled at the implications.

Calypso looked back at me, confusion etched on her face. I was desperate to reassure her, to tell her that everything was going to be okay, but I couldn't find the words. It was as though my tongue had been turned to coral and my head stuffed full of seaweed. My brain was completely muddled, leaving me unable to do anything but gape. I tried to act. I swear on my father's life, I did. Instead, I did nothing while my world unraveled around me.

Beithir's voice cut through the fog clouding my thoughts. "I apologize for the abruptness of the ceremony, but this is for the safety of the prince and the entire kingdom. Dire accusations have been brought to the queen's attention. On my advice, she has taken Lady Calypso and Headmaster Arion into custody while we conduct a thorough investigation. This will be done here, in the open, for all of you to witness."

"Mother?" I cried out, my head swiveling about. "What are you doing?"

But she didn't answer. She just stood there with pursed lips, her gaze fixed on the distant horizon, as if she could see something I could not.

"I call upon the first witness," Beithir called out. "Swim before your queen and tell your tale. No harm will befall you, so long as you speak the truth."

CHAPTER 4

CALYPSO

As I burst through the surface of the sea's dark, turbulent waters, I looked up to the heavens in awe. Medeina, the moon goddess, shone in all her resplendent glory, her radiance dwarfing the stars that twinkled in the inky blackness of the night sky. The sea rippled below with the reflection of her ethereal light, a million shimmering ripples that danced across the waves. It was nothing short of pure enchantment, as if the universe's very fabric had been woven together and placed on display for my personal enjoyment. I drew in a breath of the night's sweet, crisp air, its salty tang biting at my nose before lowering my gaze to the glistening azure expanse.

The wondrous sight of the endless sea filled my heart with awe. Shadows of sea creatures darted just beneath the mesmerizing surface; their movements infused with the magic of Medeina's luminous embrace. Their melodic calls rose in a chorus, a plea to the goddess to carry them away to her celestial home. A tremor ran through me, having been blessed to witness the full majesty of Medeina and the magnificent world she watched over.

I loved the ocean with all my heart, but there was something about taking in the fresh night air that ignited my spirit and fueled my soul.

Giving a slow, easy stroke with my tail fin, I provided just enough power to keep my head and shoulders out of the water, allowing me to scan the nearby coastline. A light breeze skipped across low rolling waves, tickling my wet exposed skin, raising goosebumps, sending shivers down my spine.

After waiting several minutes, I cast my face back to the heavens and closed my eyes in thoughtful prayer. "Great Medeina, goddess of hopes and dreams, smile down on my human this night. Bring forth the great fishes from the deep so that he might sustain his family before you flee from Pele's burning light, not to be seen again until the sun god sleeps." My words were barely more than a whisper, instantly carried away by the night's gentle breeze.

Impatience and trepidation took hold as I waited for my human to appear. He only came this way when Medeina's face fully filled the night sky, a beacon to the great fish of the deep. With a wistful sigh, I returned to watching the coastline, listening to the gentle sound of the waves lapping against the distant shore. The quiet splendor filled me with tranquility and serenity in a way that only the human world could.

My heart skipped a beat as I caught sight of him drawing near, walking with a strange gait that no other human seemed to have. I never paid it much mind, content to simply watch him from afar. He was so handsome, with his long brown hair and chiseled jaw. He had big, beautiful eyes that always looked so sad, as though he carried the weight of the world on his shoulders.

I often imagined what his life was like when he wasn't spending his nights by the sea's edge. Did he live in a fancy house with a wife and a loving family? The first night I saw him, I had heard his pleas to the sea god, speaking only of his mother and how he wanted to help her.

I wouldn't be surprised to learn he had taken a mate. Who wouldn't want to be wed to such a handsome and devoted young man? I dipped my face into the salty water, letting the tangy sea fill my mouth. I blew out a long string of bubbles, praying to Triton that he had taken no wife. Then again, maybe that was why he was sad. Maybe he had no one to love and no one to love him back.

As he started to prepare his fishing line, I dove beneath the waves and sang my song, beckoning to the mooneyes to come to the surface, to seek out this human's hook and bait, to help sustain him until the next time Medeina fully showed her face in about twenty-eight days.

"What do you think you're doing, young woman?"

My heart leapt into my throat, my blood pounding in my ears so hard I thought I might black out.

"Arion," I said, running my fingers through my long red hair. I gave him my absolute best smile, batting my long lashes at him. "What brings you up from the depths this night?"

"You do, Calypso," he said, clacking his huge pincers. I hated when my mentor, a giant red crab, clicked those cursed claws at me, treating me like I was nothing more than a guppy. "Your continued forbidden sorties bring me here, dragging me from our oh-so-uncomfortable home in the badlands to which we've been banished. I should be nestled in my cave, happily reading a book, but I'm not. Instead, I'm up here, floundering around near the surface, chasing my headstrong pupil who should be home practicing the newest spells I've been teaching her.

"What do you think Prince Draven would do if he found you here? Or worse, found *us* here? Do you think he would banish us to live even further away from the merkingdom? Maybe he'd just have us executed for breaking the most basic and most serious of laws."

"Who cares if I'm sticking my head out of the water to watch him?"

"Watch him? Him? You're following that human again, aren't you?" Arion shook his head at me, tutting all the while. "Why, Calypso? Why would you risk so much for this *man*?"

"I can't explain it, at least, not in words." I turned my gaze to the heavens, hoping for inspiration, something that might allow me to explain my infatuation with this human. "For several months now, I have been coming to the surface, seeking advice from the moon goddess. I know it's against the rules, but it's the only way for me to feel truly close to her." I took a quick look at Arion, hoping to gauge his reaction to my story. Although he looked somewhat perturbed, likely because I admitted to visiting the surface often, he appeared to be listening intently, so I continued.

"On one night, much like this, I happened to spy a young human. He struggled so hard just to make his way to shore. I found his spirit intriguing. All night, he sat over there on that very beach, casting out his line, hoping to catch the fish that Medeina called up from the depths. He had caught several small fish, but I could tell by his gloomy expression that they weren't the prize he was hoping for. So, I dipped below the waves and sang to the mooneyes, asking them to offer themselves to this poor, dejected, human fisherman."

"You forced Triton's favorite fish to bite the human's hook?" Arion's eyes widened, his long eyestalks waving about in disbelief.

"No, of course not. I *asked* them to offer their lives to the human. To my surprise, several of the smaller fishes obliged." I clutched at my breast as I recalled the joy on the man's face when he pulled that first fish from the water. As soon as he landed the mooneye, he thanked Triton for blessing him with such a rare and valuable fish. Afterwards, he took his catch and immediately returned home.

The expression on Arion's face darkened.

"And I've been coming every full moon since to help the young man. He's always so grateful and when he hobbles away, he seems so full of joy and hope. Isn't that what the moon goddess is all about, fulfilling our hopes and dreams?"

Arion groaned. "Oh, Calypso, my dearest child. I don't know what to do with you."

My teacher's words sparked a fire in my chest. I don't know why, but my emotions boiled uncontrollably.

"Nothing. That's what you do with me. Nothing at all. He's so handsome." Those last words just snuck out. I hadn't intended to say I found him attractive. Quickly, I continued speaking, hoping my mentor hadn't picked up on my tiny slip of the tongue. "I just want to watch him and help him provide for his family. That's all. Nothing more."

"Why? Why would you do that? Are you hoping he might see you? Fall in love with you? And the two of you can live happily ever after? Are those *your* hopes and dreams?"

I didn't realize I was running my fingers through my hair, instinctively combing it, trying to get my curls just right. It was only when Arion's eyes bugged out at me that I realized what I was doing.

"Bubbles and barnacles, girl. Are you so young and so naïve that you cannot see the dangers? This is real life with real-life consequences. You're not living in some fantasy fairy tale where everything works out in the end and the bliss-filled couple gets to enjoy their happily ever after."

"Why not?" I asked, swimming up to Arion, sticking my nose directly into his face. "Why can't it be a fairy tale? Don't I deserve a happily ever after? Well, don't I?"

"Of course you do," Arion said. "I know it's my fault that your relationship with Prince Draven was spoiled. You two should be married and having merbabies, or doing whatever it is that makes you happy."

The look of remorse on my teacher's face twisted my gut. It wasn't his fault that we were driven from the merkingdom at the point of a spear. The queen's advisor, Beithir, and his incessant whispers into her ear, is what landed us in the badlands, forever banished from our home. The slimy snake of a merman was jealous of Arion's appointment as headmaster of the Academy of Arcana, and he made it his life's mission to destroy my mentor. Draven's mother, the queen, never approved of my relationship with the crown prince, and she was all too happy to use the advisor's plans to ensnare me in the same net.

What really got under my scales, though, was that my love, Prince Draven, never lifted a fin to help me. He just sat on his royal throne, holding his precious scepter, while I was removed from the palace and banished to live in the darkest, most desolate reaches of the sea.

"It's not your fault," I said, shaking my head, clenching my fists. Just the thought of that fateful day drove me into a frenzy. "We stood no chance against the queen and her slithering, scaly-mouthed advisor. But the real travesty was the prince. He was supposed to be proposing to me, professing his love for me, for the entire court to witness, but he just sat there and did nothing to protect us. He seemed more than happy to cast his judgment on us and send us into this oblivion."

"There will be other mermen," Arion said. "Or, time will pass, and the prince will see the error of his ways."

All of my anger, all of my hurt, came bubbling up and something inside me snapped. I needed someone to love who would love me back, and I was going to tell Arion exactly that. "I don't want the prince. He can never make up for what he did to me, to us. I want the human!"

The words had barely escaped my lips when I realized what I had just said. I spoke of wanting a relationship with a human, and not just to myself this time. I had told Arion. My teacher. My mentor. The most powerful wizard to have ever drawn breath.

The crab's red shell darkened as his eyes narrowed. He moved in closer to me, his eyes blazing with unbridled fury.

"You can't have the human!" Arion's voice roared with the power of a tidal wave. "There is no life for a mermaid outside the sea. There is only pain, toil, and torment. You will burn under Pele's relentless heat. You will freeze when the North Sea winds blow across the lands. I've seen the damage these desires can have, and I will not allow you to swim that path. You will remove such nonsense from your mind and you will never speak of it again."

"But I... I love him! You can't stop me!"

The water around Arion shimmered as he gathered the sea's magical forces around himself. Swirls of purples and greens lit the water, bathing the crab in an unnatural light. The entire sea stilled, as though holding its breath. Panic rippled through my body as I shuddered in fearful anticipation. Never before had I seen him so angry with me.

"What are you doing? Arion, stop this." I tried to swim away, but an unseen force gripped me, holding me fast, paralyzing me.

"If I can't convince you to stay away from him or any other human, I will make it so none will ever want to see you, let alone be with you!"

Arion held his enormous pincers out to his sides. His eyes seemed to roll backward until only their whites were visible. Eerie whispers spilled from the wizard's lips. Though not of our native mermaid tongue, I comprehended every utterance, every intonation, as though Arion's thoughts were being imprinted in my mind. My entire body clenched in terror while my heart pounded against my ribs. I tried to swim away, to put some distance between us, but my tail refused to obey. The words of Arion's incantation echoed in my mind.

From depths of briny ocean's sleep,
Where secrets in the darkness keep.
I call forth beasts of strange design,
To bring about a monstrous sign.
A mermaid's beauty I will take,
And in its place a squid's embrace,
Where once were fins, now tentacles spread,
A fearsome form, the mermaid's dead.
Banished to depths and waters dark,
With monstrous shape and fearsome mark,
Her beauty lost, her fate now sealed,
A cursed existence, forever revealed.
May this spell be cast and sure,
That her form shall now endure,
The monstrous shape that I bestow,
And her true beauty will never show.

My teacher and mentor had turned his magic on me, his once gentle touch now cold and cruel. The incantation cut through me like a blade, shredding my mermaid form and remaking me into a grotesque monster. Excruciating pain ripped through me, wracking my body, contorting it into unimaginable positions. My arms felt like they were being torn apart, and my once beautiful tail fin split and twisted into slimy, loathsome tentacles.

"Why?" I cried out, my now bulbous eyes stinging with tears as my tentacles flailed about. "Why would you do such a thing to me?"

"It was the only way," Arion said, his voice and expression heavy with sorrow. "I did it to save you."

"Save me?" I echoed, confused and angry.

Arion's eyes met mine, and I could see the pain and regret etched on his face. What he did hurt him as much as it did me. I was certain of it, and I was glad for it. I hoped his actions had utterly crushed his spirit.

I released a large cloud of ink, and with a single pulse of my grotesque, gelatinous body, I surged toward my home, my hovel in the badlands.

CHAPTER 5

CALYPSO

My heart hammered in my chest as I tried to make sense of the chaos unfolding around me. Tonight was meant to be a celebration of Draven proposing to me. Why were they arresting me? Why were they calling witnesses?

"What is this about?" I shouted, my voice loud enough to echo off the throne room walls. I turned to Draven, my eyes wide, my brow furrowed. What was going on here? Why wasn't he saying something, doing something, anything? Instead, he just hung motionless in the water, his eyes blank and unseeing.

"Draven!" I called out again, desperately reaching for him. "What is happening?"

"You're being tried for your use of blood magic," the queen spat back at me, her mouth twisted into a hate-filled scowl. "You and your filthy teacher. I'll see you turned to sea foam before Pele sets in the west."

My mind raced as it tried to comprehend. Blood magic? I had no idea what that even was. I tried to get Arion's attention, but he was busy dealing with the spear-wielding maniacs who kept prodding at him, herding him towards a cage. A cage? Where did that even come from?

I turned back to Draven, looking for his support, but guards were escorting my love back to the throne, to where the newly crowned guardian of the realm would sit in judgment. His mother had taken her place at his side, her expression equal parts satisfaction and contempt.

Panic rose in my throat as I realized I was completely alone in this terrifying ordeal.

Suddenly, a voice spoke up from the crowd. It was sharp and accusatory. "I saw her and that ugly crab calling upon the spirits of the dead." A mermaid swam up to the royal dais, thrusting her finger at me. "They sacrificed the life of an innocent and used its blood in a ritual of some sort. Everything around them turned black and from within the darkness, they laughed and laughed."

I thought I recognized the woman as one of the queen's handmaidens. No, that wasn't it. She worked for the advisor. I was certain of it. A surge of anger and disbelief welled up within me, along with my magic. My chest heaved as I tried to control it. Arion's first lesson to me was to never cast a spell in anger. I didn't know why, but he made me swear to it. My hands shook as I tried to quell the desire to unleash my wrath.

Beithir leaned forward, his eyes crazed. "What else did you see?" the advisor asked, his mouth pulled back into a feral, thin-lipped grin. "Tell us everything."

The mermaid swam up to Beithir and crumpled at his feet, her big blue eyes staring up at the advisor, her hands held up in supplication. As the advisor glared down, it was at that moment I truly recognized her. She was one of the palace coral weavers. I remembered seeing Beithir berating her for having placed the wrong color coral outside his chambers. He had threatened to have her banished for her incompetence.

"I saw nothing else," the mermaid said, her entire body trembling. "I was so terrified that I swam away as fast as my tail fin would take me."

The advisor cast his gaze to where Arion was being held in his cage. "Thank you," Beithir said, running his thin black tongue over his blood-red lips. "Next witness!"

The queen eased herself from her place beside the throne and swam gracefully over to her advisor, her expression dripping with impatience. "How many witnesses will you bring before this court?"

Beithir bowed deeply to the royal mermaid, his eyes lowered in submission. "If it pleases you, Your Majesty, I have four mermaids who will give testimony. Each more damning than the last."

I didn't understand. Four witnesses? That snake had four people lying for him? To what end? Why would he be doing this? How did he even know that Arion was teaching me magic?

Again, I turned to Draven, my eyes pleading with him to intervene. He stared down at his feet, the king's scepter nestled in his lap. He refused to look up at me. Why wasn't he doing something, anything, to put a stop to this charade?

"Draven!" I bellowed out, desperation gripping my chest so tightly I feared it would crush my heart. "Speak up! Defend me!"

The man's head swung my way, his eyes vacant and unseeing. He seemed to be looking right through me, like I was someone he didn't know. Slowly, he shook his head and cast his eyes downward.

"You spineless jelly!" I screamed so hard my throat burned. "This was your idea, wasn't it? To what end? I thought you were going to propose to me! Is this what you had planned all along?"

"Silence!" Beithir boomed with an unnatural volume. He pointed his serpent-headed staff, its ruby eyes pulsing with magic, sending a stream of conjured red tentacles towards me. I struggled against the strange, disembodied appendages as they clutched onto me, clawing at my skin, covering my mouth, preventing me from crying out.

My gaze shot back to Draven. There he sat on his throne, the newly named Guardian of the Realm, and he couldn't even be bothered to protect the mermaid he loved. Hatred burned in my heart. Had I only been a pretty thing for him to swim around with, while he presented me to the court and pretended to love me?

Behind the throne swam Luna, surrounded by a team of merman guards. Her eyes were wide and wild, like she was struggling against an unseen force. She seemed to be watching me, studying me, scrutinizing my reaction to the horrible things that were being said against me.

I watched in horrified dismay as she closed her eyes, squeezing them tight. Had my best friend also abandoned me, in this, the worst moment of my entire life? Despite her appearing torn over what was happening; like her loathsome brother, she stood mute, unable to even look at me.

Luna's face contorted in pain before her eyes snapped open, her gaze filled with raw fury. "These are all lies," she yelled out with hurricane force. "Calypso would never do this! Neither would Arion! You're all liars!" With a powerful thrust of her tail, the princess burst through the mermen guards who encircled her. Like a mermaid possessed, she raced toward Beithir, her hands held out before her with deadly intent.

A brilliant flash stung my eyes, forcing me to look away.

"You will be still, sister," Draven called out. "For your own safety, you will be escorted back to your quarters."

I opened my eyes, unable to believe or comprehend what I was seeing. Draven was standing before his throne, his scepter pointed at his sister. Had he just attacked her with a spell? What magic did that accursed relic contain that would allow a non-spell caster to immobilize a person in such a way?

The soldiers who had been guarding Luna swarmed around the mermaid and hustled her off the dais. My gaze fell back onto Draven and his smug look of satisfaction. He caught my stare for a moment before turning away.

"Come, my prince," the queen called out in a sickly sweet voice. "Come, stand before your people and cast judgment on the accused. This witch and her teacher must be punished, and it will be you who will sentence them to death."

Death? Unbridled fear gripped me. Blood pounded in my ears, my heart thrumming so hard I feared it would burst from my chest. No one was ever sentenced to death, even for the most heinous of crimes.

Draven's long black hair flowed out behind him as he swam forward, taking his place between the queen and the royal advisor.

"What say you on the charges brought before you this day, oh Guardian of the Realm?" The advisor's slick voice made me want to vomit. "Have I delivered unrefuted proof of their guilt?"

"Unrefuted?" I yelled, yanking the tentacle away from my mouth. A searing hot pain ripped through my throat. I tried to continue, but the magic gripping my neck suddenly constricted, preventing me from speaking further. My eyes flashed toward Beithir and his staff. That same twisted smile pulled at the corners of his lipless mouth.

"It is time for your verdict, my son," the queen said, bowing before Draven. "Wield the power I have given you. Do it now before the sea witch casts a spell on us."

"Death is the only sentence for using blood magic," the advisor said, his eyes shifting towards where Arion was being held captive.

I held my breath, waiting for my cowardly prince to speak. Surely, he wouldn't have us executed. Not based on the word of a single lying witness.

"Make your decision," the advisor said, his beady eyes blazing. "Declare their deaths and I will carry out your command."

"Do it," the queen said, her wide and wild eyes locked on Beithir.

"They are clearly guilty," Draven said. The words came from his mouth, but they didn't sound like his own. Who was this merman standing before me? Had his lust for power corrupted him so badly that he was no longer recognizable? My head slowly swiveled to Beithir as he leveled his staff toward me. I was about to become one with the sea. If this was how I would meet my end, I wanted to watch the merman I loved speak the words.

Draven's face twisted, the muscles along his jaw rippling. He shook his head, the cords of his neck standing out against his finely scaled skin.

"You will be banished to the badlands!" The merman squinted as he spoke, like it had been some monumental effort to say the words. "I will not sentence them to death."

The prince's face seemed to relax slightly, in complete contrast to his mother's and the advisor's, who both looked ready to kill me themselves.

"No, my son. The penalty for their crimes is death. Nothing else will do."

"Am I not the ruler of this realm, mother? I have spoken and my word is law."

Beithir looked ready to attack the prince. His face contorted, becoming almost snake-like as his fury gripped him. "They should be executed," he hissed. "They don't deserve to live."

Draven cringed, as though listening to the merman's words caused him physical pain.

"Enough," Queen Morwynneth growled. "The prince has spoken, and his word is law. Take the prisoners away."

"I will see that they are never heard or seen again," the advisor said, flashing an evil glare at me. "I will send them to oblivion if I must. If they ever show themselves in the merkingdom, I *will* execute them myself for violating the prince's orders."

My eyes snapped towards Draven, who was swimming away, never bothering to look back. As he left, a group of guards grabbed me roughly by the arms.

"Gag her," Beithir said. "Don't give her a chance to curse you."

CHAPTER 6

CALYPSO

It had been nearly a full cycle since Arion and I were banished from the merkingdom. Once the royal guards had led us to the badlands, an open expanse of nothingness near the sea's eastern shore, they simply released us and swam away. My teacher and I found a large outcropping of stone that formed a natural cave. It was dark, and dreary, and cold. Like the rest of the badlands, it had no life, no color, and nothing to make it feel like home.

Plankton and algae clung to my cave's barnacle encrusted walls. They were the closest thing to life we had seen since entering these dull, gray-green waters. The minute sea creatures with which I lived filled our tiny living space with a musky odor that stung my nose and clung to my tongue.

As the moons came and went, Arion and I did what we could to make the best of our bad situation. In that time, he took the opportunity to continue teaching me alchemy and spell casting. I learned, but at a horribly slow pace. I simply didn't care enough to pay attention. The only saving grace was when Luna, at great risk to herself, visited me and my teacher. She had made herself scarce around the palace since her brother was crowned as Guardian. Under the constant scrutiny of the prince, the queen, and the royal advisor, life for the princess was no picnic, either.

Queen Morwynneth had assigned my best friend a chaperone, a miniature kraken named Octavius, who Luna affectionately referred to as her octopup. The little guy followed her everywhere, watching her like an eagle ray. The queen had expected him to report back on all the princess' misdeeds, a job he took seriously, but he rarely got the opportunity because Luna would give him the slip whenever she was doing anything that her mother would truly disapprove of.

Despite Luna's insistence that she and Octavius were becoming friends, she couldn't trust that her octopup wouldn't report on her secret visits to my dingy little cave. She was always careful to leave him behind before bringing us small pieces of home, including scraps of furniture, some alchemy equipment, and our books. Arion was always particularly excited when new books arrived since it gave him an easier way to ignore my constant ranting about how Draven's actions had sliced open my heart, creating a wound that would never heal.

Thinking it might take my mind off her brother, my best friend shared the location of our home with a mermaid in desperate need of help. She was quite young, a little less than one hundred cycles. She had a bad case of scale damage, a result of her recent tangling with a deep-water squid. My visitor extended her tail for my examination, while Arion hovered nearby, watching me like a teacher would.

I ran my hand over her blue-green scales, shocked by the array of ghastly lesions and pockmarks that covered her delicate body. She displayed all the telltale signs of mutilation caused by squid suckers, their small, jagged barbs tearing through the mermaid's scales with razor-sharp precision. It was a gruesome sight, but it also piqued my curiosity as a healer.

"You're a pearl diver?" I asked. It was the only explanation for why she would have been visiting the same waters where these squid lived. She nodded and gave me a sad smile.

"I am one of three tasked by the queen to retrieve the golden oysters, the only known source of Aurelian Pearls."

My stomach churned at her words. Of course, the queen would willingly risk people's lives so they could gather pretty bobbles for her.

"How will you help her?" Arion asked, interrupting my dark thoughts. He was testing me. I recognized his scholarly tone instantly. He only ever used it while we were in the middle of a lesson. "Is this something that requires the casting of a spell, or the use of a carefully crafted potion?"

Oh, sweet Gaia. I wasn't sure.

My mind raced as I tried to come up with possible cures. The barbs of the deep-water squid were venomous, and time was of the essence. If I didn't act quickly, the damage could be irreversible.

"Nasty creatures, those deep-water squids," Arion said, examining the wounds himself. "They are too hideous for words, with those long tentacles and bulbous eyes." The giant red crab shuddered and scuttled back, giving me plenty of room to work.

My teacher had taught me about thick potions that would cling to scales, even in the strongest of currents. I quickly swam over to my shelves where I kept all my ingredients and reagents. I scooped out a handful of seashells, some starfish powder, and a jar of nectar made from Siren's Blossoms; a rare and wondrous flower found only near the isle where our winged cousins lived. Arion called squids nasty creatures, but they were cute, harmless guppies compared to sirens.

I glanced over to my teacher for his approval, but he didn't say a word. Nor did he give me any clue whether I was on the right or wrong path.

I blew out a long stream of bubbles and got to work, crushing up the seashells into a thick paste that would form the base of my salve. When it was just the right consistency, I added the starfish powder, along with the nectar. Dark purple tendrils coiled up from my potion, tickling my nose, telling me I had mixed it just right.

The salve would likely heal the wounds, but if she was going to leave here cured, I needed to put some magic behind the remedy. As I gently applied the paste to affected areas, I quietly sang out a rejuvenation spell which would hopefully weave with the potion.

A light glow covered the mermaid's tail as my song and potion worked in perfect harmony. The young mermaid gasped as the combined magics took effect, drawing out the venom, mending the damage to her scales and the delicate skin beneath. Even in the dim light of my cave, her tail's radiance returned, reflecting the light of the tiny lantern fish who shared my dreary home.

"Good," Arion said as he peered over my shoulder. "Very good. Adding the nectar was a nice touch. Something I don't think I would have thought of on my own."

This was huge praise coming from my teacher. My face heated at his words. I hoped he hadn't seen, but the mermaid I just cured certainly did.

"I don't know how to thank you," she said. "What do I owe you for such amazing service?"

"Owe me?" I hadn't expected payment. She came in need of help, and I was more than happy to give it to her.

"I have to give you something." She touched a small pearl that hung at the end of a delicate gold chain. Before she could remove it, I placed my hand on hers and shook my head.

"If you wish to give me something, perhaps on your next trip into the depths, if it's not too much trouble, can you get me some ghost urchins?" These pure white creatures only lived where Pele's light couldn't reach. They were both rare and beautiful, and they could be used in a large number of antidotes, including a potent remedy for sea-serpent venom. Now there was a creature of nightmares. Those foul beasts had been trying to rid the Gaelinora of our kind for as long as I could remember.

My wounded visitor nodded brightly saying she would get me as many ghost urchins as she could carry. She thanked me again and again before swimming away.

The news of my having healed this mermaid spread far and wide, and before I knew it, I had a steady stream of merfolk who were seeking help. Whether it was because they thought themselves too heavy or too slight, they had afflictions that healed too slowly, or if they just needed reassurances that they were doing okay and that life would get better, they showed up at my cave's entrance, seeking my magical remedies and thoughtful advice.

I never refused those who sought me out, and I continued to only ask for small payments in return. Some brought useful items, like rare plants and sea creatures, but more often than not they brought me treasures from sunken ships. Some were quite beautiful, a tribute to human craftsmanship, but often they were useless bits of silver whazz-its and thingamabobs. After amassing several boxes, each containing twenty or more trinkets, I had to turn down the offerings, explaining how I had plenty. Even still, I never refused to help.

My life had become busier than I could have ever imagined, but it was fulfilling, and I went to bed each night exhausted and happy. Despite my newfound calling, my heart ached, like there was a piece of me missing. An affliction that could not be cured by either potion or magical spells.

That very same pain cut me deeply, when, one day, a pretty young mermaid came to see me, asking me to curse a merman who had wronged her. She described in painful detail how he had made promises of marriage, only to abandon her at the last possible moment. Her story struck too close to home, stinging worse than jellyfish tentacles.

Despite my desire to give her what she wanted, I had to politely decline her request, explaining to her that magic should never be used in such a manner. I would never cast a hurtful spell in anger or revenge. This was a lesson that Arion pounded into my head on a near-daily basis.

"I'm sorry, but I can't do what you ask. I will not bring harm to another merfolk, no matter the reason."

"I told Prince Draven you would refuse," she said, clutching at her heart. "He sent me here to test you, to see if you would use your magic to harm another. I swear, Sea Witch. I swear on my immortal soul. I told him you would never do such a thing."

The water darkened around me as my fury took hold. How dare he? How dare he send this poor girl here to test me! Was he so spineless as to fear confronting me directly? I was about to unleash my wrath on the unfortunate soul standing before me, but she was already gone, swimming away as fast as her fins could propel her.

In that moment, I was ready to call upon the full power of the sea and send it straight up Draven's tail fin, not stopping until he was nothing more than tiny bits of flotsam and jetsam.

"Breathe, Calypso," Arion said, placing his pincer on my shoulder. "Calm yourself. Spells cast in anger carry dire consequences. Don't let your hatred take you down a path from which there is no turning back. Prove to me you can control your magic even in your darkest moments."

My chest was heaving, my face burning. With clenched fists, I turned toward my teacher. His eyes were so sad, filled with a remorse I could never understand. Like a tidal wave crashing upon the shore, my fury spiked and then quickly abated. I swallowed hard, desperate to keep my emotions from spilling uncontrollably out of me. When my breathing finally calmed, my friend and mentor smiled up at me.

"Very good, Calypso. I knew I had placed my faith in the right mermaid." With supreme gentleness, he took my hands in his pincers and gazed deeply into my eyes.

"For showing me your ability to remain calm in the face of a tempest, I have a special gift for you."

A special gift? Arion had given me his time, his friendship, and most importantly, his trust. There was nothing more special than that.

"I need nothing more from you, my teacher, than that which you give freely to me each and every day."

Arion's eyestalks waved back and forth like seaweed in a slow current. His eyes became glassy and I swear, his shell became an even darker shade of red.

"I appreciate the sentiment," he said, his feet scuttling about in our cave's silty bottom, stirring up a cloud of debris as he did. "But I wish to share with you something truly special. It is a powerful counter spell, capable of breaking any magic."

"But," my words stuck in my throat. I had once read passages from my teacher's private collection, books he kept secret and hidden. I had happened upon them while I was snooping in his library. These sorts of spells were dark magic, nearing the level of evil for which we had been banished. Were the accusations made against us true? Had my teacher been dabbling in the dark arts? "Such spells are forbidden."

"They were only forbidden because Triton caught Beithir using them to break into the royal treasury. Had the queen not come to the slimeball's defense, I expect our king would have turned him to sea foam on the spot."

"But..." once again, my words lodged in my throat, and I was unable to speak my thoughts aloud.

"We are dealing with a merman who has no scruples and will stop at nothing to destroy us. I will teach you this spell for your own protection. But you must promise me, you will never use this magic out of hatred or anger."

I nodded, still unable to speak.

"To learn how to do this, we will need crimson slugs. Once you have mastered its intricacies, you will be able to cast this spell without aid of magical devices or reagents. It will awaken your power within, a strength I know you possess."

I continued to nod, my chest swelling with pride. Arion encouraged me to always do my best, but never had he spoken to me in such a way.

"The only place you can find these little creatures is on the eastern shores, beyond the boundary of the badlands. It will take you precariously close to the human worlds. It also means you are breaking the law, leaving these accursed waters. Should you be caught..."

He didn't need to say anything more. I understood the risk I was taking. The thought of going on such an adventure set my heart to racing. My mind immediately went to Luna. She'd have loved to come with me. This was exactly the sort of thing she lived for.

CHAPTER 7

CALYPSO

While I swam through the badlands towards the eastern shores, the only known place to find crimson slugs, I continued to nurse my anger and ever-growing hatred for Draven.

As I approached the outer edge of the wasteland I now called home, I came upon a large reef teeming with fishes of every imaginable shape and size. It was as though all life refused to cross the imaginary line that demarcated my territory, a place that had come to be known as *the realm of the sea witch*.

I sat on the reef watching in detached indifference as pairs of fish swam around together. A small clown fish and his mate swam past, searching for a new home among a bed of sea anemones. They seemed to be arguing about which of the stinging flower-like creatures would make the best place to raise their children. Despite their bickering, I could tell they loved each other deeply, willing to do anything to make their partner happy.

A surge of anger ripped through me. Draven and I should have been that couple but he chose to abandon me when I needed him most.

"Why didn't he defend me?" I screeched as loud as I could. The poor cuttlefish swimming next to me darted away, leaving behind a cloud of inky blackness in his wake. "You're a coward just like he is!" I screeched out again, louder than the first time. It seemed like everyone was abandoning me.

I cast my gaze towards the sky and the pale, yellow glow of Medeina's full, shining face. With a powerful kick of my tail fin, I shot up to the surface to get a better look at the moon goddess. Despite her beauty, like me, she was alone, forever searching for her true love, Pele. It seemed a cruel twist of fate that the pair could never share the sky together, one leaving just as the other arrived, forever chasing one another but never connecting.

"Triton, hear me," a masculine voice called out from the shore, drawing my gaze. "Please, don't let my mother suffer another day because of my failure. I beg of you, send me your prize fish so that I might provide for my family."

On the beach, leaning on a stick, was a young human male. He was holding a fishing line in his free hand while he petitioned the sea god for help. A gust of wind whipped across the water, sending the man's cloak lashing about his body, making him look something like a manta ray in flight. He had long black hair like Draven's, but his face was thin and gaunt. He was strikingly handsome despite appearing to be malnourished.

I stared up at Medeina's full face and smiled. The young man was smart to be out fishing under her cool, pale light. Many fish came to pay their respects to the goddess, praying that she would take them to her celestial home where they could bask in her beauty for all eternity.

One such fish that rose from the depths to worship the goddess was the mooneye; King Triton's most prized sea creature. They were bright silver, with large yellow eyes to help them see in the perpetual darkness of their deep-water homes. They were the tastiest fish in all the sea and the merfolk only ever harvested them for special occasions. For anyone else to take them was to invite the sea god's wrath.

"Let him be angry," I said to Medeina. "What additional punishment could he lay on me that would be worse than what his wretched son has already done?"

I dropped beneath the waves and swam closer to shore, nearer to the handsome human. Taking a deep breath, just like Arion had shown me, I gathered the sea's magic around me and sang my song to the open waters.

In the ocean's depths, where the seaweeds dance,
I sing my song and take my chance,
I call for the mooneyes to heed my voice,
And come to the fisherman, by your own choice.
My voice is gentle, my call is pure,
I ask for trust and use no lure,
Come closer to the shore, oh golden eyes,
And grant the fisherman, his daily prize.
I cannot promise safety, but know this well,
The fisherman will honor you, as his story will tell,
For your sacrifice is noble, and your gift is grand,
A bounty of food, to nourish the land.

I watched in awe as the magic of my voice traveled outwards, flowing like a great wave. I waited, holding my breath, unsure if Triton's bounty would heed my call. My heart swelled at the sight of the first mooneye. He was smaller than most, but he bravely swam to me.

"I have heard your call, Calypso of the never realm. If it will save the others of my kind, I will offer my life to you. But, I beg of you, do not use your powers to take all my brothers and sisters."

The small fish's words shattered my heart.

"I only wish for this fisherman to have enough food to provide for his family. I would force no one to die. I..." My words caught in my throat. "I used my magic so that you would hear me. I would not use it to compel you to sacrifice yourself."

"I believe you," the fish said, inclining his head slightly to me. "I will give myself to this fisherman. May Medeina witness my sacrifice and carry me to her realm where I may gaze upon her beauty for all eternity."

And with that, the small mooneye darted away, seeking out the fisherman's baited hook. I swam back to the surface to watch the young man's reaction to catching Triton's prized fish.

The little mooneye took the fisherman's bait. The man whooped at the sight of the fish as he pulled it onto the sandy shore. With his blade, he quickly ended the mooneye's suffering. After several moments of staring down at the fish, he raised his head to the sea.

"Thank you, Triton," he called out. "My family will suffer far less because of your generosity."

With his fish in hand, the man hobbled away from the beach. I had never seen a human this close before, and it worried me how badly he struggled to make his way from the sea's edge. Every step he took seemed to be a struggle.

As the young man disappeared over the hill, I remembered the crimson slugs I had been sent to retrieve.

⁂

After an exhausting day of training with Arion on how to use the crimson slugs, I returned the next night to find the human once again sitting by the sea, his fishing line cast into the depths. Again, I called to the mooneyes, and again, they heeded my plea. Just like the previous night, the young man left after catching a single fish, hobbling off into the darkness.

On the following night, Medeina was no longer showing her full face. I waited patiently for the young man to return, but he didn't come. Worry crept into my heart, fearing some ill had befallen the fisherman. Just as Pele was about to rise in the east and Medeina sink into the west, I dipped back beneath the waves and swam home.

Each night I returned to the shore in search of my human, but he didn't show himself until the first night Medeina once again graced us with her full presence. The young man looked different this night. His face seemed fuller and his heart lighter. Once again, he called upon Triton, asking for his help, hoping to once again be able to provide for his family.

It made me wonder if he had a wife waiting for him at home, or if he lived alone with his mother. A pang of jealousy stabbed at my heart, that he would have someone who loved him waiting for him when he returned. As quickly as the emotion had struck me, it vanished. From everything I could tell, he was a good man, and he deserved to be loved and to be happy. After all, wasn't that what we all wanted?

My life certainly wasn't turning out the way I had expected, but over the past months, I discovered more about myself than I could have ever hoped. I found joy in the smallest of things, things I had never considered important, like the company of a friend or the encouraging words of a teacher. Even the simple act of giving my time to help others brought me great joy.

If this was to be my new life, I would work hard to be the best sea witch I could be, and if the gods were willing, maybe I could find love in the most unexpected of places – in the arms of a human man.

It was a nice thought, something I could take with me to bed and dream about, something that I could wrap around myself until the next adventure came my way.

Calypso's story continues with Between Land and Sea: A Little Mermaid Retelling.

I hope you enjoyed Calypso's adventure. This tale, like all of my fantasy novels and short stories, takes place on the world of Orth in the Veil of Entropy universe. Come visit my website or check out the rest of my books on Amazon.

https://paulmouchet.ca

https://www.amazon.com/stores/Paul-Mouchet/author/B08LTL NNKH

CHAPTER 8

DYLAN

With a small bucket of bait in one hand and a dilapidated old crutch in the other, I slowly made my way across the beach. Each step was a challenge, as the heavily saturated sand swallowed up my crutch, rendering it nearly useless. The breeze coming in across the open water carried the tang of salty air, the promise of bountiful fishing, and the hope for better days ahead. Inhaling deeply, I savored the night's briny fragrance. The waves' slow, rhythmic harmonies brushed against the shore, adding to the enchanting ambiance. At the water's edge, in the still darkness, every sense sprang to life, imbuing the moment with a sense of magical splendor.

The full moon, and its pale silver halo, cast an ethereal glow across the Gaelinora Sea, its reflection rippling across the surface of the dark water. I had once heard a legend that spoke of how, on the three nights of the full moon when the goddess Medeina fully showed her face, mooneyes, the sweetest and most succulent fish in the north, would rise from the depths to beg her to take them to her celestial realm.

Filled with a sense of desperate optimism, I found myself a reasonably comfortable place to sit and unwrapped the thin strips of fish I used as bait. They were the smelly leftovers from yesterday's failed fishing trip. But this time, as I placed the strip of fish on the hook, I knew tonight would be better. The excitement was already building in me as I cast out my line, encouraged by the possibilities of what the coming hours might bring.

The chilly night air made my bad leg ache. The walk from the city to this desolate and windswept shoreline hadn't helped much, either. However, the discomfort was a small price to pay for the rewards that awaited me. In past months, with the fish I had caught during the three nights of the full moon, I had been able to earn enough gold to provide for me and my mother until Medeina returned to grace the night sky with her presence. Except tonight was the third and final night that the goddess would fully gaze upon the sea, and I had yet to catch a single fish.

The gathering night breeze whipped across the open sea, pushing waves towards me until they crashed upon the shore. The winds here were like a hungry, living thing, searching for any patch of exposed skin, just waiting for a moment to bite at it.

The dark gray clouds rolling in from the south didn't dissuade me. I didn't mind fishing in the rain. It was summer and, even though the nights were still bitterly cold, my heavy oilskin cloak kept me warm and dry – mostly. I pulled it tight around my shoulders, trying to protect what little warmth I had left in me. During the long, lonely hours waiting for a fish to bite, I needed to remain vigilant. I couldn't allow the cold to seep into my bones, leaving me permanently chilled. When vigilance failed, pure stubbornness was the key to success out here.

I exhaled heavily and watched the frosty vapor from my breath dissipate into the night air. Tomorrow, the full moon would be gone, and with it, any hope of success. Tonight was my last chance. Even if I had a good night, it likely wouldn't be enough, but some gold was better than no gold at all. If I couldn't make enough at the market, I could work the docks or find a fishing vessel in need of an extra hand. One way or another, I'd find a way to make ends meet.

Getting work wasn't easy for me, though, not with my bad leg. Standing without my crutch was both difficult and painful. Nobody wanted to hire a man who couldn't walk without aid, not when there were so many able-bodied men and women vying for the same job. My mother suffered from the same affliction, leaving neither of us in any position to find meaningful work. My mother would occasionally get a job as a cleaning lady for the local merchants, but the work was backbreaking and exhausting. It would often leave her bedridden for several days because of the pain in her leg. More often than not, she would be forced to beg in the streets and suffer the humiliation of taunts from passersby. When she returned home, she would step through the doorway, avert her gaze, and go straight to her bed. With her face buried deep into her pillow, she'd pull her blankets tight around her petite frame and cry herself to sleep. There was no hiding the tears, not in the tiny house with only a single room that served as kitchen, living room, and bedroom.

As the hours ticked by, the moon tracked its path across the night sky, and the wind never ceased, continuing to drive ever-growing waves against the shore. I had to move away from the edge lest I be soaked by a large roller. The clouds that had blown in from the south passed by with barely a drop of rain.

I tugged gently on my line, trying to give my sad piece of bait some life, hoping it might look more appealing to a mooneye. The only bites I had been getting so far were from midges, and small carnivorous fishes known as biters. They were barely bigger than a man's hand, and by all accounts, they were teeth and a tail, and very little else. Having them around was never good. They'd strip my hook clean before a mooneye had any hope of seeing it. Like the mooneyes, they, too, came up to the surface on the full moon, perhaps to say their prayers to Medeina.

Then, in the dead of the night, when the only sounds were my breath and the constant crashing of waves along the shoreline, I got my first nibble. It was tentative at first, just like a mooneye's. Tap, tap, tap, then nothing. I blew out a breath and pulled in my line. As I'd feared, my hook was bare, the bait having been stripped from it.

"Triton, help me," I called out over the vast stretch of black water, hoping the sea god might hear my plea. "Don't let me go home empty-handed. Not again." Neither Triton nor the sea answered me. They never did. I knew it was a waste of breath to pray, but when all else failed, what harm could it do? I didn't actually believe in the sea god, but it was best to not take any chances.

Trying to keep my spirits up, I softly whistled a tune while I put some fresh bait on my hook. Again, with hopeful anticipation, I cast my line into the water. The bait had barely sunk beneath the surface when I felt another tug. One sharp pull, and that was it.

"Some help you are," I said as I started pulling in my line. When I found the bare hook yet again, I shook my fist at the wind. It was blowing directly into my face, making it difficult to cast out beyond the shelf to where I knew the water was deeper, where the biters didn't congregate.

This pattern of having biters steal my chances of success continued until I was down to my last morsel of fish. With a heavy sigh, I carefully threaded my final strip of bait onto a hook. This time, I tried tying a rock to my line. I found one that was about the size of my fist. It would be heavy enough to cut through the wind, but not so heavy that I couldn't throw it past the deep-water shelf. With all my might, I cast my line out, hoping, praying that it would make it beyond where the biters amassed. I watched as my stone flew over the waves, well beyond where my earlier casts had reached. I quickly let out more line, doing what I could to help the stone carry the bait straight down.

I waited patiently for several minutes until I was certain the rock had dragged my hook down to the sea floor. It was then that I started to gently retrieve the slack line, only stopping when I felt the slightest bit of tension. It was important to make sure the line was taut, otherwise I'd never feel the gentle bite of the mooneye.

As time slowly passed, the wind continued to relentlessly sap my warmth and my strength. I pulled my oilskin cloak tighter around myself, trying to fend off the cold while stifling a yawn. I hadn't slept much in the past two days, spending every night out by the sea. But I dared not let myself fall asleep. Staying awake could mean the difference between my family surviving the month or my mother having to denigrate herself to make some coin.

A tiny tug on my line made my pulse race. Even with the wind relentlessly whistling in my ears, I could still hear the thrum of my pounding heartbeat. I prayed to the gods that it wasn't those blasted biters. I prayed to Triton. I prayed to Medeina. I even prayed to Boreas, the north wind, that the nibble I felt was not filling me with false hope. If it was, they'd strip my bait, and I'd be forced to return home with nothing to show for my efforts.

As I let out a bit of line, I whispered to the sea, "Be a mooneye." I didn't want the fish to feel the string when it took my bait. Holding my breath, another pair of tiny tugs pulled on my line. And then another. And another. It felt like a mooneye. They had a pattern when they took my line. Tug. Tug, tug. Tug, tug, yank.

Just like I had hoped, the tiny tugs turned into a mighty pull, nearly dragging me into the surf. Quickly as I could, I wrapped the fishing line around my forearm and started to drag the fish to shore. My oilskin cloak was perfect for this. It was thick and heavy, and it completely protected my skin from getting cut by the line if the fish suddenly pulled hard. There was a real danger of being dragged into the salty depths if the fish was stronger than I was, but it was a risk I was willing to take.

Each step was agonizing. With my crutch propped tight under one arm, I hobbled inland, dragging what felt like a leviathan along with me. I was working my way to where the beach was sandy, to where I could safely heave the fish ashore, but the mooneye had other plans. My catch was pulling me along the coastline to where it was rocky and the footing was precarious at best. Had I not had to use a crutch, it still would have been difficult, but in my condition, the challenge seemed insurmountable.

While the fish continued to drag me along, my heart pounded like the hooves of a charging warhorse. I had never fought anything this powerful. If it was a mooneye, and I prayed to the gods it was, this one catch could set my family for the month. Maybe more.

Panic was setting in. The longer I had the fish on the line, the more likely the biters would get to it. If they did, they'd strip it bare before I landed it. It was at that point a new fear gripped me. What if a water dragon, a Makara, saw it and decided to rob me of my prize? They were known to inhabit these waters. I pushed the notion from my mind. I was looking for problems that weren't there. I already had enough to worry about, that I didn't need to include fantastic tales of giant horned sea dragons.

While the salty surf pounded the shore, I continued battling the fish. Sometimes it felt like I was making headway, bringing in some line. Other times it was like the fish was playing with me, dragging me along, forcing me to venture near the water's edge, to where a rogue wave might come in and wash me out to sea.

It was when the rocks appeared to be getting larger, rougher, sharper, that I saw what I hoped would be my salvation. A blessedly large, flat rock jutted out into the growing surf. It was plenty big enough for me to stand on and it would provide a welcome respite from the treacherous rocks, and a good platform from which to drag in the fish.

Abandoning my crutch, I scrambled across the rocks, doing my best to not break a leg as I rushed over the uneven terrain. A sudden tug pulled me off balance, twisting my bad leg, drawing a scream of agony from me.

Just as I finished righting myself, my fishing line went limp.

CHAPTER 9

CALYPSO

I swam to the mouth of my cave, looking up at Medeina's shining face. Even through several hundred feet of water, her grace shone down, illuminating the vast sea. A cold current washed over me, cutting through my slick, clammy skin, deepening my already foul mood.

The school of lantern fish, that had been following me while I paced outside the entrance to my home, darted back inside, perhaps fearful they may be spotted by any nearby predators. We had a mutually beneficial arrangement. I let them live in the safety of my cave and, in return, they provided me with light, and they cleaned my home by eating up the plankton and algae that seemed to continuously gather here.

I swam out a little further, into the vast expanse of nothingness of the badlands. "Barnacles and bubbles. I do hope he's okay."

I had lost track of how many times I had uttered those exact same words in the last fifteen minutes. My human would be at the sea's edge, fishing for mooneyes right now. Tonight was the last night of the full moon and if he didn't catch enough, his family would suffer. "Oh, Triton, please make sure my human has a successful night. Don't let his family suffer because I'm not there to help him."

"How do you know that's what your human is doing? They're not pets, you know. And he's definitely not yours."

Startled by the voice from a dark corner in my cave, a large cloud of ink billowed out around me. "Ah, Arion, look what you made me do."

"It looks like you soiled yourself again."

"It's ink, you nasty crustacean. What are you doing out here?"

"I'm checking in on you," he said, snapping his giant crab pincers at me. "Making sure you're not gallivanting around, doing things you're not supposed to be doing."

"To make sure I don't go see my human?" I spat the words back at him, rolling my monstrous round eyes for maximum effect. "Don't worry, I'll never go back now. I mean, look at me. You turned me into some sort of horrid squid monster. It's not like he ever saw me before, but now, if he did, I'd scare the ink out of him as well."

"Humans don't ink."

"I don't care. You know what I mean. The young man's family might starve now because of what you did to me. Enough is enough. Turn me back into a mermaid. I've been like this long enough. It's humiliating. I've learned my lesson."

"I changed you so that you'd never go to the surface again. I did it for your own good." Arion scratched at the cave floor, stirring up a cloud of gray silt. "And how do you know the young man's family will starve?"

"I heard him praying to Triton. It's possible he figured that if the sea king knew why he was fishing for mooneyes, then maybe he'd help him." I swam past my teacher, a crab I often referred to as my mentor and friend, letting my overly long tentacles drag over his red-shelled body. I wanted to make it clear just how revolting I looked and felt.

"Pfft. Triton and his horrible children only help themselves. Look at what Prince Draven did when the queen and her foul-mouthed advisor framed us for using blood magic." Arion held his pincers high. "Me, the most powerful mage to ever lead the Academy of Arcana, accused in such a way. Beithir never got over Triton passing him over as headmaster, appointing me, instead."

The giant crab paced in slow circles, scrubbing his claws over his eyestalks.

"And Prince Draven did nothing to protect you. For a merman who was set to propose marriage, he sure had a strange way of treating his lady love. He knows you would never do such a thing, but still, he let the guards cart us both away like common criminals, banishing us here to the badlands, where even the sharks won't venture. There is nothing to see. Nothing to do. Nothing but miles and miles of boring nothingness. Oh, glorious starfish, how I miss the merkingdom. I used to have front row seats at the coliseum. I used to get to watch plays and listen to music from the best seat in the house. Now I've got a dank cave to call home and a surly mermaid as my company."

"I hate Prince Draven with all my heart. He's a worthless bit of flotsam who should throw himself into an underwater volcano and turn himself into sea foam. The guy is nothing more than a... scavenger."

"Careful there, sweetie. I'm a scavenger."

"You're a giant crab with an even bigger heart. And the only reason you're a scavenger is because you don't want to hurt a living thing – even though you seem to have no issue with tormenting me. You could hunt any fish in the sea if you chose to. I've seen how fast you can move when the mood strikes you. I watched you cut through a fisherman's net with your pincers like it was nothing more than seaweed."

"Those fool humans had netted a school of merchildren. What else could I have done?"

"You risked your shell to save them. Even though you turned me into this horrid monster, I still love you."

"I love you, too, my little sea witch apprentice. I'll do anything to protect you, even if it means turning you into a horrid squid monster."

"Can you change me back? Please? Tonight's the last night of the full moon. I need to make sure my human has caught enough fish to sustain his family."

"And what do you think will happen to him if Triton finds out he's harvesting his prize fish? More importantly, what do you think the sea king will do to you if he finds out that you're helping him?" The crab's eyestalks swiveled towards the cave's entrance. "Here comes the princess. Watch what you say around her. None of the royal family is to be trusted."

As quickly as Arion had arrived, he scuttled back into the shadows.

Luna, my best friend, came swimming into my cave, rapidly tapping her throat. Her skin was pale, her long flowing hair a sea-foam green. The mermaid's sapphire blue eyes were wide, bulging out of her head. At first, I thought it was because she was struggling to breathe, but then I realized that the sight of me frightened the cockles out of the little princess.

"Luna, it's just me," I said, swimming nearer to my friend. She threw her arms up in an attempt to ward me off, her blue tail fin kicking to maintain her distance from me.

"Luna, it's me, Calypso." I stopped moving forward, giving her a chance to process what she was seeing. "Arion did this ... as punishment."

My friend's wide-eyed fear changed to wide-eyed shock, which quickly changed to giddy laughter. Her head seemed to weave side to side, likely because she was looking for my overly enthusiastic teacher. The princess understood what it was like having a chaperone lurking at her side all the time. Where I had a giant crab hovering over me, she had Octavius, an annoying little octopus who resembled a miniature kraken, who followed her everywhere she went.

"Let me guess. You lost your voice again?" Luna nodded and rapidly tapped on her throat. "When are you going to learn, girl?" The little mermaid was nodding furiously. She had a penchant for fire-shrimp. Perhaps an addiction was a more appropriate word for it, the way she risked life and fin to steal them. All too often, she had a bad reaction from eating them, causing her to lose her voice; a condition that could last many days. The bright-red creatures were a species of crustaceans carefully cultivated and farmed by sirens. My skin darkened at the thought of those cursed winged mermaids. They were the reason land dwellers feared our kind and killed us on sight. The sirens used their magical voices to lure ships towards their rocky island homes. What those vile creatures did to the humans afterwards was too gruesome to think about without making me shiver.

Luna blew out a few bubbles, her way of pleading with me to hurry.

"This is the last of the remedies I made. I don't have the ingredients to make any more." I swam close to my friend, cringing when she shied away from my grotesque form. If my best friend was frightened by my appearance, there was no way a human wouldn't be absolutely terrified. "I have a favor," I whispered. "One that could get both of us into deep water."

A smile crept across Luna's face. I knew exactly how to manipulate her. She might have been Triton's daughter, but she was a free spirit, an adventurous soul who would do anything for fun, even if it meant angering her father. If it meant infuriating her brother, then all the better.

"You can't tell anyone that you're doing this for me, especially Draven. And you need to make sure Octavius knows nothing of this. He would report us in a heartbeat if he knew." The girl scowled and blew out a stream of bubbles, making her hair swirl about her head. Of course, she understood. Luna gave her octopup the slip all the time. It was the only way she could visit the sirens' shrimp farm without her brother finding out. I held up my hands defensively, giving her a big smile.

I pressed my lips close to Luna's ear, breathing out my words, barely loud enough for her, and only her, to hear. After I finished explaining what I wanted her to do for me, she pulled away. Her eyes were as wide and shocked as when she saw my horrific new body for the first time. The girl suddenly blushed scarlet and nodded furiously while a mischievous grin pulled her cheeks wide.

"Thank you. You're the best friend I've ever had." And with that, I fluttered to my wall of potions and scrolls and retrieved the last of my fire-shrimp cure. "Please hurry. The night is nearly gone, and it will be the last time Medeina fully shows herself for a long time."

Luna snatched the bottle from my hand and, with a flick of her tail, disappeared in a cloud of bubbles.

"What were you two whispering about?" Arion asked, creeping out from his shadowy hole. "Please tell me you didn't send her on a fool's errand?"

"I didn't send her on a fool's errand." The words came out too quickly and my body turned a horrid shade of green.

"You're lying to me, Calypso. You know how I feel about that."

"I only did what you asked." My body switched from ghastly green to pathetic pink. "You told me to tell you I didn't send her on a fool's errand, so that's what I did."

"What am I going to do with you, child?" He snapped his pincers at me. "If she gets caught, we'll be shark bait for sure."

CHAPTER 10

DYLAN

I stared down at the limp, lifeless fishing line in my hand. My salvation had been so close. That single fish might have been enough to see my family through until the next moon. But like so many other times in my life, I was forced to swallow down the bitter taste of disappointment.

"Triton, why?" I bellowed at the gathering clouds that threatened to blot out the moon. "Why would you give me hope, only to dash it against the rocks?" Yelling at the sea god was a waste of breath. It's not like he ever listened. My heart ached, my lungs burned, and the pain in my leg had become so acute that I feared I was going to pass out. So what if I did? I was useless. My mother would suffer because I was an incompetent, wretched bag of bones. She would be better off if I just left. I could stow away on a merchant ship, travel across the sea, and get as far away from this gods-forsaken town as was possible. There would be one less mouth to feed. One less body to clothe. One less pathetic waste of skin.

I despised giving in to setbacks. "Get a hold of yourself, Dylan."

I spoke the words aloud. They sounded like something my mother might say to me. If she had heard my thoughts of running away, she'd have been ashamed of me. My mother and I waged a daily war against life's challenges. We knew no respite, but we never wavered in our determination to overcome every obstacle that lay in our path. Even when we were belittled and oppressed by overbearing merchants, deceitful fishmongers, bullies, and cutthroats, all of whom discriminated against us because of our disabilities, we never surrendered to defeat. Today was just another struggle, even if it felt so much harder to bear.

I finished making my way to the large flat rock that jutted out into the sea and began the task of pulling in my line, wrapping it around the sleeve of my oilskin cloak. As I did, I moved closer to the brink, doing what I could to stop the line from dragging over the platform's sharp edges. Even if I was going home empty-handed, I needed to protect my line and hook. They were expensive and the only way I had to make any gold.

The wind suddenly picked up. The waves became larger, crashing upon the shore. The icy sea-spray stung my face, drenching my hair, filling my mouth with briny water. The tiny hairs on the back of my neck sprang to attention. Lightning danced across the skies like fiery serpents, turning the clouds into great beasts, their bellies swollen with the deluge of water they were about to unleash.

A bolt of lightning struck the water with a deafening crack that echoed across the waves, sending shockwaves through my body. In that brief moment of blinding brightness, the monstrous windswept whitecaps became visible with perfect clarity. Driven by howling winds, the onslaught of rain followed immediately after, pelting my skin with icy shivers.

Panic surged through me. I was staring directly into the teeth of a monster that would devour me whole. I needed to get myself off this rock before Triton's sea dragged me to its murky depths. My heart sank as I looked back to where I had thrown my crutch, suddenly regretting my short-sightedness for having cast it aside.

As quickly as I could, I continued to bring in my line, wrapping it around my arm as I did. A wave broke over the top of the rock on which I was standing, nearly taking my feet out from underneath me. As the water receded, it made the stone slick. If another wave, a larger wave, were to come before I could get off, it would surely sweep me into the water.

With my heart hammering in my chest, I continued gathering in the line. Regardless of its value, I considered just throwing it away, but it was so tightly wound around my arm that I'd never be able to get it off. I reached for the knife that hung at my side, beneath my cloak. While I worked my way past the heavy metal clasps, the fishing line suddenly went taught.

A heavy pull on my line threatened to drag me off balance. Footing was difficult on the now too-slick rock. Another crack of lightning split the sky, illuminating a massive wave hurtling towards me. As terror gripped me, my throat seized and my muscles froze. I watched and waited in hopeless desperation, knowing what fate had in store for me.

The fish suddenly yanked me forward, toward the edge of the rock and the raging sea below, toward my doom. Was it all some sort of cruel joke? I finally hooked the fish of a lifetime, and in retribution, the sea decided to try to kill me for it. I don't know why, exactly, but I barked out a laugh at the absurdity of the situation.

"I will not go quietly," I bellowed at the waves. "You will not have me this night."

Triton and the Gaelinora Sea laughed right back as a massive wave crashed over me, sending me heels over head, tangled in the tenacious turbulence. While the water pushed me against the shore's sharp rocks, the great fish was trying to yank me into deeper water. Caught in a tug-of-war between two forces, my body was banged and battered across sharp boulders.

My lungs were burning from exertion, desperate to gulp fresh air, but the sea continued having other plans for me. The water began to recede, threatening to help the great fish drag me into the deep. Hoping against all odds, I jammed my foot between two rocks in an attempt to anchor myself in place.

Another tug from the fish pulled me seaward, twisting my ankle to an unnatural angle. Fully submerged beneath the waves, I screamed out in agony. When the bubbles I had released from my lungs dissipated, I was nose to nose with the most beautiful vision I had ever witnessed. Just before I lost consciousness, I saw the face of an angel – perhaps the true face of Medeina, the moon goddess, herself.

CHAPTER 11

LUNA

Swimming leisurely away from Calypso's lair, I sucked back the last of the potion she had given me. Oh, what blessed relief the bitter-sweet liquid provided. It slid down my throat, calming the urchin-like needles that seemed to perpetually bite at me. I don't know why I couldn't resist stealing the siren's divine, delicious, delectable, fire-shrimp. I swear to Gaia, those crunchy crustations called to me, begging for me to snack on them. It seemed like one in ten came with more than just spicy flavor, causing me the horrible affliction of losing my voice. Too bad I couldn't stop at nine. If I could, I'd likely be fine.

Turning my head to give silent thanks to my friend for her cure, I caught sight of Octavius swimming after me. Lately, anytime I snuck off without him, Calypso's home was the first place he looked. Some months ago, he managed to thwart my best efforts to evade him and followed me there. As I was leaving, I found him waiting for me. I begged him to not tell my mother, or my brother, explaining that the sea witch was my best friend and that she needed me. Even though he tattled on me more times than I could count, the octopup kept my secret. Even if Calypso didn't trust him, I did. The little guy had a good heart, even if he took his job as chaperone far too seriously.

But this time was different. I couldn't let him follow me to the human. There would be no excuse I could give him that would justify breaking my brother's laws. I shooed him away and darted off as fast as I could. I knew he couldn't keep up with me, not while I was swimming at top speed. Of course, I'd pay the price for this when I got back home because, sure as the tides, he would tell my brother, the oh-so-noble Prince Draven, mother's favorite, that I had run off without him – again.

I certainly wasn't going to let my barnacle-brained brother dictate my life. If I wanted to go help some human or even, heavens forbid, to visit the human world, then that's exactly what I was going to do.

I gazed in wonder at the colors that became more visible as I rose up from the depths. Where we lived, very little light penetrated so deep, casting my bone-chilling world in deep blues and near-black greens. As I ascended, I basked in the warmer water and marveled at the vibrant shades of oranges and yellows. I had never come this close to the surface before, and I was reveling in it. A school of small fish raced past me, dodging and weaving, perhaps fearing I might choose to make a late-night snack of them. Where there would have been little more than shadows at depth, here brightly colored scales reflected the moon's pale light, mesmerizing me with flashes of silver, red, and gold.

Gold! I was supposed to be looking for mooneyes. That's the fish Calypso said this human coveted more than any other. I wondered if he realized they were my father's prize species, which he farmed and cultivated. The old man might not be around much, but my brother was, and he was quick to deal out punishment to anyone who broke our father's laws. Even Calypso, the mermaid he had once planned to marry, wasn't beyond his wrath.

Cockles and Corals, what a spoiled guppy. As soon as he was given our father's royal scepter, the symbol of power over the merkingdom, my brother went mad. It seemed he had spent his entire life seeking affirmation from our parents, desperate to prove his worth. Then, when the world was laid at his fins, the night he would gain both the scepter and the hand of the woman he loved, Prince Draven lost his mind. All he needed to do was stand up against the false accusations being leveled against his lady love and her teacher. Instead, he listened to the steaming pile of lies that were being hurled about them, sucking up each and every one, faster than I could munch down a handful of fire-shrimp.

As I neared the top of the water, the moon shone brightly overhead, casting a silvery glow across the ocean's surface. The pale light penetrated the dark waters, creating a wondrous world filled with reds, yellows, and marvelous shades of oranges. Everything in sight was vivid, and the currents here were, oh, so pleasantly warm.

The water suddenly darkened. Medeina's face no longer shone down upon me. I gazed up in time to see a series of large waves roll overhead, no more than two body-lengths above. With each passing wave, a powerful current swept me inland. In the deeps, we never experienced anything so intense or so violent.

I broke the surface, looking to get a better view of where I was in relation to where Calypso had said I needed to be. I took a deep breath, the cool night air filling my lungs, setting my heart ablaze. I had never felt so free, so alive. If this was what the humans experienced every day, then, surely, they were living in paradise. The sensation of rising from the water was nothing like the crazy songs Octavius sang that told of how the humans toiled and strained beneath the burning hot sun. No wonder we were warned about leaving our sea homes. If the merfolk knew how wonderful this was, they'd leave in droves to live on dry land.

While I marveled at the sheer magnificence of breathing air, I completely lost track of my surroundings. Turning my back to the turbulent water was a mistake, a potentially life-threatening one.

A huge wave crashed over me, sending me tumbling head over fin. I choked on the sea water while I tried to expel the night air from my lungs. It burned so badly I feared I was about to pass into the Beyond. Maybe my chaperone was correct. Perhaps life on land wasn't everything I'd hoped it would be.

Regardless of the fear that gripped me, I had a task to complete. In the short time I had surfaced, I hadn't taken a moment to search for Calypso's human along the shoreline.

With the powerful surge pushing me towards shore, I picked up speed and leapt from the water, making certain to hold my breath this time, searching for the fisherman. The light of the moon wasn't quite as bright as it had been moments ago, likely obscured by clouds. Although the light was dim, my ability to see in the dark was excellent, and I easily made out the young man standing by the water's edge, struggling against a line he had wrapped around his arm.

With a few quick kicks, I raced towards where the man was standing, searching for the mooneyes he so desperately needed to catch. I couldn't believe my eyes as I watched a huge fish, the biggest mooneye I had ever seen, struggling against the man's fishing line.

It seemed Calypso's human wasn't as helpless as she had described him. Without any aid, he had managed to hook a massive prize. Just as I was about to turn around and return home, the fish spit the hook.

I guess he needs my help after all.

The great fish was about to speed back off to the depths before I called upon my magic.

Oh, blessed fish with fins so fine,
Your sacrifice will be divine.

For in the bellies of the men,
You'll give them strength to live again.
I know it's hard to give your life,
But through your death, you end the strife.
The humans need your flesh to thrive,
To keep them going, to stay alive.
So take the bait, my little friend,
And make your mark, until the end.
For in this game of life and death,
You'll be the one who gives them breath.

The mooneye paused long enough to listen to my song. It seemed to be considering my words. I would not use my magic to force him to give up his life, but I did my best to make the plight of the human convincing. After several long moments, he nodded his assent and returned to the fisherman's hook, clamping onto it with his powerful jaws.

"Thank you, noble fish."

I stayed nearby, watching as the great fish slowly made his way towards shore. Not that I would have stopped him if he'd chosen to leave, but I wanted to ensure that Calypso's human got what he needed until the next time Medeina shone upon the world.

An enormous swell took hold of both me and the fish, hurtling us towards the shoreline. With wide eyes, I looked down at the sharp rocks against which I was about to be slammed. In the depths, the seas were never this violent. Even in the strongest of currents, I would have had no trouble resisting. But here, in the storm-swollen waves, I was powerless to resist. My best choice was to stay clear of the largest, most dangerous rocks.

With the fish only an arm's length from me, I continued to be pushed into dangerously shallow water. My powerful tail was now nearly useless. There simply wasn't enough room to fully kick. Despite their relatively useless abilities, I thrashed with my arms, desperate to keep myself above the razor-sharp edges of the rocks.

Anchors and albatrosses! Calypso's human was neck deep in the water, struggling to keep his mouth from submerging. I knew very little about humans, except for one simple fact: they couldn't survive beneath the water for more than a few precious moments. I couldn't for the life of me understand why he was staying where he was and not swimming to safety.

Gritting my teeth, I made my way nearer, holding onto the rocks as I moved, trying to guide myself towards the man amid the swirling currents. Moments before the next wave broke, I dove beneath the surface. I gasped in horror at the sight of the human's leg trapped between two large stones. Another huge swell propelled me towards him, pushing my face mere inches from his.

Oh, heavens above, he was terrified!

I dug my nails into the rocky surface, fighting desperately to not let the wave wash me away like a bit of rogue flotsam. Another vicious wave broke across my back, thrashing me and the human about like limp-bodied kelp stalks. Whether it was an incoming tide, or the relentless waves crashing upon the shore, the human was now fully submerged. Panic-stricken, he yanked at his leg, screaming out in panicked agony when it wouldn't come free.

I blew out a deep breath and tried to calm my racing heart. I tore my gaze away and went to work trying to free his trapped leg. But in the shallow water, these rocks were far too heavy for me, even with my natural mermaid strength. I tried blowing bubbles into the crevices, hoping they might help dislodge the huge rocks. It was when I watched the air-filled spheres rise up towards the man's panic-stricken face that I had an idea.

If he couldn't breathe beneath the waves, and I couldn't get him out of the water, I needed to find a way to buy him some time. Expelling every bit of my air reserves, I created a bubble that completely encased the two of us. My lungs burned as the bubble expanded around us. I anchored it to the sea floor, using what little water magic I could wield, creating a protective shell around us both. As soon as the last of my breath left me, dizziness took hold, and the world swam around me in slow, nauseating circles. Just before I succumbed to the increasing darkness enveloping me, I saw a vision, a hallucination most likely. My beautiful tail was gone, replaced by a wonderful pair of spindly, knobby-kneed human legs.

CHAPTER 12

CALYPSO

My brain was a jumble of conflicting emotions. On one tentacle, I was happy that Luna had agreed to help me help the human. On another, I was worried that she would be sidetracked along the way, lured into following a bright bobble or a school of dancing clown fish. On yet another, I was furious with Arion for having turned me into this disgusting creature, making it impossible for me to help the human myself.

I was thankful for not having a mirror in my home, so I wouldn't have to see the wretched creature I had become, but the sight of nasty black tentacles, where I used to have a luxurious blue-green tail, was enough to make my stomach pitch. It was bad enough being relegated to this cold, barren land, but having to live here looking like a thing of nightmares made it unbearable.

Wrapped in a blanket of self-loathing, I swam out of my cave, for what was likely the tenth time in the past hour, hoping to see Luna's smiling face as she returned with good news. Like every other time I checked, I was met with a wide expanse of nothingness. Even Medeina's shining face seemed to have disappeared into the gloom, heightening my sense of dread. Even at these depths, I should have been able to easily see the moon goddess high above. There were still a few hours before Pele would chase her from the night sky, forcing her to retreat to wherever it was she disappeared to when the sun god took his place in the heavens.

"Arion?" I called out as I drifted back into my cave. I knew I was being shallow, worrying so much about my outward appearance, but this was too much. Even Luna, my best friend in the whole world, was repulsed when she saw me. How was I going to be able to help other merfolk when just being in my presence was enough to terrify them? "Please, for me. Turn me back into myself so I can check on Luna. I'm worried about her. She's been gone far too long."

The great red crab came scuttling out from his hole. He was holding a thick tome between his pincers, his eyes glued to their pages. He muttered something unintelligible under his breath.

"Arion, please. Medeina will be gone from the night sky very soon. I need to make sure..." The way my mentor's eyes were bulging at the end of their stalks stopped my words. I was about to ask what was wrong when I felt a change in currents, the temperature in my cave dropping rapidly.

"Where is she?" a voice boomed from behind me. An enormous cloud of darkness erupted from my body, enveloping both Arion and me. Despite my embarrassment for having inked myself, yet again, I could definitely see the benefit of such a defense mechanism. "Where is Calypso? Where is the sea witch?"

I peered through the sweet, metallic-tasting cloud that swirled around me. My smooth, leathery skin turned pink at the sight of the merman lurking outside the entrance to my cave.

Prince Draven's chiseled physique glistened, lit by the hundreds of tiny lantern fish who rushed out of my cave to greet their ruler. His body rippled with power as he swam out from the ocean's depths, filling my cave's entrance with his considerable bulk. His hair, a tangled mass of dark waves, framed a ruggedly handsome face with piercing blue eyes that seemed to stare right through me. The merman's broad chest and muscular arms were adorned with intricate tattoos, each one a symbol of his fierce strength and unwavering loyalty to his father, King Triton.

As he moved through the water with effortless grace, his merman tail shimmered a deep emerald green that seemed to change color with each passing moment.

Sweet Gaia, he was so beautiful – and I wanted to smash my fist – make that my tentacle – into his face.

"You are not welcome here, Prince Draven," Arion said, stepping past me, thrusting his book out in front of himself, wielding it like a weapon. "Leave."

"Not until I've spoken to her. Get out of my way, old crab."

My heart leapt into my throat. Draven was pointing his scepter at my mentor. I didn't know what it could do, not exactly, but I could feel its power pulsing. Even if Arion's magic was potent, I wasn't going to put his shell at risk for my sake. At that moment, it dawned on me. Draven was the reason for Medeina's grace being absent from the night sky. He was conjuring a storm, fueling the scepter's magic with his rage.

"You have no say here, Draven," I said, my skin erupting into a deep red. "These badlands exist outside your domain. Go home and leave us alone."

The merman's face twisted as he sucked a breath through clenched teeth. It took me a moment to realize that I was the reason for his reaction, or, more accurately, the hideous thing Arion had turned me into, was. His repulsion barely lasted a heartbeat before he regained his composure, his unbridled fury once again bubbling to the surface, turning his already sharp-featured face into a block of granite.

"Get me Calypso. Now!" A wave of icy current hurled me across the cave, slamming my body against the wall. With his scepter raised, he slowly swam toward me, threatening to unleash his wrath within the confines of my too-small cave.

"I *am* Calypso, you ponderous oaf." With a burst of speed I didn't know I possessed, I raced forward, my beak-like nose pressed up against his, my overly large bulbous eyes glaring. Gods above, I wanted to wrap my tentacles around his throat and squeeze the life out of him. "You've got a lot of nerve showing up here, after everything you've done. I'm sure seeing me like this pleases you. You treated me like I was some sort of monster, and now I am one."

His throat bobbed as he swallowed, his eyes locked onto mine. For a heartbeat, I saw sadness and pity in his swirling sapphire pools. His full, bottom lip quivered for a moment, just before his expression, once again, turned deadly serious.

"Where did you send my sister?" Draven used his massive body to corral me, forcing me to back myself into a corner, the sharp bits of coral and barnacles digging into my delicate squid skin. The heavy muscles in his arm flexed as he leaned in close, his hand pressed flat against the wall beside my head. The faint crimson glow of his scepter lit the side of his face, giving him an even more menacing appearance. Through clenched teeth, he seethed. "Where is she, Calypso? What ridiculous quest have you set my witless sister off on this time?"

"Back off, Draven," I spat back at him, slipping four of my tentacles between us, using the other four to push me towards him. The merman was being a bully, using his muscular frame to intimidate me. I knew he would back down if directly confronted. So, I tried calling upon my magic to help me appear more aggressive, hoping to force him to cower away. I hadn't expected him to grasp my tentacles in such a powerful grip, twisting and squeezing until I squealed in pain.

"Let her go," Arion said, his pincer wrapped around Draven's wrist, just below the scepter. "I don't care what your father will do to me, but if you don't release my apprentice, I'll sever your hand from your body."

The pressure on my tentacles immediately lessened, but the burning hatred in Draven's expression didn't. The prince's jaw twitched while his chest heaved.

Arion removed his claw and shuffled himself close to my side. "Where is she, Calypso?" my mentor said, his eyestalks trained on me.

"She was swimming towards the human city of Cormorant," Octavius said, appearing from behind the merman's bulk. "My prince. I tried to tell you, but you swam off before I could finish speaking."

The tiny black octopus followed Luna everywhere, whispering in her ear like some sort of external conscience. *Don't do that, Luna. Your mother wouldn't approve. Don't listen to her, Luna. She's going to get you in trouble.* Even though my friend could swim a dozen times faster than her chaperone, he always seemed to find a way to catch up to her. Even though Luna had given him the slip, he seemed to know everything about what she was doing and where she was going.

"I asked you a question," Draven growled at me. His long black hair swirled around his head, framing his angular features, his sapphire blue eyes, his coral-red lips. "Calypso! Why did you send her towards a human city? What business do you have there?"

"She's going to see a human," Octavius said. "She's helping him catch mooneyes." He let out a small cloud of ink when Draven's hand shot out to grasp him, but the tiny cephalopod was quicker than he looked, darting away before the prince's fingers could wrap around his soft little body.

Screaming starfish. How did he know that? Had he been using his natural camouflage skills to lurk nearby, spying on Luna and me while we spoke in private? I glared at the tiny kraken, only to have him give me a crooked smile in return.

"Take me there," Draven said, directing his wrath at me again. "By the gods, sea witch, you will take me there or I will show you my true wrath." His words were pushed out through clenched teeth, small bubbles leaking out with them. Whatever his threat might have meant, my mentor took exception, shoving the prince away, moving closer, and shoving him yet again.

"I won't tell you again, Draven. Speak to her like that one more time and they will be the last words you ever utter."

"You would dare threaten your prince?"

"Except you are no longer my prince. You banished us from the merkingdom, forced us to find refuge out here in the badlands where nothing lives, and nothing grows, except for my burning desire to rend you limb from limb, you spineless jellyfish."

Arion's words made Draven's lips curl into a cold, heartless smile. "Tell me where she is, old crab, and I'll restore your place in my kingdom. Continue with your current actions and you will witness a wrath unlike anything you have ever experienced before."

Arion glanced over at me, stroking what passed for a chin on the giant crab. "Well, if you did reinstate us as members of your kingdom, and returned us to our previous stations, you would be within your rights to place demands on us." My mentor's eyes narrowed as he continued speaking. "But we can never return home so long as the people believe we wield blood magic. I don't know what happened to you, but you've known me since you were no bigger than a seahorse. You know I would never do anything like that. You know the mermaid you once loved could never do anything so evil. Even now, outcast beyond your realm, she strives to help others. Either you grow a backbone, or you can leave."

Draven seemed to be thinking over my teacher's words; his rage-filled eyes softening.

"Call off the storm," I said, using what appeared to be a moment of vulnerability in the prince. "Your anger may well be the death of your sister. If she is near the shore, you're just as likely to kill her as the humans that you despise."

The scepter in Draven's hand glowed red. Whatever hint of softness I had seen in him instantly vanished.

"That I despise? It's they who despise us. If you hadn't been so caught up in your own fantasies, you'd have understood that. Bringing harmony between merfolk and the humans is everything I've been working towards."

Cockles and coral. Could that be right? Had I been so tied up in wanting to be his bride that I never bothered to consider the significance of what he was doing? I had believed his actions were to impress his parents, in order to be given the royal scepter and rulership over the merkingdom.

"Perhaps you're right; it's possible I was so caught up in our relationship that I couldn't see beyond that. I've had a lot of time to think out here in the vast nothingness; about who I was, but I've also had a lot of time to think about you. I used to love you. I loved you so much it hurt. But you threw me away at your first opportunity and now – I hate you with every fiber of my being."

That single comment broke through the sea prince's rigid exterior, his puffed-up chest instantly deflating. The face of the man I had fallen in love with resurfaced, melting my frozen heart. The temperature in the cave returned to its normal chill.

"Please, Calypso. Help me find my sister. She is not equipped to deal with humans. Luna is too naïve and too kind-hearted. She will follow her adventurous heart, no matter where the danger leads her."

The roundness of his eyes and the gentleness of his words cut through me. Seeing Arion swallow hard told me he was also moved by the merman's pleas.

A tiny glint in Draven's eye hardened my heart. I realized that he was playing me, using my emotions to get what he wanted. But two could play that game, and I would not allow this backstabbing piece of pond-scum get the better of me.

"I would help you, my prince," I said, bowing low. Speaking kindly to the man brought sour bile into my mouth. He was despicable, but in this moment, I saw an opportunity to escape this grotesque body I was trapped within. "But in my current state, it would take me two days to travel to where we need to go."

His scepter glowed red once again. I hadn't fooled him. Not at all.

"Then tell me where she went. I will go myself."

"Alas," I said, waving my tentacles about, rolling my overly large hazel-green eyes. With a pulse of my body, I circled the prince, my words coming out in a sing-song sort of way. "There are no clear markers that I could use to describe her location." I slowly turned my gaze to Arion, my skin's color morphing into a pale blue. "I will need to come with you if there is to be any hope of finding her before Pele returns to the skies."

"Change her back," Draven demanded. His voice was low and threatening, but there was a palpable undercurrent of fear in his words. I believed he truly feared for his sister's wellbeing.

"No," Arion said. "I won't."

I gave my teacher the saddest look, desperate to have him undo what he did to me. I couldn't spend my life like this. It wasn't my fault I fell in love with a human. Arion was the one who sent me to search for crimson slugs, which could only be found very close to the human settlement. He had been using those very same slugs to teach me specialized incantations. It was only a few days ago that we had used up the last of the red worms. Arion had said that once I mastered the magic, I wouldn't need them anymore.

"Let me break the spell myself," I said. "You taught me how, now let me use what I've learned. Please, Arion." I wanted to promise that I wouldn't try to see my human again. Even though doing so might have been enough to get him to agree, I simply couldn't. I would not lie to get what I wanted.

"We have no more slugs," my teacher said, shrugging at me – or at least what passed for a shrug for a giant crab. "But if you want to try to break the spell I put on you without them, I won't try to stop you."

"No magic!" Draven bellowed. "I forbid it."

I leveled a stare at the merman. "Fine. Then you can leave. I can't help you in my current state, so I guess we'll just have to hope that Luna is safe."

Draven pointed his scepter at me, its jewel-encrusted head glowing with the same fury that filled the merman's eyes. His jaw was clenched tight enough to shatter his teeth.

"I should vaporize you," he growled. "I should have followed the recommendation of the royal advisor, Beithir, and executed you on the spot for your use of blood magic. Mother told me. She said I would regret staying your execution."

"Well, you didn't execute us. You cast your judgment on us without any proof, other than the lies of Beithir's lackeys. You chose to banish us instead. Execute me now and you're committing murder. Is that what you've turned into, a murderer? I guess it's true what they say about power and how it corrupts. You're pathetic."

Draven roared and unleashed a bolt of magic across the cave, exploding every scroll, potion, and bit of decoration I had in my home.

"Then do it! Change yourself back to a mermaid and help me find my sister." The merman's chest was heaving. He seemed a hair's breadth from completely unraveling.

"Get out of our home," Arion said to Draven. "Take the little kraken with you. If this spell goes wrong, I don't want any of you hurt. I wouldn't want to give you an actual excuse to take your wrath out on us."

The prince spun around, and with a kick of his tail fin, was gone. There was only a small cloud of ink suspended in the water where Octavius used to be. I guessed that he had squirted out of here as soon as Draven lost control of himself.

"Okay," Arion said to me. I could tell he was still rattled, but he was trying his best to remain calm. The fact that he hadn't attacked Draven while he was laying waste to our home told me just how strong my teacher's self-control was. "Before you begin, release your anger. Let it all go. You must be at peace if you're going to have any hope of success. Remember what I taught you. To break a spell, you need to feel for it. The energy of its magic is a real, tangible thing. Once you've located it, draw upon the power of the sea. Harness it and funnel it at the spell you're trying to break. The enchantment I put on you was very strong, so you're going to need to gather and hold on to a great deal of energy if you are to have any hope of undoing what I did to you."

I tried to not ink myself. Just the thought of gathering so much power into my body was terrifying. Holding magic hurt. It stung my skin and made my chest burn. When I was first learning to cast this spell, Arion gave me easy targets that needed very little power to unravel them.

But if I wanted to be rid of this monstrous squid form, I needed to try.

With a deep, cleansing breath, I cast my tentacles out, feeling for the sea's power, pulling on it, drawing it into me. The cave shimmered in an unearthly light, its walls reflecting luminous swirls of red and yellow. My heart raced as I continued to fill myself with the magic that seemed to stretch out into the Beyond. A cacophony pounded in my ears as my delicate skin struggled to contain the tempest building within my body. My mind reeled as it struggled to keep its tenuous grip on reality. I threw my head back, fighting to maintain my concentration. I wanted to scream as my soul was being torn from my chest.

"Good," Arion bellowed. I was barely able to hear him over the torrents of blood rushing in my ears. "Very good. You're ready. Release the power you're holding and break my spell."

The power within had become a raging hurricane desperate to be free of the confines of the tiny crucible that was me. With a primal scream I released the gathered magic, focusing it on the enchantment that was infused in my body.

A sudden vortex swept around me, spinning my tentacle-laden body at a dizzying speed. When it stopped, my long red hair was wrapped around my face, threatening to smother me. I gave my head a shake, freeing my locks, allowing them to gracefully land across my shoulders, chest, and back. I tried not to smile at the sight of my glorious blue-green tail and iridescent scales. By the seas, it was good to be myself again.

Arion snapped his pincers in front of my face to draw my attention to him. "You understand the only reason I allowed you to undo my spell was so that you'd help the princess, right?" Before my smile had time to register in my expression, he pressed forward, his eyestalks locked firmly onto me. Whatever joy I felt at being returned to my normal state was quickly washed away. "Next time you disobey me, I'll wrap you so tightly in an enchanted state that you'll never be able to undo the spell. Do I make myself clear?"

I knew my teacher's threats were not something to take lightly, but through his actions, he only showed me how much he cared, even if his lessons were like a spiny urchin – good for me but difficult to swallow.

Draven came bursting back into my home, his eyes roaming up and down my body. "You are back to your mermaid form. No more excuses. Take me to my sister!"

"I will see you back at the palace," Arion said. "I've got a lot of work to do, lugging my library and alchemy equipment back to my residence."

"You're not going anywhere, except with us, old crab. If anything has happened to Luna, you'll both pay."

CHAPTER 13

DYLAN

I tried to roll over, sending a shock of pain up my leg. My brain was foggy, struggling to make sense of what was happening. My bed wasn't comfortable, not by any stretch of the imagination, but it was never this hard and lumpy.

My eyes snapped open. A pink-tinged horizon signaled Pele's imminent arrival. Directly above, the sky was still a vast expanse of deep blues and purples, adorned with a myriad of twinkling stars. My waterlogged body and the salty scent of the Gaelinora penetrated my senses, quickly reminding me of where I was, and how I got here. I raised myself up enough to get a look at my surroundings, noticing first the vast sea stretched out before me, its surface a perfect mirror, reflecting the last of Medeina's face before she disappeared for another twenty-eight days. Another burst of pain in my leg reminded me that my foot had been trapped between two rocks, a circumstance of my own making. I had used the rocks to prevent myself from being washed out to sea in the storm, but now I was paying the price for surviving the raging waves.

I carefully maneuvered myself, adjusting the angle of my leg until I could slip my foot out and escape the rocky prison. With gritted teeth, I slipped off my boot and gingerly prodded my ankle, searching for any signs of a fracture. The pain was excruciating, but, as best as I could tell, my leg was intact. However, the walk home was going to be even more agonizing than usual. In addition to the physical pain, the heartbreak of returning home empty-handed was unbearable. I knew that failing would cause my mother to suffer, and the weight of my shortfall weighed heavily on me.

I blew out a breath and closed my eyes. I pictured the look of dismay my mother would have, knowing that she'd be forced to beg on a street corner to earn enough to sustain our family. The thought of it made my stomach churn. I decided, at that moment, that I wouldn't go home, at least not immediately. I'd go to the docks first to see if I couldn't sell my services to a fishing boat before they left the harbor. Although, with the way my leg was aching, the trip would be slow going and Pele would likely be high in the sky by the time I arrived.

I hung my head low, my chin resting on my chest. "I'm sorry, mother. I'm sorry I failed you."

What made this situation even worse was knowing my mother wouldn't make me feel guilty for coming home empty-handed. She would embrace me and tell me everything was going to be okay. She'd make me a hot bowl of porridge and send me off to bed to get some sleep. She would stroke my head and tell me to rest.

I needed sleep, that much was true. But there was no way I was going to let my failure become her burden. As carefully as possible, I slipped my water-soaked boot back on. I braced myself for the stabbing pain in my leg, accepting it as punishment for my failure. I expected it would continue to remind me for a few more days, driving me to ensure my mother would never again be forced to suffer for my incompetence.

With a wince, I stood up, searching for my crutch, hoping beyond reason that the storm hadn't washed it out to sea. My heart leapt into my throat at the sight of a young woman entangled in a thick blanket of seaweed, almost from head to toe. Her skin was terribly pale. Concern gripped me, driving my own worries from my mind.

"Sweet Gaia, are you okay?" I stumbled toward her, desperately hoping she wasn't a drowning victim. I pulled some of the seaweed away, revealing her beautiful face and porcelain smooth skin. "Miss? Wake up. Please wake up. Oh Triton, please don't let her be dead."

My heart rejoiced when her eyes fluttered open, and she coughed up a large amount of seawater. I dropped down close beside her, ignoring the shooting pain in my leg, and continued removing her seaweed coverings. I stopped immediately when I realized that, beneath the smelly tangle of wet greenery, the girl was stark naked.

She smiled up at me from her place among the twisted strands of kelp and bits of flotsam and jetsam. Her bright green eyes beamed at me, filled with awe and innocence, like she was looking upon the world through the eyes of a child.

"Are you injured?" I asked again. I wanted to avert my eyes, but when her gaze locked onto mine, I couldn't bear to look away. "Miss? Are you well?"

She didn't say a word. Instead, she chose to silently stare up at me.

I tried to avert my gaze, but my eyes kept flicking down to her exposed body. I couldn't tell if she didn't know that she was nude, or if she didn't care.

"Here. Take my coat." As I spoke the words, I began peeling off my oilskin cloak. Even waterlogged like it was, it was still warm, and it would at least cover her up. As I pulled my arm out of a sleeve, the girl's head tilted to the side, like she was perplexed by my actions.

"You aren't wearing any clothes," I said, trying to sound sympathetic. "I'm giving you my cloak to cover yourself. I can't be seen walking a naked woman into town."

The girl stared down at herself and let out a startled gasp when she realized she was completely nude. Her skin, which had been so pale just moments earlier, turned a brilliant shade of pink as she quickly gathered the seaweed around herself, covering up as much of her exposed body as possible. A heavy wave of shame and guilt washed over me, for having not taken immediate action to cover the poor girl.

"I'll take you home," I said, holding out my coat to the shivering woman. "My mother might have something for you to wear. In the meantime, this should do."

Wariness crept into her gaze as she studied me, her eyes widening with fear. Growing up in a world where kindness was a rarity, I understood what it was like to be mistrustful of others. But I had to try. I draped the oilskin over her shoulders, hoping to offer some small comfort. All I could do was hope that she felt safe and warm beneath the folds of my cloak.

Her initial fears suddenly vanished, replaced with a look of curious fascination. She sniffed my cloak's heavily oiled leather, seemingly puzzled by its heady scent. After a moment, she pulled the cloak up under her chin and smiled brightly. A sense of relief washed over me, knowing that she was no longer afraid of me.

"Go ahead and put it on. I'll turn around while you do." I kept my voice calm and gentle, trying to maintain the bit of trust I had built up. While I waited, I stared out across the sea, wondering how my life had taken such a strange turn. After waiting for what I thought had been a sufficient length of time, I turned. The girl had put the cloak on backwards. She had her arms through the sleeves, but, undoubtedly, her backside was completely exposed to the elements and shameless prying eyes. My hand flew over my mouth, fighting back a chuckle, while my entire body involuntarily shook with silent amusement.

"You need to turn it around," I said, motioning to the cloak. "You've got it on wrong." She stared down at the coat for a moment before returning her perplexed gaze to me. I wasn't sure if she didn't understand my language, or if she had a head injury, or if she was *a few fish short of a school*. Without another idea on how to describe what she had done wrong, I realized it was easier to demonstrate, so I peeled off my soaking wet linen shirt, shivering as a gust of wind hit my damp skin.

"Here," I said. "Like this." I quickly, but methodically, showed her how to put my coat on, using my shirt as an example. As I did, I couldn't help but notice her intense gaze roaming up and down my exposed skin. When I finished, she nodded briskly and pulled off my cloak. I quickly turned around to hide my blushing face and give her some privacy. After a few moments, she made a small noise, hopefully inviting me to face her once again.

Relief flooded through me when I saw that the girl had finally managed to put on the cloak properly, with its belt firmly tied around her waist. I let out a deep breath I didn't even realize I was holding, grateful that she was now fully clothed. As I turned my attention to the rocks at her tiny bare feet, my mouth flopped open in awe. There, lying in all its glory, was the biggest mooneye I had ever caught. Its shimmering silver scales reflected the light of the rising sun, and I couldn't help but run my fingers over its slick, cold skin. My heart swelled with pride, knowing that I hadn't failed my family and better days were ahead of us.

⁓

"Mother," I called as I pushed open the rickety salt-stained door to my home. The morning light was leaking in through the cracks in the walls and roof, highlighting the still wet floor after last night's rains. I couldn't help but feel a pang of embarrassment over the shabby exterior and the equally dilapidated one-room interior, but this was my home, and I was proud of what we had, despite the abject poverty in which we lived.

I needed to find a way to repay the kindness the castaway had shown me. When she had seen how badly injured my leg was, she offered to let me lean on her while we walked. Even with her help, it was a struggle for us to make our way here. We must have been quite the sight – a man with a badly mangled leg, a barefooted girl in a full-length cloak supporting him, all the while managing to share the weight of a huge dead fish.

As we had slowly made our way into town, I had asked her many questions, perhaps too many, because she remained silent the entire time, except to tell me – if I understood her correctly – that her name was Luna. She had spent a good deal of the trip staring down at her bare feet and legs. On the rare occasion that she had looked up, she eagerly took in the sights, her eyes wide, smiling the entire time. The way her gaze darted from one thing to the next, I could only assume she was new to the area. Perhaps she had come from across the sea, from southern Berrathia or maybe even Lycos.

"Mother?" I called out again as I stood outside, looking into our one-room home. Relief washed over me as my mother stepped out from behind a small privacy screen, the remains of an old door that served as a divider between our beds and the rest of the house. She flashed a smile at the sight of me and the pretty young girl who was holding me up.

"Stars above," she called out, bustling over to greet us, smoothing out the wrinkles of her simple white linen dress. She gasped when she beheld the enormous fish in my hand, obviously relieved that I had finally seen some success from all my efforts.

"Mother, this is Luna. I found her washed up on shore." I dropped my voice down to a hushed whisper, which was pretty useless since Luna was standing right next to me. "She was completely naked, so I gave her my cloak."

"I see," my mother said, eyeing the young woman's hair. "Likely a shipwreck survivor in last night's storm. Why she might have had no clothing is a mystery to me, even if I have my suspicions."

"Can you give her something to wear? I need to take this fish to market right away. I lost my crutch in the storm, but Luna seems willing to help me get it there."

My mother looked the castaway up and down and clucked her tongue. "I might have something she can fit into. Go gather some firewood and leave her with me and I'll see what I can do." She waved her hands at me, shooing me toward the door. "Come with me, child. I'll do my best to help you out."

I loved my mother dearly. Even though we had very little, she was always quick to help others, even strangers who washed up on our shores. Luna seemed happy enough to accept my mother's help, giving me a warm smile as I left the two women alone.

CHAPTER 14

LUNA

Dylan's mother was much smaller and slimmer than her son, and significantly shorter than me. I very much liked her midnight-black hair. It was far more dramatic than my sea-foam green locks.

"Thank you for helping my son," she said to me. At least, that's what I understood. The human language wasn't so different from the language we spoke in the merkingdom. As much as I believed I was understanding, I was too nervous to speak aloud, fearful that I might look foolish if I spoke poorly.

"I'm afraid I don't have anything pretty for you to wear," she continued. She looked sad. It was as though not having something pretty to give away was hurting her. "None of my clothing is as beautiful as you. The only dress I have might be a bit small. I'm neither as tall nor as shapely as you, but even if it's snug, it's got to be better than wearing my son's ratty oilskin cloak." At her words, my skin turned a bright shade of pink. I tried to look away, to hide my embarrassment, but the overly kind woman had already noticed. "I thought maybe you were from someplace far away, and that you spoke a foreign language, but I think you understand me well enough." A tiny hint of a smile brightened her drawn out face.

I gave a tiny shrug and grinned at her. I didn't understand why, but the woman clutched her breast and smiled warmly.

"My name is Angelika," she said. It was so fitting. Dylan's mother had the heart of an angel. It shone like a beacon of hope, drawing me in, welcoming me. As poor as they were, she was so quick to offer what little they had. Truly, life on land was wondrous. Everyone was so kind and giving. I felt a little ashamed of myself. I grew up wanting for nothing and I never made this sort of effort to help those who were in need. Not that there was poverty in the merkingdom, but there were some who struggled more than others.

"Hello, Angelika. My name is Luna." The words came out strained, like they didn't fit properly in my mouth. I couldn't believe how lucky I was to have met such wonderfully kind-hearted humans. "It is I who should be thanking you."

Dylan's mother beamed at me and, leaning on a wooden stick, hobbled over to a small piece of furniture tucked away in the corner of the room. She rummaged through the bottom drawer for a moment before pulling out a small, pale-blue bundle of fabric. As she unfolded it, the cloth revealed itself to be a delicate piece of linen, intricately embroidered with a pattern of flowers and vines.

"I made it myself," she said with a shy grin, clearly proud of the fine garment. "It took me ages to find enough thread to embroider the pattern on it. I know it's not much."

"It's beautiful." The two words barely escaped my rapidly constricting throat. My eyes were stinging, but I didn't know why. "You are an angel."

Angelika lowered her eyes, perhaps trying to hide the tears welling up in them. With a loud sniff, she cleared her throat, straightened her back, and smoothed out the simple gray shirt she was wearing.

"Okay, if that's what you think, then you're definitely not from around here. Maybe you can come back with Dylan after you visit the marketplace." Excitement lit Angelika's eyes. "I would so enjoy talking to you. I don't hear much about what happens outside my little district, and I would so enjoy having a chance to chat with a woman for a change. Dylan doesn't have much to offer in the way of girl-talk. I would love to hear news of where you come from."

Oh, thank Gaia. This was exactly what I had hoped might happen. What better way to learn about the human world than by having a conversation with someone as kind and worldly as this wonderful person? I didn't understand the strange wistfulness in her voice when she asked about where I came from, but I nodded frantically at the suggestion, eager to spend time with this woman.

"I would be honored."

Slipping into the wonderful dress was easy enough, but the buttons proved to be a challenge. I was substantially curvier than Angelika, and this bit of fabric strained to contain me. The dress was also shorter than she expected, causing Dylan's mother to tut and express concern that it didn't cover my knees. I couldn't understand why she'd want me to hide them. I loved my legs. They were so much more interesting than my mermaid tail. Angelika said that if her legs were as beautiful as mine, she'd wear shorter dresses. It was only then that I noticed her left leg appeared twisted. She had been walking with the aid of a wooden stick. I hadn't really thought much of it until just now. Dylan, too, struggled to walk, perhaps for the same reason. She gave me a warm smile as she offered me the wooden device. "For Dylan. He won't make it to the market without it."

I accepted the stick with a nod of gratitude, impressed once again by Angelika's thoughtfulness. As I made my way towards the door, I paused and turned back to her. "Thank you again for everything. Your kindness means the world to me."

Angelika smiled, her eyes crinkling at the corners. "Of course, dear. Safe travels." I was just about to step out the door when the woman called out to me. "Here, for your head." She held out a plain piece of rough cloth. "Your hair color is... uncommon in these parts. You had best cover it up so as to not draw too much attention to yourself."

She had to help me with it, having never worn a *headscarf*. I hadn't even heard of the term before. After a short while, she had all my hair tucked away, safely hidden from view.

With a final wave, I stepped out into the bright sunlight and began to search for Dylan. The street was bustling with activity, and it took me several minutes to spot his familiar form carrying a bundle of wood.

⁘

As we approached the marketplace, Dylan's body seemed to stiffen. His head swiveled like he was on the lookout for sharks. "Be wary of the people here," he said, his words clipped. He was definitely nervous. "Just stay close to me, and everything will be okay."

I was puzzled. Humans were so kind, much nicer than merfolk. What did I have to be concerned about? What unseen dangers were there?

The wind shifted and a cacophony of unfamiliar scents greeted me, carried on the sea breeze. I didn't know what they were, but they were making me salivate. It made me wonder if this happened in the merkingdom as well, but I couldn't tell because, beneath the waves, my mouth was always full of water.

"After we sell this fish," Dylan said, breaking me from my reverie, "I'll treat us to some fresh bread. It's not something we buy very often, but I think it's a good day to indulge a bit."

I had no idea what fresh bread was, but the way his eyes lit up at the mention of it, it must be something truly extraordinary. As we wended our way through the swarming crowd of humans and the little structures filled with mouth-watering scents, I couldn't help but notice the amount of attention we were getting. People stopped their activities to gawk at us. It gave me an uneasy feeling, but I couldn't explain why. My heart raced as I realized this might be the danger that had Dylan so concerned.

"Don't worry," he said, inviting me to stand closer to him. "They've just never seen anyone so beautiful before, especially in my company."

"Your mate isn't beautiful?"

The young man's eyes lit up at my words. He was quite handsome when he was excited.

"So, you do talk. Other than telling me your name, you haven't said a word since we first met." I shrugged in response, my face heating. "I have no mate. I don't even have a girlfriend." Dylan's expression sagged, his chin dropping to his chest.

"Why? You're very... handsome. Is that the right word for a pretty human man?" I must have said it correctly, because Dylan's skin turned bright pink. His obvious shyness made me giggle. "I don't know your language very well, but I am learning it. It's not much different from Aquarian, the language we speak at home."

"Aquarian? I've never heard of such a language."

"It was the only one I knew until today. What is yours called?"

"There are three dominant tongues in this area: Berrathian, Arnnorian, and Common. Most people speak Common, especially in the marketplace. I've been speaking Common with you, but I can speak Arnnorian if you prefer. Where is Aquarian from?"

"It's the language of merfolk," I said, like it was the most normal thing in the world. "Everyone in the merkingdom speaks it." I didn't understand why, but Dylan's mouth flopped open like a goliath fish trying to swallow me whole. As quickly as his mouth had opened, he slammed it shut. His gaze darted about like he was trying to avoid a predator. I did the same thing, fearful that there were land-sharks or something as equally frightening.

"You can't say things like that. Not here, and especially not in the fish market. Mermaids are hated here and so is anyone who associates with them. We need to hurry and get this fish sold."

Fear gripped me as Dylan rushed us through the crowds. I also didn't understand why my kind might be hated. We rarely had interactions with humans. If my brother had his way, and he usually did, we'd avoid them even more than we stay clear of sharks and sea dragons. I wracked my brain, trying to find some reason for what Dylan had said. Then, like a slap from a tailfin, it dawned on me.

"Oh, Gaia. You're talking about sirens. They're winged mermaids who lure ships to the rocks and make them crash. We merfolk don't like them any better than humans do."

"Stop talking about mermaids and sirens. Please!" Dylan was frightened, terrified even. Had my speaking of my kind put us in danger?

We continued pushing our way through the people until we came to another area, one that smelled of death and decay. My stomach churned. I held my hand over my nose and mouth, desperately trying not to inhale whatever was making that horrid stench.

Gaia, save us all.

It wasn't until the crowds opened up that I saw the source of the stomach-churning aroma. My heart shattered at the sight of fish, crabs, and shrimp, piled in great heaps of death. People were using strange devices to carry them out by the dozens, while even more dead sea animals were arriving in gigantic boxes, overflowing the sides, pulled by enormous land creatures. All the while, people clambered over each other, offering tiny pieces of copper, silver, and gold, in return for the lifeless carcasses. Did they have no sense of the damage they were causing to my home? Many of these animals they were harvesting were critical to the sea's balance. Some were cleaners, while others were the only food source for some of the larger species. Destroying them would force the large predators to change their habits and...

"Hey, boy. Where'd you get that fish from?"

I turned to see an unsavory-looking man with rotten teeth, bad breath, and a patch of cloth covering one of his eyes. The other visible eye was red and bloodshot. Perhaps he, too, had been crying over the death of so many of my father's creatures.

"Boy. Yes, you. I asked you a question and I want an answer."

"From the Gaelinora," Dylan replied. He didn't seem to want to talk to the man. "Stay close to me," he whispered, his breath warm on the shell of my ear. I could feel the wave of fear emanating from him. Even though I had only known this human for a short while, I had come to trust him. If he was afraid, there was likely a good cause.

From behind us, the angry voice grew louder and with each passing moment, more voices were joining in.

"How much will you give me for this fish?" Dylan said to an extremely obese, sweaty man standing amid piles of dead sea animals. "I'll bet this is the biggest mooneye you've ever seen."

I didn't catch the full conversation between Dylan and the fat man because I was too busy watching the growing school of angry humans surrounding us.

"I asked you a question, boy." It was the man with the patch of cloth over his eye. He had a weapon in his hand, something that looked like it was made for cutting.

"How much will you give me?" Dylan said. As he continued haggling with the fat man, more people continued to gather around us.

"Leave him alone," I yelled, putting myself between Dylan and the angry crowd. "He caught this fish fairly; not like you net-wielding maniacs who strip my home of every living creature beneath the waves."

A nasty human male reached out and snatched the cloth covering my head. As my hair fell down over my shoulders, the man's eyes widened. "I knew it. I knew she was a mermaid! Get her!"

CHAPTER 15

CALYPSO

It was invigorating to be back in my mermaid scales, swimming through cool morning currents, reveling in the vastness of the sea's cerulean blue water. If only I didn't have to deal with the icy waves that were flowing off Draven. The sour-faced merman seemed determined to leach out every drop of joy within me, making me think there was more to his dour mood than just me sending his little sister off to help a human.

"You're stalling," he growled. "Pele has already risen and we still haven't found my sister."

It's true, I was stalling. Despite my concern for her safety, I had been taking us off course, trying to give Luna as much time as possible to help my human before Medeina left the night sky. Hopefully, by now, she had helped him hook up several mooneyes, giving the man what he needed until the moon goddess was once again in full view. I cast a hateful glare at the prince and surged forward.

We broke the surface a safe distance from shore. We'd be close enough to observe the human fishing if he was still there, but not so near that he'd easily be able to see us.

"There's no one here," Draven growled. The merman's long black hair was plastered across his face, clinging to his cheeks and neck. It gave him a rugged, almost feral appearance. "What games are you playing, Calypso? If you think banishment was harsh, wait until you find out what I'll do if I discover you've been tugging my tail."

"No. I swear. This is where I usually find him. Perhaps he's already left?"

"Then where's Luna? Why didn't she return?" In a heartbeat, the prince was in my face. "If she's gone on land. If your insane mission to help a human has—"

"Yes, yes. A fate worse than banishment." I pushed myself away and swam closer to shore. From behind, I could hear Draven yelling at me, but the words were washed away by the wind and the waves. When I neared the beach, the spot where my human preferred to hunt for fish, I swam harder, giving myself enough speed to fully leave the water.

By the time I was on the beach, I had already changed my scaled tail into human legs. All of my kind could control their transformation between merfolk and human form, although, if we were out of the water for too long, our tail would vanish and legs would appear, whether we wanted them to or not.

I couldn't help but smile as the waterlogged sand beneath my feet came squishing up between my toes. The scent of salty air tickled my nose, inviting me to breathe more deeply. I found it strange how the water smelled so different, and how Pele warmed my skin in a way that it never did below the sea's surface.

The roar of a great wave drew my attention. I turned just in time to see Draven being carried by a wall of water and deposited, with an annoying level of regal elegance, onto the beach. As he gracefully emerged from the water, I couldn't help but notice the way his bare feet landed lightly on the sand. For a brief moment, he stood there dripping, his well-muscled form glistening in the sunlight. The familiar flutter rose in my chest, the one I experienced back when we were together – before he betrayed me. As I felt that pull towards him, I berated myself, furious for letting his beauty cloud me to the self-serving, ego-maniacal man he had proven himself to be.

His royal scepter glowed for a moment, wreathing him in a pale red aura. When the spectral light dimmed, Draven was wearing well-fitted clothing that shimmered lightly in the morning sun. He had a pair of tight-fitting leather breeches and a white, puffy, long-sleeved shirt that seemed to cling to his chest muscles while still leaving him plenty of room to move.

I was thankful for having read some of Arion's hidden collection of books. One of them discussed human customs and their clothing in great detail, including an array of colorful images depicting men and women spread out across a polished stone floor, engaged in some sort of stylized ritual known as *dancing*.

His eyes lingered on me longer than I had expected, his gaze suddenly making me feel uncomfortable.

"What?" I asked. "You're staring like you've never seen me before."

"I haven't," he said, turning away. "Not as a human. Cover yourself. You can't be among them without clothes."

I stared down at my naked body, completely devoid of scales or any other covering. Thinking back to the books I had seen, and the wonderful clothing the human women were wearing, I muttered a quick spell and conjured a snug fitting outfit that hugged my hips but left my legs unencumbered. It wasn't exactly the same as the pretty images, but it made me feel comfortable, like I still had my mermaid tail.

Again, Draven raked his gaze over my body. This time, his expression was different; an angry scowl drew his mouth downward at the corners.

"What are you doing? Do you have any idea how dangerous this area is? The humans here hunt merfolk."

The unexpected harshness in his words made my pulse race. I wanted to say something back, but my throat had completely locked up. His scowl deepened, and he shook his head at me.

"Why would you choose to conjure an evening gown? Are you expecting us to attend a formal gathering, or do you literally want to look like a fish out of water?"

"An evening gown? What's that?" I looked down at my shimmering clothes, marveling at how even the smallest of movements caught the morning sun, reflecting it into a dazzling display of colors. The merman shook his head yet again, seemingly unable to look me squarely in the eyes.

"What you're wearing is called a *dress*. And this particular style is suited to parties held by wealthy humans. Change your clothes into something more practical, like what I'm wearing. Most of the people who live near here are fishermen and laborers. Outside of the town's lord and a few merchants, nobody would be clothed in such finery."

My eyes narrowed as I took a few shaky steps towards him. "You seem to know an awful lot about humans and this town. If I was a gambling mermaid, I might bet heavily on you having spent a good deal of time on land – even though you preach that the rest of us must stay away from it." My stomach twisted when he cocked an eyebrow and raised his chin to me. His condescending air of superiority made my blood boil. It was like I didn't know this merman at all anymore. Ever since he was given the title, Guardian of the Realm, and his father's infernal scepter, he was a complete stranger to me. But I had

had quite enough of him and I wasn't going to let him push me around. "Go ahead, look down your nose at me all you want, but I've just proven that you're a charlatan."

"I am no charlatan. I am your prince, and in my position, I must walk among the humans to learn their ways and assess their threats to our domain. If you had ever paid attention when I told you of my dealings with them, you'd know this. But it seems this is all beyond your comprehension. You cannot fathom the depths of my role, and how I must degrade myself, carrying the weight of keeping our kingdom safe and thriving. You must trust me to do what's necessary, even if it means going against the rules I set out for the rest of the kingdom. My actions are for the betterment and safety of all, and my decisions are above reproach."

I rolled my eyes at the man. "Oh, mighty prince, thank you for lowering yourself to protect us." I crossed my arms over my chest. "Do you really believe you're the only one capable of walking among the humans to discover their intentions towards us and the sea? Are you really that arrogant?"

"Why do you choose to see my actions as arrogance? Can you truly say that you understand the dangers that lurk beyond our borders? I doubt you do, otherwise you'd be grateful for the risks I take to keep everyone safe."

I sucked a breath through clenched teeth. Had he just shown me a crack in his self-righteous façade? Was he truly acting selflessly, and I was choosing to see otherwise?

"Now, change into something less idiotic and let's go search for Luna. I swear to the seas, if any harm has befallen her because of your actions..."

Nope. He's still a royal jerk.

Nevertheless, I had to assume that his comments about my *dress* were correct and, with a simple spell, I changed my clothing into a bright-red shirt and trousers that nicely matched my hair. I added a cloak that was similar in style to the one I had seen my human wearing while he was hunting fish.

"How is it that you were able to clothe yourself the way you did?" I asked, shifting my weight to one leg and placing a hand on my hip. "Considering you banished me from the kingdom for being a witch, I find it interesting that you can so easily cast such magic."

That angry scowl that had twisted him up appeared once again. This time, it was accompanied by a full dose of loathing. "My scepter grants me great powers. And, for the record, you weren't banished for casting spells. It was for practicing blood magic. You were tried and found guilty. Be glad I didn't have you executed like the queen and her royal advisor wanted."

"You're an imbecile," I shouted, my hands clenched in tight fists at my sides. "We were together for over four years. You were prepared to propose to me that night. How could you possibly believe the lies Beithir and your mother told about Arion and me? How? In all the time we were together, did you ever witness me doing anything that might make you believe the so-called witnesses that were brought up to testify against me?"

Draven's expression softened for a moment before his scepter glowed red. Muscles rippled across his jaw as he spoke through clenched teeth. "You cannot use your magic to dissuade me from the truth, not like you did all the time we were together. I know who you are and what you are capable of. When we find my sister, you will return to your lair. I will pass a law that will ensure you never practice your witchcraft on my citizens ever again."

"Have your mother and Beithir poisoned your mind so completely that you actually believe what's coming out of your mouth?"

The merman's nasty expression remained, like it was carved into his face with a hammer and chisel.

"As Guardian of the Realm, I am entrusted with my father's royal scepter. Your paltry spells are feeble in comparison to the magic I wield. But I will say that I was surprised by how easily you conjured up your clothing. I understand that you're a witch, but it seems beyond your skills." He turned and gazed over the sea, his head swiveling as he searched the coastline. "Is Arion here performing this enchantment on your behalf?"

I laughed. Well, scoffed might have been a better description of my reaction. Truth was, the spell came easier than I had expected and I found myself scanning the shoreline for my teacher. On Draven's orders, my mentor had followed us, but I had been so happy to be back in my mermaid form that I never bothered to see if he had managed to stay close behind.

I couldn't let Draven have the upper hand, so I went on the offensive. "For someone who purports to know so much, you have very little understanding of our species' inherent magical abilities. Perhaps you're a poor choice to speak to the humans on our behalf, considering how much you have to learn about your own kind."

A definite pink hue colored Draven's cheeks. The minor victory, such as it was, gave me far more satisfaction than it should have. It made me wonder if I didn't have a petty streak. I tried to suppress the grin I knew was pulling at the corners of my mouth.

"Oh, mighty prince, which way to the dangerous people? Let's go find your little sister."

"Conjure yourself some footwear." Draven shook his head and started walking away. After a quick look, I saw he was wearing boots that covered his feet, stopping just below the knee. I muttered a spell under my breath and gazed down at my own *footwear*. Like Draven's, they covered the lower half of my legs. I didn't like how they muted my connection to the sea, but if it's what I needed to blend in, so be it.

CHAPTER 16

DYLAN

With each passing moment, the attention we were getting made me increasingly uncomfortable. My instincts told me we were in a dangerous situation. People were gathering nearer, staring at Luna, pointing at her. I needed to sell my mooneye and get her away from here as quickly as possible.

"How much will you give me for this?" I bellowed at the vendor, holding up my fish by its gill plate, showing that it was easily four feet long. "I'll bet this is the biggest mooneye you've ever seen." The fat vendor's eyes widened at the sight. He rubbed his double chin thoughtfully as he considered how little he could offer me and still make the sale. The man blanched as his gaze drifted past me, over my shoulder.

"I asked you a question, boy."

My guts twisted at the words. As best as I could, I ignored the sailor, a scoundrel I recognized to be Lachlan, the first mate of one of the deep-water trawlers. I had worked on his boat once, and he had been nothing but cruel and condescending during the entire voyage. By the time we returned to shore, I had been convinced that the only reason he had hired me was to have a private punching bag to keep him amused while his crew fished the Gaelinora.

"How much will you give me?" I repeated, my voice growing more urgent as I shook the massive mooneye, desperate to regain the vendor's attention. As the crowd closed in around us, the first mate's gaze burned into my back. I couldn't let him catch us here, not after what had happened on his trawler. The fat vendor hesitated, his neck-rolls jiggling wildly as he weighed the risk of angering the sailor against the potential profit. He was afraid, and he had good reason to be. The first mate and his captain were notorious for their cruelty, and anyone who crossed them was likely to end up on the receiving end of a beating, or much worse.

Luna threw herself in harm's way, waving her arms, drawing even more attention to herself. "Leave him alone! He caught this fish fairly; not like you net-wielding maniacs who strip my home of every living creature beneath the waves."

Oh Gaia, what has she done?

I threw my mooneye onto the vendor's table. "Sell the fish for what you can. I'll split the earnings with you. You'll never see a better deal than that."

I didn't wait for a response and quickly drew Luna away from the growing crowd. Before I could get her clear, a sailor snatched her headscarf from her head.

"I knew it!" The foul man motioned with his heavy short sword to the gang of sailors who had gathered around him, signaling them to move forward. "I knew she was a mermaid! Get her!"

"Get away! Back off, all of you!" I thrust my crutch at the nearest sailor, catching him neatly in the belly. The brigand let out a whoosh of air while he grasped weakly at the empty space in front of him. In my youth, I often used my crutch like a make-believe sword, pretending to be a swashbuckling sailor, fighting off evil pirates, saving the princess, and winning the day. I'd have never imagined myself using my feeble skills in real life.

A second sailor, a squat man with large meaty hands, wrapped his fingers around Luna's wrist and pulled her away from me. With all the strength I could muster, I swung my crutch like it was a great-ax, trying to break the man's hold on the woman. Even though my strike had connected cleanly with his wrist, it didn't even slow him down. My heart was literally thrumming in my throat as the sailors continued to swarm around us, their faces twisted into grotesque masks of anger and fear. Before I pulled my make-shift weapon back for a second attempt, a fist caught me squarely in the face. The impact was so sudden and so jarring that, for a moment, everything went black.

When I opened my eyes, I was lying amidst a pile of tiny flopping fish, their pungent scent filling my nostrils, jerking me back to reality.

"Let her go," I yelled again while trying to dig myself out of the surrounding sea of dead fish. "I swear to Gaia, let her go or I'll..."

"Or you'll do what, boy?" the first mate said, hovering over me, his yellow, rotted teeth visible through his mangled smile. "You'll do nothing, that's what. You think you've got it hard now? Just wait until Cap'n Roberts has a chat with Lord Vayne about you bringing another mermaid to our marketplace. How do you think that'll go for you?"

Another mermaid? What did that even mean?

Before I had a chance at a retort, his boot crashed into the side of my head, driving me beneath the piles of dead fish.

"You heard me, boy. Stay out of this and I'll even let ol' Fester, here, give you a fair price for your mooneye. Won't you, Fester?"

I could neither see nor hear the fish vendor's response. Between being kicked in the head and the piles of dead fish covering me, I couldn't really make out much of what was happening. Somewhere in the distance, frightened, angry screams drew my mind from the depths. Driven by my fury, and the thought that I had led the poor woman to her doom, I pushed past the pain and dug my way out of the heap of sardines that covered me. In the briefest of moments, I saw Luna hanging over the shoulder of a sailor while she ineffectually beat at his back with her fists. A moment later, a wave of bodies swallowed up the entire lot of them.

I tried to stand, to extricate myself from the mass of sea creatures, but all I ended up doing was flopping about like a fish out of water. My crutch was nowhere in sight. It was impossible to see much at all amid the forest of legs surrounding me. It took me several moments to even realize that a crowd had gathered, and from the sounds of it, they wanted to lynch me for having brought a mermaid into their marketplace. Several times I tried to stand, and with each attempt, I was knocked back to the ground.

"I had no idea she was a mermaid! She fooled me. She showed me kindness. How was I to know?" The words blurted from my mouth, instantly filling me with shame for having used the woman who saved me as a scapegoat for my situation. My words did little to appease the mob, but eventually they grew weary of their taunts and insults and returned to their own business.

"I'll take your fish as compensation for the damage you caused to my stall," the vendor said, a hate-filled sneer raking across his face. "Be lucky I don't ask for more."

"I didn't cause this," I said, finally getting myself upright. Fish scales clung to my cloak and skin, adding to the disgusting situation. "And that one mooneye is worth more than all your smelly fish combined. We both know it."

"Take your complaints to Lord Vayne. I'm sure he'll side with you and force me to pay the two hundred gold pieces this fish is worth." The fat thief laughed at me while he held up my fish, offering it as a one-of-a-kind oddity of nature, caught by a mermaid. If I hadn't been desperate to help Luna, I'd have dealt with the man and given him a sound thrashing.

Who was I kidding? Had I tried to take my fish back, I'd have been the one on the receiving end of a beating. I watched helplessly as someone kicked my crutch, sending it skittering across the ground. With my head hung low, I hobbled through the crowd towards my staff, finally retrieving it after being knocked down several times.

With it tucked up under my arm, I pushed my way through the throng, working my way towards the docks, to where the first mate had surely taken Luna.

As I forced myself into a limping run, my bad leg screamed in protest, making it impossible to put any weight on it without buckling. But in this critical moment, pain was irrelevant. I owed my life to the young woman, and I was determined to repay that debt, no matter the cost. The agonizing jolt that came with every step I took was a reminder of my mortality, and of the fact that I was living on borrowed time. It drove me forward. It filled me with resolve and blinded me to the couple who were crossing my path as I slammed into a young woman with long, flowing red hair, sending us both to the ground in a tangled mass of arms and legs.

CHAPTER 17

CALYPSO

From my prone position, I stared up at the human male who had just knocked me over. Despite the discomfort in my side where he had elbowed me, and the pain in my backside from falling on it, the mortified contrition on the young man's face told me the collision was purely accidental. The way Draven grabbed him by the front of his shirt and hoisted him off his feet suggested he thought differently.

"Watch where you're going," he growled, pushing him back, knocking him to the ground. A wooden stick tumbled from the man's hand as he fell flat onto his back. It was at that moment that I recognized this person. He was my human, the one I had been helping to catch fish, the one I had sent Luna to help. I rarely prayed to Gaia or the Sea God, but in this moment, I'd have kissed their feet if they were responsible for this stroke of good fortune.

"Leave him alone," I shouted up at Draven. "It was an accident. He might be able to help us."

"The man's nothing more than a pauper. How could he possibly help?"

I pushed myself up to my feet, still unsteady on my new legs. I snatched up the young man's crutch and offered him a helping hand.

He cringed away from my offering, his dark brown hair splayed haphazardly across his face, barely hiding his wide, blue eyes.

"I'm sorry for my friend," I said, thrusting my hand forward. I gave a quick glance at the sea prince before turning back to the prone man, offering him a crooked smile. "He means well, but he lacks manners. Please, let me help you up."

The man hesitated, eyeing my outstretched hand like it was a spiny red urchin. "No, I'm good staying where I am. The way my day is going, I'll likely just get knocked down again, anyway."

I shot another glare at Draven, who appeared ready to step over him like he was a piece of garbage.

"Please," I said again, pushing my hand even closer. "We're looking for someone, and I'm hoping you can help." He just stared at my offering, his eyebrow twitching. "Please."

The man's expression shifted slightly. Finally, he took a firm grip on my hand, his skin warm and rough against mine. With a tug, I helped him to his feet and offered his crutch back to him. "My friend is missing and I'm really hoping you might tell us where she is."

The young man's brow furrowed at my comment. He shot Draven a wary eye. "I'm sorry, I can't help you."

"You didn't even ask who we were looking for," Draven said, pressing his much larger, significantly more heavily muscled body forward. His sheer size was enough to make most people cringe in fear, but this young man held his ground, defiantly thrusting his chin up at him.

"I don't need to ask, because I don't know any women. Now, be on your way. I've got pressing business to attend to."

"And what sort of business does one, such as yourself, need to get to?" Draven pressed closer. He was easily a head taller than my human and he was taking too much pleasure in lording himself over the young man. "I'm guessing you don't have two coppers to rub together, so I doubt you have anything of any importance to get to. You will either answer our questions, or you'll be picking yourself up off the ground a second time."

"Draven," I yelled, attempting to push him aside, but it was like trying to move a mountain. "Leave him be. If he's going to help us, it won't be because you're intimidating him."

The young man glared up at Draven. "Intimidate me all you like, oaf. I'm not helping you. Not now. Not ever."

"Draven! Back off!" I laced my words with what little magic I could muster this far from the sea, hoping to calm him down. He turned his smoldering eyes on me, and I immediately knew I had gone too far. Not that I cared. My human was our best chance of finding Luna, and Draven was spoiling everything.

"Please," I said to my human, ignoring the raging storm in the sea prince's eyes. "We're desperate, and I believe you have seen my friend. She'd be about the same height as me, sea-foam green hair, and incredible blue eyes. If you've seen them, then you understand exactly what I mean."

His body stiffened at my description of Luna, which absolutely told me he knew exactly who I was talking about, but he refused to acknowledge having met her. It was at that moment that I realized he was a good person, willing to go to any length to protect my friend. I needed to give him more information, more proof that we were in league together and that we were there to help. I dropped my voice low and placed my mouth near his ear.

"She helped you last night, just like I've been helping you when Medeina's full face has been in the night sky. We have been helping to bring mooneyes near, guiding them to your thin strips of bait." I pulled back to gauge his reaction, and sure enough, his eyes widened.

The young man's eyes flicked between me and Draven, his expression shifting from defiance to confusion.

"I've seen you before." His voice was filled with awe and wonder. "Your red hair. That's what I saw, out in the waves. I believed it to be an illusion, a trick of the pale moon's light, or fatigue fooling my eyes." I nodded slightly and lowered my gaze.

"You prayed to Triton and Medeina and I answered."

Draven groaned loudly at my words, shaking his head. I completely ignored his annoyance with me and pressed on. "My name is Calypso. The other *person* who helped you; her name is Luna. She is my best friend, and this oversized leviathan's younger sister. It's imperative we find her. She has never... visited this village before." I raised my eyebrows, hoping the man would catch my meaning without me having to speak specifics. He swallowed hard, his eyes darting around, fearful. He definitely understood.

"My name is Dylan. They took her," he whispered. There was a mixture of terror and profound sadness in his voice. "I tried to stop them."

Before I could speak a single word, Draven's hand flashed forward, grabbed the man by his shirt – again – and picked him up off the ground. "Who took her? Where did they go? If you value your life, pauper, you'll tell me everything and you won't leave out a single detail."

Dylan stared intently into Draven's eyes, his look fierce and defiant. Slowly, he glanced down at the prince's meaty fist, the one holding him aloft. When he raised his chin, he cocked an eyebrow. To my surprise, Draven slowly lowered the man, giving him a curt nod as he did.

"The first mate of the *Abyssal* took her. Him and a gang of his deckhands. No more than ten minutes ago, I think. I might have been unconscious for a while. I swear, I tried to protect her, but there were too many of them.”

Draven’s expression darkened at the man’s words. “One of Lord Vayne’s ships. Are you sure?” When the man nodded, the sea prince scrubbed his hand across his forehead and blew out a breath. “Not good. Not good at all.”

“What’s not good?” I asked. Draven never looked worried. He was always confident to the point of arrogance, and he never showed a crack in that façade. “Tell me what’s going on?”

“There will be no reasoning with him. He’s obsessed with killing mermaids. If he had his way, he’d kill every one of us.” The big man ran his fingers through his long hair. “One of his ships was lured onto a shoal by sirens. When it ran aground, none survived. His wife had been traveling on the ship that day. She was coming back from Ravenlord, in southern Berrathia.”

My stomach churned at the news. Even if Lord Vayne’s anger towards mermaids was misplaced, I understood it. Had someone murdered Luna, I’d never give up looking for the person responsible. I wouldn’t stop until my anger was fully sated.

“Surely he understands that mermaids and sirens are different, right?” I dropped my voice low, but I couldn’t keep the panic from my words. “We would never do something like that.”

“The man’s hatred is beyond rational thought. He cannot be reasoned with, not about this.”

“What do we do?” Dylan asked, his jaw set tight. “How do we get her back?”

“There is no *we*,” Draven growled. “You’re the one who got her tangled in this net. Go home.”

"I'm helping," Dylan said, clutching his crutch up under his armpit. "With or without you. Unless you know exactly where they took Luna, you're going to need all the help you can get."

"You can barely walk. How do you think you'll be anything but a burden here? Go home."

"He wants to help," I said. "And he's going to try whether you like it or not. We're better off with him than without him." Dylan's chest puffed out at my words.

"Are you familiar with the docks?" Draven asked. He looked ready to bite off Dylan's head. "Can you find the *Abyssal*?" The young man simply nodded to his questions, jutting his chin out while he did. "Take Calypso there. Make sure the ship doesn't leave the harbor. Wait for me to get back."

"Where are you going?" I asked. "How long will you be?"

"I'm going to Lord Vayne's manor. If Luna's there, I'll free her. If she's not... I'll meet you at the docks. Go! Now!"

CHAPTER 18

DYLAN

My eyes were drawn to Calypso like a drowning man seeking a life preserver. She walked with a fluid grace that made my heart skip a beat, but at the same time, her presence felt heavy on my chest, as if the air had been sucked out of my lungs. We weaved through the crowded marketplace towards the docks, where I both hoped and feared Luna would be. Calypso's questions tumbled out one after the other, like waves crashing on the shore. She wanted to know everything about life on land - our joys, our struggles, and how we managed to keep going despite it all. Her surprise was palpable when I told her about the simple pleasures that filled my days - like watching the sunrise or sharing a humble meal with my mother.

For a moment, the weight on my chest lifted, and I found myself smiling at the memory.

A pang of disappointment cut through me each time Calypso clammed up when I asked her about her life below the waves. It was as if she feared revealing too much, afraid that I somehow wouldn't understand. I don't know what changed, but as we walked along the beach, our feet sinking into the soft, waterlogged sands, her eyes lit up and she began to talk about the sea in a way that I could never have imagined.

With wide eyes, she made swimming motions with her arms while she spoke of how the water was always in motion. She described in vivid detail the cool currents that flowed around her skin, invigorating her as she swam through the vast open waters, filling her with the ultimate experience of freedom.

A somber, profound expression crossed her face as she described the deep blues and dark greens that filled the depths. I laughed at how her expression suddenly changed, her eyes wide and sparkling like the sun glistening off the water. She couldn't contain her excitement as she spoke of the riot of colors in the shallows and the vibrant reds, oranges, and yellows of the coral reefs.

With perfect clarity, I envisioned the enormous schools of tiny fish she described, traveling together in a shimmering, silver mass that caught the sunlight and reflected it in a thousand different directions. She swayed as if caught in the memory of their movements, mesmerized by the breathtaking sight.

She spoke of the silent predators that lurked in the shadows with their razor-sharp teeth and lightning-fast strikes. But even as she spoke of the danger, I could hear the awe in her voice, her sheer love of the oceans. To her, these creatures were not evil or cruel - they were simply living their lives as best they could, just as she was. In that moment, I had glimpsed a world that was both beautiful and terrifying, and I knew that the sea would never be the same for me again.

As we limped into the harbor, sharp, shooting pains radiated from my bad leg with every step. I had been so enthralled in my conversation with Calypso that I had hardly even noticed, but now that our destination was in sight, my reality came crashing back with a vengeance. My breaths became shallower as I tried to fight back the tears that threatened to spill over. The weight of my body on my twisted leg was becoming an unbearable burden. I needed to rest, to give myself a chance to recover, but Luna's life was likely in mortal peril, and that was infinitely worse than what my physical challenges forced me to endure.

"Are you injured?" Calypso asked, seeming to notice my limp for the first time. "Do you need to rest?"

"No. I'm fine. My leg gets sore if I walk for too long. This wet sand seems to make it worse." I blew out a breath, trying to will my pain away. I didn't want my challenges to give her a reason to leave me behind. "I'll be okay. Let's keep going." I really wish I could have said that without wincing.

"I cannot heal your affliction," Calypso said, taking a knee beside me. "But I might be able to ease your discomfort some." A shiver ran up my back when she pulled my cloak back, exposing my twisted leg. She looked up at me expectantly, waiting for me to give her the okay. With a shrug, I nodded lightly.

She slowly wrapped her long, slender fingers around my calf and quietly sang a haunting melody. It was as though the power of the sea was welling up from the wet sands, enveloping me, carrying my pain away like a receding tide. When she stopped, sweat glistened on Calypso's face, her long red hair plastered against it.

"Are you okay? You look..." I struggled to put into words the exhaustion etched into her face, her eyes drooping, and her shoulders slumped. Beads of sweat glistened on her forehead and cheeks as she took a deep breath and closed her eyes, seemingly lost in thought. For a moment, the only sound was the gentle hum of the ocean waves and the distant cry of seagulls, as if even the world around us knew to give her a moment of peace after the incredible effort she had put into helping me.

"Drawing upon the power of the sea was more difficult than I expected," she said, her voice barely above a whisper. She swayed slightly, and I reached out to steady her. Her eyes flickered open, and I saw a flash of gratitude before they closed again. "My connection to it is limited here on the shore," she continued, her words punctuated by ragged breaths. "I expect that it was the seawater in the sand that allowed me to pass my strength on to you. Had we been inland, I likely would have been powerless to help." She paused, and I could see the effort it took for her to keep talking. The slightest hint of a smile pulled at the corner of her mouth. "Does your leg feel better?"

I put some weight on it, pressing it into the wet sand. It still ached, but it was dull and manageable now. "Yes," I said, testing it further by jouncing on it. "That was amazing. Thank you."

"Good, let's get moving then." Calypso slowly stood and brushed the sand from her knee. She was still a bit wobbly, but she already seemed to be recovering from the exertion. "Where is the Abyssal? We should hurry in case they try to leave port with Luna."

"It's over there," I said, pointing to the far side of the harbor. "It's the only place where the water is deep enough for a ship that size to dock." I limped forward, tucking my crutch under my armpit. Even though my leg wasn't hurting nearly as much, I still needed the support the crutch offered.

Calypso slid in next to me, slipping her head under my arm. The scent of salty sea foam wafted up from her hair, drawing me closer. Her fragrance was that of the sea, personified. "Let me help. Take the pressure off your leg and lean against me. I don't think I have it in me to help with your pain again. We'll get there faster if you don't need to rely so heavily on your crutch."

I hesitated. This was the second time today a mermaid was offering to bear my weight because of my infirmity. I hated being a burden on anyone, but I knew she was right. I gave her a quick thank you and let her assist me across the harbor.

As we continued on our way to the ship, people gawked at us. Some pointed and sniggered. I'm sure many more kept their thoughts to themselves. At this point, I didn't care. My mission was critical, and if I needed help to make it happen, so be it.

Truth is, I was enjoying the warmth of having Calypso so near. Even with my oilskin cloak on, I had a chill that didn't seem to want to leave me. Since it was a pleasantly warm morning with clear skies and bright sunshine, I could only assume it was my nerves getting the better of me. Somehow, this woman wasn't just bearing my weight, she was also sharing her internal strength with me, bolstering my resolve, giving me the courage I'd need to follow through with rescuing Luna.

As we neared the vessel, Calypso hissed and drew me to the side, pulling me away from a small group of sailors dragging fishing nets behind them. "What's wrong?" I asked. "They're just fishermen."

"They're not fishermen. That net they're dragging behind them, it's laced with iron."

"That helps it go deeper," I said, confused by Calypso's concern. Weighted nets were normal. "It's the only way to catch fish in deep water."

"They're not weighted. The iron strands woven amid the ropes are designed to catch and hold mermaids." Calypso's voice was now a harsh whisper. "We're susceptible to iron. If mermaids were caught in such a net, we'd never be able to free ourselves. Being near iron saps us of our strength and our magic. Touching it can be fatal. We can't even cross over it unless there is enough water between us and the metal."

"Okay, I think I get it." I nodded my head, but in truth, it didn't make any sense to me.

"No. You don't get it." Calypso's eyes were blazing. "I think they're going to use Luna as bait to catch more mermaids."

CHAPTER 19

CALYPSO

I tried to hustle Dylan along, hoping to get close enough to the net-wielding sailors so as to listen in on their conversation. Fortunately, the noise of the iron trap dragging along the sand masked our footfalls. Unfortunately, it also made it impossible to understand what they were saying until we were only a few feet behind them.

"This isn't what we signed up for," the taller of the two men said. He was thin and swarthy, with greasy brown hair that hung down well past his shoulders. "We're fishermen, not monster hunters."

"We do whatever da cap'n says we do," the other shorter, rounder sailor replied. "We've made more gold workin' wid dat guy in da last moon than we did all of last season."

"Yes, but that was catching fish, not mermaids." Though his voice was barely more than a whisper, I caught every word.

"What difference do it make to us?" the rotund man said with a shrug. "Mermaids is just fish wid pretty voices. Da gold in our pockets jingles just as good no matter what we catch."

"Because the sea god won't try to scuttle our ship for catching fish, but if he or Prince Draven found out what we're doing, they would drive us up on a reef and the mermaids would skin us alive."

"Bah. Triton ain't been seen in many years and dat Prince Draven's in for a big surprise da next time him visits Lord Vayne. Big surprise. Ya. Dat hoity-toity merman gonna git his. Da lord's house is going to be as good as da cage we made for dat mermaid we gots now."

My heart raced at the news. Not only had they confirmed they had Luna, they also said that Draven was walking into a trap. I so desperately wanted to say I told you so to Dylan, but what good would that have done?

"Hush!" the tall man said, his head swiveling about. When he caught sight of Dylan and me directly behind him, he glared at his cohort and the pair of them sped up, quickly putting extra distance between us.

"I told you, didn't I?" I couldn't help myself. The words fell from my mouth before I could stop them. I couldn't blame Dylan for not understanding the danger those nets posed to my kind. It was exactly the same net that had trapped a school of merchildren on a field trip. If Arion hadn't been present, had he not been able to cut through the iron-laced mesh with his pincers, the loss of life would have been catastrophic.

Barnacles and bubbles! Why didn't I think of Arion sooner?

Draven and I had left him at the beach, figuring it was safer for him to stay behind while we searched the town for Luna. A giant crab wandering through the humans would simply have drawn too much attention to us. "Come with me." I said, as I led Dylan closer to the water. "I'm going to call for some help."

The young man's body tensed as I started walking him towards the water. I wasn't sure if it was the sea that worried him, or the fact I was going to call for help. It was clear to me that he preferred to be self-sufficient, which I totally respected, but sometimes it took an extra set of claws to get the job done. But the way his eyes remained fixated on the two sailors, I decided it was neither. He was upset that we weren't following the two humans back to their ship.

"I have to go help Prince Draven," I said, turning the young man to directly face me. "You're going to have to save Luna, but I'm going to get you some help. Do you understand?"

Dylan's head swiveled toward the two sailors who were now running full out down the beach. When he turned back, his eyes were brimming with sorrow.

"It's my fault she's in trouble. I'll do anything to help her."

The worry in his voice broke my heart. I, too, was frightened for Luna, but Dylan had nothing to do with her predicament. She willingly helped him, and the young man was not responsible for the evil others did. All we could do was stand up against it and do our best to break it.

"I know you will, and so will my friend. Wait here." I saw no need to drag him into the water as well, so I left him on the sand while I waded into the surf. I dipped my hand into the water, relishing the sensation as its coolness enveloped my fingers. As I closed my eyes, a rush of power surged through me, replenishing the energy I had depleted while easing Dylan's pain. I focused on the rhythmic ebb and flow of the currents, letting the immense force of the sea carry away my thoughts as I let them flow across its vast expanse. *"Arion. I need your help. Hurry!"* The sea became a conduit for my message, carrying it to him without the need for spoken words.

Time passed at a glacier's pace while I waited for my giant crustacean teacher to show up. I turned away from the sea to check on Dylan. His eyes were glued on the *Abyssal*, perhaps watching for signs that the ship might be leaving shore. At the sound of a large splash, he turned towards me, his eyes suddenly going wide, while his mouth formed a large 'O.'

"What in the name of Triton are you doing with this human?" Arion's voice sounded completely different when he wasn't underwater, but I'd have recognized it anywhere. "Girl, what are you up to? Did you not learn your lesson? Do I have to *change* you again?"

"Get your shell up here," I hissed, searching the area for any humans who might be near enough to watch, or worse, listen. "Luna's been kidnapped and Draven's walking into a trap. You need to help Dylan to free the princess while I go help our prince."

"Oh. My. Tentacles!" Octavius leapt down from Arion's shell and glided towards me, his body undulating through the shallow water in a bizarre, flowing dance. Even though the annoying octopup hadn't been invited, he had managed to hitch a ride with my mentor.

With a tentacle pointed directly at my nose, his round, bulbous eyes narrowed. "If anything happens to my charge because of your fanciful plans, I will give a whole new meaning to the words *Release the Kraken*!" Even if the little guy was being a major pest, he seemed to care deeply for Luna and would literally do anything to protect her.

Forgetting the seriousness of the situation, I found myself wanting to laugh at the octopup who so desperately wanted to be thought of as a true kraken. Notwithstanding his fierce expression and overbearing behaviors, he could also be utterly adorable. Although, the way he was glaring at me suggested he might be far more formidable than I had previously considered.

My shoulders sagged under the weight of the problem we were facing. "Can we put blame aside for now and concentrate on saving our people? Dylan is going to show you where to go. He's dealt with these fiends before, and he knows their ship. Listen to him."

"Do you expect us to just march up to the boat and rescue the girl?" Arion asked. "If that's the plan, we're doomed."

Up until this moment, I had no plan except to just walk onto the ship and save Luna. However, hearing my thoughts spoken aloud, it became painfully evident that I was not well suited to being a rescuer. I was a mermaid, a sea witch, a…

"No!"

The word flopped from my lips as an idea coalesced in my mind. "Not by land. You will go by sea. The fishermen are not going to expect anyone to board their vessel from the water. Not while they're at port."

"I don't swim so good," Dylan said, scrubbing the back of his neck. I hadn't considered his humanness in my plan. "I'll likely drown before I make it to the ship."

I blew out a breath, unsure what to do next. I didn't think there was any way Dylan would let Arion and Octavius try to rescue Luna without his help. If I couldn't devise a solution quickly enough, he'd probably try to march onto the ship and into their waiting hands.

"Kiss the boy," Arion said, rolling his eyes on their extended stalks. My look of confusion prompted him to continue. "Kiss the boy. Give him some of your magic." My eyebrows continued to climb up my forehead. Arion snapped his pincers at me, as though trying to rouse me from a deep slumber. "Use your natural merfolk magic to let him breathe underwater…"

My gaze shifted over to Dylan, whose skin was turning a beautiful shade of pink. A lock of his long black hair fell across his face, lightly brushing his full red lips. My heart fluttered at the prospect of pressing my mouth to his, finally being so near to him after watching from afar for so many nights.

CHAPTER 20

DYLAN

My heart was racing out of control as Calypso drew near. Sure, the woman was attractive, likely the most beautiful creature I had ever seen, but there was something more to her, an intangible quality that I couldn't explain. I tried to swallow down my growing fear as she reached out and cupped my cheeks in her hands.

"Relax," she said to me, her voice soft and warm like butter over fresh bread. If only my body was listening. My muscles immediately turned rigid, and my hands clenched into tight fists at my sides. I had never been kissed before, except by my mother. Calypso was trying to draw me down to her, but I had stiffened so badly, I couldn't even bend over.

"I promise," she said, her hazel-green eyes widening while the slightest hint of a smile graced her soft, inviting lips. "This won't hurt a bit."

Oh, gods above. I was about to be kissed for the first time, and I was petrified beyond comprehension. If I stayed like this, behaving like an unyielding piece of driftwood, she'd change her mind and we'd have to find some other way to get me onboard that ship. A small whimper escaped my lips as I tried to let her pull me closer. I wanted her to kiss me, and I wanted to kiss her back, but mostly I wanted to curl up under a nice slimy rock and disappear.

Calypso's hands dropped from my face and wrapped around the back of my neck. Rather than pulling me down, she changed tactics and drew herself up to me, forcing me to either bear her full weight or yield to it and bend over. My sore leg only left me with one option and I finally, reluctantly, leaned down, letting the mermaid place her warm, moist mouth over mine.

At first, I just stood there like an idiotic statue, but as the warmth of her embrace took hold, my fears and inhibitions melted away. My hands relaxed and found their way to her waist, cradling her while I leaned closer. Her gentle pressure on my lips invited me to reciprocate, our tongues suddenly becoming intertwined in a strange, enticing dance.

She must have been pushing her water breathing magic into me. My face was heating and my skin tingled all over. My heart was rapidly beating; no longer out of fear, but from something profoundly different. It was a longing unlike anything I had ever before experienced. I was overcome with a desperate desire to press my body against hers.

A sharp intense pain exploded in my leg, causing me to screech, yanking me from my moment of overwhelming pleasure. I looked down to see Arion's pincer wrapped around my thigh and a threatening look in his overly large eyes.

"That'll be quite enough, lover boy."

As I pulled away, the giant crab released me from his grip. I stumbled backwards, my body feeling like it had just been slammed by a rogue wave. My head was swimming, leaving me disoriented and confused. When I caught sight of Calypso's bright pink face and heaving chest, I feared I had somehow angered her. Had I kissed her badly? Did I hold her tighter than I should have?

"I'm sorry." I didn't know what else to say. My heart sank when Calypso turned away and ran her hands through her long red hair. Her body trembled before she turned back to me, her eyes wide and shiny.

"You did nothing wrong," she said, her cheeks reddening further. "It was... I..."

"The transfer of magic can be an intense experience for humans," Arion interjected. "It can result in confusing emotions for both the mermaid and the human. I suggest, young man, that you dunk yourself in the cool sea water and take a deep breath."

Calypso's chest was still heaving as she nodded in agreement. She swallowed hard and smiled. "Arion's right. You need to test my magic to make sure it worked. Otherwise..."

"There will be no more kissing," Arion interrupted. "If the magic didn't take hold, we'll find another way."

Secretly, I desperately hoped the magic transfer had failed and that Calypso would try again.

"Get," the crusty crab said, snapping his pincers at me. "Get out there, dunk your head, and suck it in."

Reluctantly, I waded out into the surf, my long oilskin cloak dragging on me as each wave rolled over my thighs. The coolness of the sea seemed to lessen the tingles that were still coursing through my body. I plunged my face into the water, ready to breathe, but my lungs refused to obey.

"I can't," I said, throwing my head back, letting my water-soaked hair fall down the back of my neck. "I don't know how to do this."

Arion scuttled into the surf and disappeared beneath the waves. Suddenly, his pincers seized the hood of my cloak. "I'm sorry," he said. "But I know of no other way to get this done in a short period of time."

Before I could react, he dragged me under the surface and pinned me to the sea floor. It was a strange sensation, being held flat on my back, looking up at the surf rolling in above me, casting undulating shadows across the water. The sun looked so bright and inviting from beneath the waves.

For a moment, the peacefulness of the underwater world enveloped me, filling me with awe and wonder. Then, abruptly, the peace was shattered, replaced with a desperate desire to breathe. My pulse quickened as I thrashed under the weight of this oversized crustacean, while my lungs burned with extreme pain. My chest tightened as my thrashing turned into punches and kicks while I instinctively tried to free myself, to swim to the surface, and take a huge gulp of fresh air.

Darkness crept into my vision as the burning in my chest grew more intense. My pulse pounded in my ears as terror gripped my soul. My gaze darted about frantically until it settled on Arion, his massive form a steady anchor amid the chaos. His eyes, filled with empathy and understanding, locked onto mine and held fast. I could have sworn he felt the same pain and fear I was experiencing. He conveyed infinite emotion in that passing glance. For an instant, the world around me stilled, and a surge of emotion that transcended panic and pain enveloped me.

That single instant of peace that had crept into my consciousness vanished, turning into unbridled terror. My miserable life passed before my eyes in less than a heartbeat. But, in that fraction of a second, I realized my life had actually been quite wonderful, regardless of its difficulties and setbacks. It hadn't been miserable at all. It had been filled with love and belonging, and that same sense of belonging filled me right now, even as my lungs screamed for air.

I sucked in a breath, filling my mouth and lungs with the cool, salty sea. While the briny taste would take some getting used to, the sensation of breathing water was a surprisingly pleasant, refreshing experience. The panic and fear that had gripped me earlier receded, replaced with pure peacefulness.

As I exhaled, tiny bubbles tickled as they escaped my lips and floated towards the surface. A grin split my face as I drew another breath. It was more difficult than breathing air, sucking in, and expelling water, but there was an unexpected thoughtfulness to it.

My eyes widened as I seemingly saw the sea for the first time. There were multitudes of fishes, their rainbow colors flashing as they moved in and out of the coral, playing among thin green grasses that swayed with the current. The sunlight filtering down to the silty bottom, dancing across tiny rocks and seashells, casting everything in an ethereal light.

"Welcome to the undersea world," Arion said, spreading his pincers wide, his gigantic eyes gleaming with excitement. "Calypso's magic will last no more than an hour. We best hurry."

I nodded, still entranced by the awesome beauty surrounding me.

"Wait," I said, grabbing onto the giant crab's sharp, boney leg. Talking underwater was truly bizarre. I could actually feel the words forming in my mouth before I expelled them into the never-ending current. "I wanted to thank you."

"Thank me?" Arion held out his claw, offering to help me up off the seabed. "Whatever for?"

"I couldn't have done this without your help. I couldn't have breathed the water in. And not just that, you helped to quell my fears."

"You're welcome," he said with a warm smile. "And I should warn you, if you do anything to hurt Calypso, I'll cut you in half and feed you to the sharks."

I laughed at his joke. The smile on my face melted away when I realized he wasn't kidding.

"Like I said, we need to hurry. You have one hour before this magic fades and you become just a regular air-breathing human again."

CHAPTER 21

LUNA

The two sailors standing watch over me paused their heated argument as I cried out in distress. The iron cuffs around my wrists burned with a searing agony that shot up my arms. I gritted my teeth and tried to steady my breathing, but the agony was becoming unbearable. The salty scent of the sea wafted through the air, mingling with the stench of sweat and fear. As I trembled involuntarily, waiting for the next wave of pain to hit me, drops of perspiration dripped down my forehead.

"I beg of you, remove these manacles." My throat stung with each word. "They burn. I promise I won't fight. Please, they hurt so badly. I cannot be in contact with iron for this long. It's poisoning me. Whatever you hope to do with me won't work if I'm dead."

As soon as they had dragged me aboard their boat, I knew I was in trouble. The first mate, a man named Lachlan, wasted no time in having me restrained with these torture devices. Instead of just fastening me to a beam, he ordered his men to throw me into an iron cage, one of many that lined one side of the ship's hull. The cages themselves were three-sided, with the fourth side being the hull wall itself.

I knew being in contact with iron for an extended period would kill me, but these humans didn't seem to care. Had they understood our species better, they'd have known the way the metal affected us. The bars were superfluous, a cruel addition to my already miserable predicament. A simple band of iron on the floor would have been enough to hold me, as mermaids are incapable of willingly crossing over the disgusting ferrous metal. But instead, they threw me in this cell alone, leaving me to suffer in agony. While the heavy bars slowly leached away my strength, my skin felt as though it was being stung by thousands of jellyfish.

I held out my trembling arms, showing the two guards the black lines snaking up from the manacles and winding around my arms like vicious sea-vines. The pain was a constant burning, pulsing through my veins and seeping into my bones. My strength was ebbing, my body growing weaker with each passing moment. Ferrous poisoning was a death sentence for my kind, and my fate hung in the balance.

I had never seen anything like this before. In the merkingdom, we had no use for iron, preferring instead to use noble metals like silver, gold, platinum, and palladium. I had heard stories of the dangers of iron, but they paled in comparison to the reality of it. In desperation, I pleaded for their help.

"Please. Look at my arms. If those black lines spreading up from where the manacles are touching me reach my heart, I will die."

"Get Lachlan," the hairy guard barked, puffing out his chest in a display of bravado. "He should see this. If she dies, he'll blame both of us."

I swallowed hard, fear clutching at my breast. Lachlan was the last person I wanted to come down here. If he saw what was happening to me, he would surely take pleasure in my suffering. I could only hope that these guards would find some mercy in their hearts and would remove the manacles before it was too late.

"You get the first mate," the other guard said, his mouth turned downward. "I'm not going anywhere. Lachlan will skin me alive if I leave my post."

The guard's threat of Lachlan flaying him sent a shiver down my spine. Could the man truly be that cruel? These men were nothing like Dylan and his mother, who were both so kind and loving. These were horrible, disgusting people.

"Fine. We'll both stay here," the hairy man said, "and when she dies, I'll tell Lachlan that you refused to inform him she was being poisoned. Which do you think he'll be more upset about? That she dies, or that you left your post? If she's dead, we can't use her to call the other mermaids."

They want me to call other mermaids? What good could that possibly do?

It was only then that I fully understood why they had taken me. I had thought they wanted me to help them catch more mooneyes, like the one Dylan had brought to the market, but these were not fishermen. They were mermaid hunters.

"Fine," the sailor said to his hairy partner. "I'll get Lachlan, but I'm going to say you sent me. If anyone is going to catch his wrath, it won't be me."

The man scampered up the ladder to the deck above like he had sat on fire coral.

"I'm sorry," the hairy man said. "I don't agree with what my cap'n is doing, but I have little to say in the matter. I'm just a deckhand."

A melancholy swept across the man's face, seeming to mirror the weight of his burdened heart. I knew it all too well, having shed many tears since my capture.

"What's your name?" I asked, hoping the conversation would take my mind off the growing pain traveling up my arms. "My name's Luna."

The man stole a glance over his shoulder towards the ladder his shipmate had climbed. "Hakon." He ran his hand down his long brown beard, tugging on it as he did. "Can you really call other mermaids?"

"I can, but I don't see why it matters." The thought of these humans capturing more of my kind gnawed at my soul. As a wave of exhaustion passed over me, I dropped my chin to my chest. "Why are you hunting us? We don't hurt sailors."

When I watched the man's body visibly stiffen, I realized I had spoken the wrong words. His demeanor suddenly shifted, his eyes turning fierce, his hands clenching into tight fists at his sides.

"You sing songs that draw sailors to you, driving our ships onto rocks and reefs," he said, storming forward, his nostrils flaring. He gripped the bars of my cage like a mad man. The heavy corded muscles in his thick arms stood out while his knuckles turned bone white. "As soon as the ship sinks, you swoop in and kill us all."

"Not us mermaids," I said, shaking my head adamantly. "Sirens do that. They're the ones who choose to wreck your ships and steal your supplies. We help sailors in distress, so they don't drown."

The color of the man's hands returned to normal, while the expression of hatred on his face subsided. "My father's ship was taken by your kind. All but three perished and those who survived spoke of mermaids who feasted on the bodies of the captured sailors."

Ugh. Bile rose from my belly at Hakon's words, the sour flavor twisting my mouth into a horrendous grimace. I knew sirens lured ships to crash on their rocky islands, but I had no idea what they did with the humans once their ships were destroyed. I had always thought they robbed them of their food, and any precious metals and trinkets they had, before casting them back into the sea.

"Every member of this crew has lost people they cared about to mermaids. It's why Cap'n Roberts picked us." Even with his thick brown beard, I could see his jaw tense.

"Not mermaids," I corrected, swallowing down the vomit that was desperately trying to find its way up my throat. "Sirens. They have wings, but we do not."

"The survivors of my father's ship said nothing about anyone flying." The man's brow furrowed; his thick bushy eyebrows pinching together until they were touching. He rattled the door to my cage. The light streaming in from the small porthole window cast his face in dark shadows.

My heart sank at the man's words. What if he was speaking true? It was possible the survivors of his father's ship had not seen the siren's wings. I knew from personal experience that being frightened could cloud a person's perception of reality.

"My people..." the words snagged in my throat like the spiny barbs of an urchin. "They'd never do that. We're not... that's just not who we are."

"Are you suggesting that the survivors of my father's ship were liars?" The man's knuckles started turning white again.

"No," I said, casting my eyes down to the salt-worn floorboards. Much of the wood on this vessel seemed to be rotting away. Mustering up as much courage as I could manage, I locked my gaze on to his. "I... I can only tell you that in my experience, my people are kind and helpful. My brother would never allow that sort of heinous act, not while he rules the Gaelinora."

Hakon's hands dropped from the cage while he warily eyed me, his eyes roving up and down my body, resembling a shark ready to devour its prey. From outside, I could hear the hull creaking, as if a lumbering beast was climbing up the ship's side. With any luck it was a kraken wrapping its long tentacles around the boat, ready to crack it open and feast upon the foul men within. What a sight that would be, watching these sailors clamber over each other like crabs over dead coral, desperate to escape.

"Your brother is Prince Draven, son of Triton?" When I nodded, one eyebrow cocked high on his forehead. "How far do you think he'd go to get you home safe and sound?"

"There isn't a sea, a lake, or an ocean that he wouldn't scour from shore to shore to bring me home. When he finds out I'm on this ship, he'll rip it to shreds."

A sly grin tugged at the corner of the man's mouth. I suddenly realized he wasn't being friendly with me because he cared. He was tricking me, fooling me into giving him information to use against my people. A wave of fury ripped through me. Using what little remaining strength I had, I lunged forward with the ferocity of a sea lion protecting her pups. I reached for the bars of my cage, intent on tearing them from the rotted floor.

As I grabbed hold, my hands sizzled with intense heat. The biting pain forced me to release my grip and back away. I stared down at my badly burned hands in disbelief. The thick black lines climbing up from my manacles had doubled in size and now extended past my elbows.

"Unless these manacles come off right away, I won't last much longer, and you won't get what you want. If these lines keep creeping up my arms, the ferrous poisoning will become irreversible." I raised my eyes to find the bearded man hustling up the ladder. I was going to die alone here in an iron cage. I would turn into sea foam and leak down through the floorboards, never to return home.

As I wallowed in self-pity, I dropped to the floor and leaned against the ship's hull. Almost instantly, a searing pain shot across my lower back, sending me scrambling forward into the middle of my cell.

More iron!

Even though the wall was wooden, the hull must have been clad in that loathsome metal, like a hulking warrior whose loins had been girded for battle. These monsters had taken every precaution to ensure that any mermaids they snared could never escape.

"Luna!" a high-pitched voice called from somewhere behind me. "Luna! Up here."

Although I could barely raise my head to look up, joy surged in my heart. "Shiver me fins! Octavius? How'd you get here?"

"He had some help," Dylan said, peering in through the porthole, his face pressed firmly against the glass. Octavius seemed to have a death-grip on the young man's neck. "We're here to break you out."

CHAPTER 22

DYLAN

My seawater-saturated overcoat weighed heavy on my shoulders. I had wanted to shed it, but it was the most valuable thing I owned and I feared losing it. My fingers were aching and the muscles in my forearms were burning from the exertion of climbing up the outer surface of the Abyssal. Even with the thick heavy bands of iron that ran the length of the trawler that provided handholds, I'd have never made it to the porthole window without Octavius' help. Despite the little octopup's diminutive size, he was able to carry most of my weight while we scaled the side of the boat. Although, if he didn't let up on his grip around my neck, I would pass out from lack of oxygen.

When Luna caught sight of my face in the window, her eyes lit up with a glimmer of hope. Slowly, she picked herself up off the floor, barely able to keep herself upright on her wobbly, unsteady legs.

"I'm going to try smashing the porthole," I yelled. "Back away so you don't get sprayed with glass."

Luna's expression of joyous excitement vanished, instantly replaced with fear and doubt. Her once vibrant green locks hung limp around her face. She fell to her knees, her body trembling badly. "I can't go out that way," she said, barely loud enough for me to hear her. "I can't cross over iron."

"What does Luna mean she can't cross over iron?" I asked Octavius.

"Merfolk are like all fae creatures," the octopup said, his overly enormous eyes glistening in the morning sun. "They're allergic to the metal and for reasons only the gods can explain, they cannot intentionally cross over it. That thick iron band running under the porthole is an impassible barrier for her."

"If she can't cross iron, how did they get her onto the ship?"

Octavius' brow furrowed. "They'd have dragged her onboard and it would have been incredibly painful for her. In her current state, crossing over iron would likely kill her."

The idea that they had hurt this sweet woman twisted my stomach into a tight knot. How could anyone be so cruel? I peered in the window again, my eyes widening at the sight of Luna's condition. Her skin was pale and clammy, and her once vibrant green hair hung limply around her face. She was wearing iron manacles that dug deep into her flesh, leaving deep red welts on her wrists. Thick, dark lines covered her hands and arms. Fury ripped through me as she flopped down to the floor, her body trembling and spasming in agony.

"I'm going to get you out," I yelled, my heart racing with fear and determination. "I'll find a way."

"Just leave," Luna yelled back, her voice weak and defeated. "I'll be dead soon, anyway."

"I won't let you die," I shouted, my voice shaking with emotion. "We'll find a way to get you out of there. Trust me." But as I spoke, my grip on the iron band was already starting to give out. The strain of holding up my own weight, along with my seawater-saturated overcoat, was too much to bear. My grip was slipping, and even with

Octavius' best efforts to hold me up, we both tumbled back into the briny sea with a resounding splash.

My oilskin cloak immediately dragged me to the sea floor, sending me into a panic. It didn't matter that my brain knew I was able to breathe underwater. My body refused to acknowledge this fact, and it desperately wanted me to surface and breathe air instead.

Now was not a time to let fear rule my actions. I got this poor girl into this mess and I was going to get her out of it. Mustering all my courage, I ignored my baser instincts and sucked in a breath, filling my lungs with the cool, salty seawater. A moment later, after my chest finished spasming, I breathed normally again.

"They've got her in manacles," I said to Arion. The giant crab had stayed behind while I searched for the girl who had once saved my life. "The upper hull of the ship is wrapped in bands of iron, and Luna said she can't cross them. If we don't rescue her quickly, she's going to die."

Arion swore under his breath. His words were harsh, but I couldn't make out what he said. "I can't help you. Like Luna, I'm unable to cross over iron."

"Why not?" I asked. Octavius seemed unaffected by the metal, so why couldn't a crab cross it?

"Because, even though I look like a crab, I'm a merman. I had a... mishap while casting a spell. Somehow, its magic reflected back on me and now I'm this bizarre abomination." The giant red crab's body shook, his eyes filled with regret. "It's a mistake that I will be reminded of for the rest of my life."

I blew out a breath, sending a curtain of bubbles up in front of my face.

"Ok, then. It's going to be me and Octavius on our own." I looked up at the hull of the Abyssal. Everything in my world was so different when viewed from beneath the waves. From below, the trawler resembled a huge black log. There were no iron bands on the bottom of the ship. It seemed that they had only installed them above the waterline.

"We can do it," Octavius said, waving his tentacles around in a frantic display. "We just need to get her on the ship's deck and then jump into the water. She'll fall past the bands so fast they shouldn't hurt her. At least I hope they won't."

"I'm not sure if that will work," I said, pulling my cloak tight around my body. Despite the relative warmth of the shallow waters, I was shivering uncontrollably. It was likely my nerves, but it might have been the water drawing away my body heat.

I was suddenly concerned about how much longer I'd be able to breathe underwater. My bad leg had made swimming to the boat extremely difficult, causing my journey to take more time than it should have. Had it not been for Arion towing me along, I'd have likely never made it. In hindsight, I should have accepted his help sooner rather than insisting I do it all on my own.

"I don't walk very well on land and there are going to be ship's hands on deck. They'll spot us immediately as we come up through the hatch. Besides, I have no idea how I'll get on the boat in the first place. I'm not sure I can scale up the side again. And if we make it all the way to the deck, the deckhands will see me as soon as I climb over the railing."

"We'll go in through Luna's porthole window." I loved how confident the octopup sounded. The risks didn't seem to matter to him. All he cared about was freeing his charge. "Once we get inside and unlock Luna's manacles, we can figure out our next move."

"I don't know if I can break the glass. Porthole windows are very thick." I ran my fingers through my hair. "And there is still the matter of me climbing the side of the ship again. I'm not sure I have the strength for it."

"No worries," the little octopus said. "I'll pop that window like a clam shell. I just need you to do your part once we get there."

"Do you have enough strength left to help me climb up again?" I asked, flexing my hands to loosen them up. The cool water seemed to ease their stiffness, but I wasn't sure how well my arms were going to hold out.

"Hey!" Octavius' expression brightened. "Maybe Arion can change you into a sea creature like he did to Calypso? If he turns you into an octopus, you'll have no trouble climbing up the side of the boat."

"Sorry," he said, shaking his body. "I can only transform mermaids. That's not the way my magic works. If I was in my home, I might be able to brew up a strength potion, but even then, I'm not sure it would work on you."

I was glad Arion couldn't change me into a sea creature. The thought of being anything but myself was giving me the creeps. Then again, if it would mean rescuing Luna, I'd gladly do it.

"If you can help me climb up," I said to Octavius, "I'll find a way to get Luna free."

"Get going then," Arion said. "I have no idea how much time you have to breathe water, but there can't be much left." It seemed I wasn't the only one who had that concern.

As best as I could, I pushed off the seabed and swam to the surface. Octavius quickly climbed up on my shoulders and wrapped a leg under each of my armpits. Using the suction cups on his remaining six legs, he latched onto the ship's hull and started lifting me from the water. As soon as I could, I grasped one of the iron bands that ran from front to back and pulled myself up. Using them like a ladder, I found a toehold for my good leg and dug in. With a push of my leg and a pull from Octavius, we started our ascent.

With the muscles in my arms screaming in protest for having been put to work again, we slowly made our way up the side of the ship until we were within reach of the porthole.

"Can you hang on without me for a few minutes?" the octopup asked. "I'm going to need all my legs to pop that window out."

I grunted my acknowledgement and tightened my grip, making sure my toehold was secure. A moment later, I was on my own while Octavius was positioning himself over the porthole; his legs splayed out all around it.

With extreme effort, he yanked at the frame and a moment later, there was a satisfying, grinding pop as he dislodged it from the vessel. All I needed to do now was squeeze myself through the small hole and pray to Gaia that I could figure out a way to get Luna free.

CHAPTER 23

CALYPSO

It didn't take me long to discover where Lord Vayne lived. Several people had pointed out his enormous home, which sat atop a hillock overlooking the town. The building was massive, rivaling Prince Draven's palace in the merkingdom. However, unlike the elegance and artistry of the prince's grand abode, this home was stark and gray, completely lacking any sort of esthetic design. It did, however, strike an ominous chord in my heart as I approached its front gates.

"State your business," a burly man dressed in heavy armor demanded in an overly officious tone. Standing an arm's distance away, the iron that covered his bulky body stung my skin, forcing me to take a step back.

"I am here to see Lord Vayne," I said, trying my best to sound confident, like I belonged here and these humans were beneath me. I held my chin high while I waited for these men to open the gate for me.

"She's prettier than his last *guest*," a second guard said, giving his cohort a nudge with his elbow. "Do you think we should search her?" The burly guard chuckled at his smaller companion's joke.

I called upon my magic, ready to protect myself if need be, but it didn't respond. I was too far from the sea to draw upon its power. With no better option, I decided I'd try talking myself past these two humans. There was no time to waste.

"I am Calypso, agent of Prince Draven and the royal house of Triton." I paused for a moment to gauge their reaction to my assertion, smiling internally as the men exchanged a wary glance. My declaration of being from the merkingdom seemed to have had the desired effect, so I quickly pressed my advantage. "I bring dire news of the *Abyssal* to Lord Vayne, and time is of the essence."

The two men swallowed hard and continued to stare wordlessly at one another.

"Rather than wasting time gawking, perhaps you should escort me to your master. It would be unfortunate if Lord Vayne's ships were scuttled because you were too slow to react to my urgings. Who do you think he'll blame first when I tell him you stalled rather than taking decisive action?"

The two guards shifted nervously, their iron-clad feet shuffling on the hard stone walkway. I inhaled deeply through my nose, letting the tangy sea air fill my lungs.

"I suppose I could just sing a song and put you both to sleep." I gave the guards a coy smile. "If you think that would make it easier on you." Truth was, my voice would have no effect on these men. I wasn't even sure I could sing without being in contact with the sea. The way their faces were twisting up as they tried solve to this quandary was entertaining, but I needed them to hurry.

I gave them a shrug. "Okay, sleep it is." As I opened my mouth in mock preparation, the first of the two guards held up his gantlet-covered hand, sending a pulse of discomfort across my body. I feared that I might have winced, but I don't think they noticed if I did.

"There'll be no need of that, now," he said, motioning for the other to open the gate. "We will need to check you for weapons."

I threw my hand up to halt the man's progress. I was counting on him not knowing anything about my species, like the sailors I had overheard speaking on the beach.

"To touch a mermaid uninvited is to court death," I said. "As unpleasant as the smell of your iron covered body is to me, you would find that touching me would go very badly for you." I cocked an eyebrow and motioned with my chin to his cohort. "For both of you."

The man's face visibly paled, and he swallowed hard. He gave a wide-eyed glance at his partner, who frowned in response. "The clothes she's wearing don't really have any place to hide a weapon," he said. "We'll just tell Lord Vayne we thoroughly checked her."

"It can be our little secret," I said with a warm smile. "Lead the way, gentlemen."

As we climbed the winding stone path that led to the manor's front entrance, my heart raced with excitement. I was far better at dealing with humans than I would have ever expected. It made me question our laws about interacting with them. It also seemed obvious to me that Prince Draven's ramblings about how important his work to solidify merfolk-human relations was a much simpler task than he let on.

The guard's iron-clad knuckles rapped on the home's entry, each strike booming like a drum. A small pane in the door slid off to the side, allowing a man from within to peer out at the visitors.

The guard cleared his throat and spoke in a loud, authoritative voice. "I have an emissary from the merkingdom with me. She insists on speaking with Lord Vayne on a matter of extreme urgency."

The man peering through the tiny window grunted, his eyes narrowing as he turned his gaze upon me. "One moment," he said before sliding the tiny pane back into place. After several excruciatingly long seconds, the door slowly opened.

"Please, my lady," said the man from within. He was dressed all in white, with gold trim and embroidery patterns woven over his shoulders and down both sleeves. The man's nose resembled that of an elephant seal, hanging well below his mouth. No wonder he hid behind a closed door when he spoke to people. He had a face that could scare eels. However, even with his repulsive outward appearance, he was quite civilized in how he addressed me. I gave him a respectful nod and stepped into the manor.

I gasped at the sheer beauty of the home's interior. Where the building's outer appearance was harsh and austere, the décor within its drab gray walls was spectacular. Noble metals, like silver and gold, gilded every ornate surface. The morning sun glittered across the floor; its blue-green surface reminiscent of the Gaelinora Sea. The wavelike patterns that were inlaid with flecks of glistening stone reflected a multitude of colors and hues.

"What a lovely..." my words were cut off when a large, iron-laced net was cast over me, sending me crashing to the hard floor. The netting against my skin was like a thousand knives cutting into me while lying on a bed of fire coral and being stung by jellyfish. I wanted to cry out in pain, but my body was convulsing so badly I could barely control my bodily functions.

From somewhere beside me, a harsh voice called out. "Tell Lord Vayne we've got another trophy for his wall. These stupid fish are practically jumping into the boat." It was the last thing I heard before darkness enveloped me.

"Hey, wake up."

The words were soft like butter, warm like hot springs. I wanted to open my eyes, but they were so heavy. Sleep beckoned to me. I wanted to pull the darkness around myself and drift off into oblivion.

"Calypso, wake up."

Ugh. This time the words were sharp, and they were accompanied by a most uncivilized shaking of my shoulder. The mists that had enveloped me slipped away long enough for me to rouse myself from this unnatural slumber. My eyes opened to Prince Draven hovering over me, worry etched deeply into his face.

"Oh, thank Gaia," he whispered, his head snapping up, swiveling. "When they threw you into this cage with me…" The man slipped his hand beneath my back and hoisted me into a sitting position. I had to swipe away a mass of red hair that had drooped over my eyes. "I feared you were dead."

I shook my head and swallowed. My throat felt like it was filled with tiny sea urchins. Except for Draven's face, which was much too near to mine, the rest of the room was a complete blur. I rubbed my eyes and tried blinking repeatedly to clear my vision, but to no effect.

"Doing that won't help," he said, gently pulling my hands away. "We're in a cage of some sort. There is a fine mesh hanging over it, making it difficult for us to see what's beyond."

The man's hands felt smooth and warm against my skin. I watched, dumbfounded, as he carefully caressed the back of my hand with his thumb.

"I don't understand. I had come to tell you that Luna had been taken…" It was as though my memories were muddled, my head filled with silt. I had stepped inside the manor's front door. There was a peculiar-looking man with an overly large nose. I was about to comment on the interior. The memory of the net dropping on me, the excruciating pain, and the blackness that enveloped me, came flooding back into my consciousness. I thrashed, pushing away Draven's hand, and stumbled to my feet. I never quite made it to being fully upright, collapsing when the world suddenly listed heavily.

The man I had come to hate caught me before my body fell to the stone floor. His natural salty fragrance cut through the stench of mildew that filled the room.

"Give yourself a few moments," he said, propping me up. "Breathe."

"What's wrong with me?" I pushed myself away from the man's embrace, unsteady on my feet.

"Your body has been sapped of its strength. They left the iron net on you for too long. It almost killed you." Draven tucked an errant lock of his black hair behind an ear. "I thought you were dead when they threw you in here with me."

"How long have I been here? Wherever here is?" Despite Draven telling me it would do no good, I found myself rubbing my eyes yet again. Looking at the netting that held us in place had a mesmerizing effect on me.

"You've been asleep for three or four hours. It's hard to know for sure. Time passes very slowly down here. I tried to wake you, but you wouldn't respond. This is Lord Vayne's larder; except he's calling it his dungeon. It's like an underground prison."

"We're below ground?" A surge of excitement ran through me. If we were deep enough, it was possible we were near water, an underground stream, or maybe even the sea itself.

I fell to my knees, pressing my hands against the cold stone floor. I closed my eyes, feeling with my senses, desperately reaching out for any water source. With any luck, there would be enough to allow me to replenish my depleted magic stores.

"Nothing," I said, dropping my forehead to the ground. "I had hoped there might be water beneath us."

Draven offered me a hand up from the floor. "There is a sizeable stream running beneath this house, but we're too far away to make use of it. Either that, or it's this mesh covering our cage that's blocking our ability to connect with it. I can't even call my scepter from the ether."

I blew out a breath, refusing to accept Draven's assistance. "For people who don't seem to know anything about mermaids, this lord seems to have done an excellent job thwarting us."

Draven's square jaw clenched hard enough to make the muscles on the sides of his face twitch. "Lord Vayne has done his homework. The man is driven by hatred. I knew he had no love for our kind, but I had no idea his loathing ran so deep."

CHAPTER 24

DYLAN

It was with extreme effort that Octavius was able to drag me through the porthole. Perhaps if I hadn't been wearing my oilskin cloak, it would have been easier, but I still wasn't prepared to leave it behind. If I got in a fight with the sailors, and they had swords, at least I would have a bit of protection against their blades. The cloak's leather was thick and strong, and with any luck, it might be able to absorb a strike or two before they killed me.

I flopped onto the deck-boards with a resounding thump, sending a spray of water across the floor. I rolled over onto my hands and knees, gasping, trying to fill my lungs after the landing knocked the air out of me. My heart stopped when my gaze fell onto Luna, whose hair was a sad shade of gray and her skin appeared almost translucent.

"What's wrong with her?" I asked Octavius, who had just finished climbing down from the porthole. He had waited outside until I was safely on the boat, in case I needed any assistance.

"The iron bars are slowly sapping her strength, but the real danger are those manacles. Being in contact with them for so long is poisoning her. In time, they will kill Luna."

The black lines I had seen on her skin earlier were now raised welts that ran up her arms and disappeared beneath the short sleeves of her tattered dress. I scrabbled near, scooping up Luna's body in my arms. She was cold, so very cold.

My stomach twisted into a tight knot as I examined her wrists. They were completely black, covered with nasty, festering blisters. I tried pulling the manacles over her tiny hands, but they were too tight and the iron was much too thick for me to break it.

"What do we do? I can't get these off her without a key."

"I might be able to help," Octavius said, clambering over me. "Keep holding onto her arms while I try to work some magic."

"You can do magic?" I asked, my eyes widening. The octopup just shook his head and rolled his large eyes.

While most of Octavius' legs were wrapped around my forearms, giving him unfettered access to Luna's manacles, he got to work on trying to remove them. I had never seen an octopus before, let alone had one clasped onto me. His little body shifted and morphed into bizarre shapes as he tried a multitude of ways to slide the cuffs off Luna's wrists.

With each failed attempt to free the girl, his grip on my arms grew tighter, threatening to break my bones if he squeezed any harder.

"You can do this," I said, trying to offer whatever support I could. "I have faith in you."

By the way his grip tightened further, I was guessing my words were not of benefit to him.

"There's a lock mechanism," I said, motioning to the keyhole on the manacle. "If you can stick a tentacle in there, maybe you can pop it open."

The octopup nodded and immediately jammed the tip of a leg into the opening. He made something of a grunting noise as he twisted his body, contorting himself as he worked the internal mechanisms. He let out a squeal just before the cuff popped open.

"It's simple," Octavius said as he immediately got to work on the second manacle. "Now that I understand how they operate, all I need to do is..." His face twisted in concentration as though he was envisioning the cuff's internal workings. "Find this small bolt inside, slip my tentacle behind it, twist, and push it over."

As soon as he finished the words, the second cuff popped off, and the shackles fell to the floor.

"We need to get her back in the sea," Octavius said, sliding off my arms and curling up on Luna's shoulder. Her breathing was shallow and rapid. She groaned softly with each exhale. "Seawater will help her fight the poison, but I don't know if that will be enough. She looks..."

"Are you sure we can't push her out through the porthole? She's tiny. She should fit easily enough."

Octavius shook his head while he gently tucked an errant lock of hair behind Luna's ear. His skin color changed from dark gray to deep blue as he carefully caressed her skin. "I fear she wouldn't survive, but we may be left with no alternative."

Tears rolled down my cheeks, joining the seawater dripping from my cloak's sleeve. As a droplet fell onto Luna's hand, hope burst through my body, my heart instantly hammering with excitement.

"My cloak," I said, as I quickly peeled it off my body. "It's saturated with sea water. It's not much, but it's a start."

"It might help," Octavius said, helping me pull the heavy leather off me. "Wrap it completely around her. It may even slow the effects of the iron bars surrounding us."

My hands were shaking so badly, I had trouble getting out of my cloak. Of course, it might have had something to do with the octopup who was aggressively yanking on my sleeve. After what felt like an eternity, I wrapped Luna in the soggy, make-shift blanket, covering her from head to toe.

"That's going to help," Octavius said, "but we need to get her in the water if she's to have any chance of surviving."

As fast as I was able, I jumped to my feet and yanked on the cage's door. It was locked, but with Octavius' newfound skill, it wouldn't be a problem to circumvent. Then again, opening the door was just the first step in getting Luna off this boat. I'd have to carry her up the stairs to the main deck, and that presented a multitude of problems for which I had no solutions.

First, there was no way my bad leg would let me carry Luna up the steep staircase, even if I had a crutch. Second, there would be sailors up on deck. As soon as they saw me, they'd be on me like flies on a dead fish before I made it anywhere near the railings to throw her overboard. Third... I didn't bother trying to list any other obstacles. Not when numbers one and two were already more than enough to thwart any attempt to escape.

"We need to hurry," Octavius said, clutching onto my leg. "She doesn't have long."

"I know. I'm working on a solution." I wanted to scream the words at the octopup, but he was only trying to help. He clearly loved Luna, and he wanted to see her safe and sound. I turned, hoping to scan the area for ideas on how we could proceed, but my feet got tangled in the little guy's tentacles, sending me crashing hard onto my face.

In frustration, I slammed my fists against the deck-boards, furious with myself for not being able to think my way through this problem. A sharp pain shot into the heel of my hand. I grimaced at the sight of a large splinter jammed into my skin. As I removed the thin wedge of wood, a steady stream of blood poured out and fell onto the badly damaged floor where my fists had struck it. My pulse quickened as an idea slowly formed in my mind. My plan, such as it was, wasn't great, but there was a small chance it might actually work.

"This wood is rotting," I said to Octavius. "Do you think you can squeeze your tentacles between the cracks and yank out a board?" The little guy stared blankly at me. I couldn't tell if he was considering my question, or if he was wondering why I'd want him to do such a thing.

"Below this deck is the ship's bilge. It holds a great deal of water. A ship this size will use the extra weight for ballast." The octopup continued to stare at me while he considered my words. "It's filled with *sea water.*" I said those last words slowly, hoping he wasn't as dim as he looked right now.

Octavius' blank expression vanished, instantly replaced with wide-eyed wonder and a bright, albeit peculiar-looking, smile.

As he slid the tip of his tentacle between the cracks, I urged the little guy to try to pull the boards up intact. I showed him where they were fastened to the ship's beams, identifying those as the critical points in each plank. He nodded his understanding and quickly went to work. The nails squealed in protest as they were pulled through the rotting wood. In no time, he had the first of the planks lifted, releasing the heady scent of fresh bilge brine.

"Can you pull up three? I need enough space to fit Luna through."

The little guy nodded and returned to his task, lifting two more boards and piling them over the first. I peered in through the opening, and as I expected, the bilge was filled with what looked like six feet of water. It was overfull, almost all the way up to the floorboards.

Once the way was clear, Octavius and I set to work, rolling Luna toward the hole in the floor. Just before pushing her into the drink, I gave the octopup a quick nod. "Gently lower her in. I don't want the water to slosh onto the deck. If the floor is soaking wet, it might give them a clue what we've done."

Anchoring himself to the deck with four legs, Octavius took hold of Luna and slowly lowered her into the water below. As soon as she was submerged, he followed her into the bilge.

As quickly as I could, I dragged the three floorboards beside the opening. My plan was to put them back in place, to hide any trace of what we had just done. I instinctively took a deep breath before lowering myself into the smelly water, doing the best I could to cover the hole with the loose planks. Even though I was able to get the first two into position, pulling them tightly to the framing, the third slat was conspicuously loose. As soon as someone came down the stairs, they'd notice it and immediately realize what we'd done.

Loud voices from the upper deck announced sailors were approaching.

"Octavius," I hissed. "Help me put this board in place. Someone's coming." He didn't respond. The octopup was underwater with Luna, caring for her, making sure she was okay.

I needed his help, and I needed it now. I didn't know how much time had passed since Calypso's kiss. I didn't know if I could still breathe underwater, but I needed to speak with Octavius, and this was the only way to do it.

My heart was thudding against my chest as I submerged. I desperately tried to inhale, to intentionally drown myself, but my lungs refused to listen. Within the bowels of the ship, the sound of footsteps pounding on the stairs echoed like I was trapped within a great drum. I was out of time and out of options. I cast a quick glance at Luna, whose face was still deathly pale, and quickly inhaled the salty seawater.

CHAPTER 25

CALYPSO

I forced myself to stop staring at the netting over our cage. After considering the problem, I decided that it must be magical in nature, and whatever enchantment that had been woven into it was creating this disorienting effect.

"How was I so easily fooled?" I asked. The words were directed at Draven, but they were also being offered up to the universe as well. The human world had deceived me. Looking at it from a distance, safe within the waves, it had appeared to be so serene and peaceful. It was anything but.

It's not like evil didn't exist beneath the sea's sun-drenched surface. Merfolk are not perfect by any stretch of the imagination, and sirens, our winged cousins, are evil personified. But up close, it became obvious that humans could be cruel, heartless creatures; wreaking havoc for the sole purpose of watching others suffer. I swore they got pleasure from it.

"We both were," Draven said. His voice sounded distant, as though lost in his own thoughts. He blew out a long breath that ended with a deep, throaty groan. "I should have seen this coming. I've met with Lord Vayne several times. I knew he was unhinged, but..."

I turned to look at Draven. He sat hunched over, with his back against the wall and his face buried in his palms. Never before had I seen him like this. He typically exuded arrogance and overbearing confidence, but now he appeared deflated and defeated.

"I thought I could get through to him," he continued, still talking into his hands. He sat motionless for several long moments before raising his face, showing me just how beaten he truly was. As much as I hated his self-important, cock-sure attitude, it broke my heart to see my prince in this light.

"It was worth the risk," I offered. "If you can remove the sick fish from the school before they all get infected..."

"That's what I thought, too." He smiled and reached out towards me, but I flinched and drew back, refusing his contact. His smile quickly melted away, leaving behind a deep melancholy.

"I wanted to fix the merfolk-human relations here, to make my father proud of me and to prove myself worthy of his respect after what happened to my brothers and sisters in the wars."

"Your family sacrificed everything to save the humans; the same ungrateful bastards who seek to annihilate us now."

"I never got to meet any of them. They were all sea foam before I was even born. But I heard about their heroism, their great deeds, how they were able to turn the tides against a great fleet of enemy soldiers."

He offered a wane, apologetic smile. "I'm sorry."

"Sorry? For what?" I asked, folding my hands across my lap. "Even if you knew this man wasn't stable, what you set out to accomplish was a good thing."

Draven closed his eyes and turned his face to the heavens. "That's not what I meant. I'm sorry about what happened to you, to us. I know it was my fault."

I sat in silence, staring at the person I had once loved. The same one who had thrown me away and banished me for a crime I could have never committed. I wanted to hate him, to tell him he was getting what he deserved, but I just couldn't.

In all the time I'd known Draven, even in the quiet moments when we were alone, he always needed to impress, to build himself up, to appear more than he was. He never stopped being the faithful prince, the son of Triton, God of the Seas. But seeing him in this vulnerable state made me think that, perhaps, he believed his father expected him to present that persona. Only Gaia knew for sure, but that was how Triton behaved whenever he chose to grace his children with his presence. Like father, like son, I guess.

Draven shook his head, sending a lock of hair across his face. "I'm sorry I banished you to the badlands. I should have done something to stop it."

I stared at the man, fire rising in my belly. Damn right you should have done something. You should have fought for me, for my teacher, for *us*. I wanted to scream. I so desperately wanted to jump down his throat with both feet and unleash all my anger, and hurt, and... sadness. But seeing him crushed like this, his eyes welling up, his hands trembling – I just couldn't do it.

"Why?" I asked, shaking my head. "Why didn't you stop it?"

The man's throat bobbed as he looked at me, his big green eyes welling up. He suddenly looked so young and so vulnerable.

"The power," he said, staring down at his empty hands. "When mother gave me the scepter that day, its enchantment coursed through me."

He threw me away because he experienced real magic for the first time? Was he so weak-minded that, in an instant, it clouded his judgment to the point of being moronic? I knew Draven sought the mantle of rulership, but I could have never guessed his lust for authority went so deep. A sneer crept up at the corner of my mouth. All those hate-filled words I had wanted to say earlier were on my lips, just waiting to come screaming out of me.

"I can't explain it," he continued, perhaps trying to cut me off before I went on a tirade.

"Try." The word came out through clenched teeth. It was a good thing we were not close enough to the sea for me to draw on its power. I was seething, and I was more than willing to break Arion's first rule of magic and cast a spell in anger.

"There was a voice." Draven's brow furrowed, and he returned to staring at his empty hands. "The scepter was talking to me, whispering things to me. The words crept into my mind, my heart, my soul. It twisted my thoughts."

I scoffed. I was well aware of how badly power can corrupt, but it was ludicrous to suggest that the magic in his father's scepter could force him into acting against his will. Only cowards placed blame for their actions on other people, or in this case, an inanimate object.

"Congratulations," I said with a huff. "You've sunk to a new low. Of course, it wasn't your fault. Your father's royal scepter made you do it."

When Draven lifted his head to look at me, terror filled his wide eyes. He quickly grasped his hands together, trying to stop them from shaking.

"No," he said, shaking his head. He leaned toward me, swallowing hard. "I swear to you, there was a voice. It hissed at me when I held my father's scepter. It told me to kill you and Arion. I tried to fight it, but it was so strong. When I banished you instead of sentencing you to death, it sent wave after wave of excruciating pain through me. It demanded I take back my words and have you immediately executed.

It didn't matter how hard I tried, there was no way to silence whoever was speaking to me."

I didn't want to believe him, but the remorse in his voice and the fear in his eyes told me he was speaking true.

"I wanted to get rid of the scepter, to send it into the ether, but I couldn't. It wouldn't let me relinquish my grasp on it. Even when I slept, I had to hold on to it."

"So, where is it now, then?" I asked, suddenly becoming skeptical again. "If you couldn't let it go, why are you not holding it now?"

"When we came on land. As soon as I was away from the sea, the voice went silent. Its grip on me vanished, and I got rid of it."

"You threw it away? What if someone else picks it up?" Apparently, I had completely bought into his story.

"I sent it to the ether, the nether realm. Father taught me how to hide important things there, so that they would always be accessible to me, no matter where I was. Calypso, I swear on my life, I did the best I could. I love you. My soul is forever bound to yours. I would rather die than hurt you."

I stared at the man, unblinking. I spent the last year loathing Draven. If what he was saying was true, then what happened between us wasn't his fault. Even still, I couldn't find it in my heart to forgive him. I spent too many nights crying myself to sleep, and too many days feeling like I was an empty shell. I could see no path back from where he'd sent me.

"I see," he said, his brow furrowed. He nodded slowly and looked away. "You have found another merman to love."

I laughed, even with the crushing weight on my chest. "There isn't much room for romance in the badlands. Beside Arion, the only people I've seen are the poor unfortunate souls in need of my magic, and the human I sent Luna to help."

I hadn't intended to mention Dylan or the merfolk who sought out my assistance.

"The human." Draven turned my way, tilting his head to the side slightly. "He must be very important to you if you sent Luna to help him."

Damn. Oh, how I wish I hadn't mentioned him. A dozen eels seemed to be swimming around in my belly.

"Do you love him?" Draven moved beside me, close enough that I could feel his body heat against my skin.

Barnacles and bubbles. Why were we having this conversation? I stared at the merman who I had once so desperately loved, and it made my heart ache. My gaze locked on to his, waiting for Draven's next words. When they never came, I shrugged and turned away.

"I thought you were finished with me, or at least, I was finished with you."

"Do you love him?" He asked again, cupping my cheek in his large, calloused hand. He gently turned my head until I was facing him again. "You would choose a life with him, among the humans, and forsake your own kind?"

"I don't know how I feel about Dylan." The words came spilling out, but as they did, I wondered if I had just lied. "He's very handsome and there is something strangely appealing about him. When I kissed him..."

Draven's face crumpled. I hated myself for hurting him when he looked so vulnerable, but he asked me a direct question, and, at that moment, I did my best to answer. Even though I spoke the truth, my feelings toward the human were unclear. In these past few minutes, conflicting emotions swirled inside me, leaving me unsure of how I truly felt about anything. As I gazed upon the broken-hearted man sitting beside me, I saw a glimpse of the young merman I had fallen in love with, and it had nothing to do with his warm smile, broad shoulders, and narrow waist.

My finger feathered across my mouth as I recalled the heat of Dylan's lips. When I had given him my kiss, our connection was like a lightning bolt ripping through my core. The intensity of it made my toes curl. However, when Draven asked how I felt about the man, I couldn't be sure if my excitement was real, or if it was merely the fulfillment of a wishful crush. It was a moment that left me breathless, yet empty.

"No," I said, the realization crashing into me like a tsunami. "I don't love him. I think…" My words stuck in my throat at the sight of Draven's overly glassy eyes. "I was drawn to him by his willingness to fight insurmountable odds for the betterment of his family. I respected how dedicated he was to his task." I dropped my gaze, unable to continue holding the prince's. "I also found him extremely attractive and the thrill of potentially having a human mate was… exhilarating."

"I understand. At least I think I do."

I had no idea what I was expecting Draven to say or how he might have reacted to my confession. Truth was, I hadn't intended to share any of this. Mostly because it was only at this moment that I had enough clarity of mind to understand it myself.

"Thank you," he continued. The hitch in his words plucked at my heartstrings. "It's been a long time since you shared yourself with me like that. I know it was my fault. I had been so wrapped up in trying to impress my parents, I lost sight of how important you are to me. I cannot rule our kingdom without you by my side. At least, I don't want to. Even with the never-ending insidious voice in my head, I never stopped thinking of you. I never stopped loving you."

I gave him a shy smile and shrugged. I didn't know how to respond to those words. Ever since being banished from the merkingdom,

I had dreamed of hearing them. I had wished Draven would come to his senses, rush to my side, and tell me that everything would be okay. But every morning, the reality of the situation came crashing back, leaving me stuck somewhere between loathing the merman and wanting vengeance for what he had done to Arion and me. I wanted to say something smart, or witty, but when nothing meaningful came to mind, I blurted out the first words that popped into my head.

"It's understandable. I am very lovable."

Draven laughed. It was a genuine, warm laugh that made it all the way to his beautiful blue eyes. I couldn't remember the last time he laughed like that. It was likely when he first asked me on a date. He was nearly sixteen when he first came to visit me at the Academy of Arcana. The merman had waited outside the classroom, hoping to impress me with his charm and smooth words.

"You are a precious pearl," he had said, holding out a bouquet of sea lilies. "Would you consider accompanying me on a swim to the western shallows?"

I had crossed my arms over my chest and cocked an eyebrow at him. "Did you know pearls are created because of something irritating the oyster? Are you suggesting that I am irritating?" Draven's fin had reddened horribly at my comment. I knew who he was, and I was more than a little surprised that he had come to see me, a literal nobody in the merkingdom.

"Well," he'd said, rubbing the back of his head. "You're being pretty irritating right now."

We had stared at each other for several excruciatingly long seconds before we had both burst out laughing.

"What's in the past can't be changed," Draven said, taking my hand in his. "But if I die today, I'll still be grateful for having had a chance to spend this time with you – even under such unpleasant circumstances."

"I'm glad for it, as well, but I don't plan on dying and I don't plan on you dying either. We'll figure it out, one way or another."

I wasn't really sure how it happened, but I found myself wrapped tightly in Draven's arms with my face resting on his chest. I ran my hand over his silky shirt, marveling at its smooth texture. I sighed quietly while I listed to the rhythm of his beating heart. It was beating so fast. Much too fast.

CHAPTER 26

LUNA

Heavy footsteps on the lower deck's floor echoed through the bilge. Each thump made my heart skip, fearful that they'd find me hiding, wrapped in Dylan's smelly leather cloak. Despite the stench of the oils used to impregnate the hide, it couldn't completely mask the young man's heady scent. I snuggled my face deeper into the rough clothing, inhaling deeply, filling my nostrils with the intoxicating fragrance.

"Are you feeling better?" Dylan whispered, sending a string of bubbles into my ear. It was likely the tenth time he had asked me in as many minutes, and the twentieth time he pulled up the sleeve of the cloak so he could examine the progress of the ferrous poising the iron manacles had infected me with. The way he ran his hands over the scales of my tail fin skin tickled me nearly as much as the bubbles he was blowing into my ear. He seemed mesmerized by my mermaid form. I had switched to it shortly after entering the bilge, hoping it would allow me to heal more quickly.

I nodded lightly and grinned. I didn't dare open my mouth, fearing I might burst out laughing and alert the mermaid hunters to our location.

"It looks like she escaped out the window," a harsh voice said from above. "But it makes no sense. Those window frames are pure iron. There is no way she could have gotten past them. I don't even understand how she had the strength to knock out the porthole."

"I'm guessing it was her last act as a mermaid," a man said. His voice was so distinctive, I had no doubt it was Lachlan, the first mate. "See that puddle of water on the floor? My guess is, she succumbed to the iron and turned into sea foam. If we go into the bilge, we'll find her there. She'll be the thin slick of scum floating on the surface."

Four men laughed at the first mate's joke. It made me want to burst up through the floorboards and drag them all below. I'd show them what it was like to deal with a mermaid in her domain, with the full power of the sea at her disposal.

A leathery tentacle slipped around my neck and gave me a light squeeze. Octavius maneuvered his gelatinous body over my shoulder and slid upwards so that his enormous bulging eyes were directly in front of mine.

"It's not worth it, Luna. First, we get you free, then we deal with these miserable humans. Once the hunters go back on deck, we'll find a way out of here and tell Prince Draven what these people are up to."

I couldn't see anything with the octopup's face pressed against mine, but I could feel Dylan thrashing beside me. I immediately recognized what was happening. He was out of air, and no longer able to breathe water. I had seen it before while rescuing sailors who had inadvertently fallen into the sea. There was no place for him to surface, not with the bilge water filling the entire space right up to the floorboards.

The first mate and his crew were still directly above us and, at any moment, we were going to reveal ourselves to them. I had no idea if I was able to use my mermaid magic to help him, but I saw no other option. My pulse raced out of control as I gripped Dylan by the sides of his head and drew him to me for a kiss. I pressed my mouth over his and blew air into his lungs.

I didn't know if it was enough to free him from the panic that was actively gripping him. His body stiffened in response, his eyes wide and wild. He gripped my arms, squeezing hard enough to leave bruises, but I continued breathing for him, filling him with life-saving air.

After several excruciatingly long moments, Dylan's grip on my arms lessened, and he began breathing on his own. I tried to pull away, but he held me tight, pressing his lips against mine. His eyes, once wild with panic, now burned with an intensity that I didn't quite understand.

His hands dropped from my arms and slid around to my back, pulling my body tight against his. The thrumming of his heart pounded against my chest. My own heart kept perfect rhythm with his as I slid my hands to the back of his head, running my fingers through his long hair, pulling his face hard against mine.

"Luna, you can let go of him," Octavius said, tapping me on the shoulder. "He's breathing fine on his own now. The humans have left."

I blinked several times. I was disoriented and confused. It took a moment for his words to register, and when they did, I reluctantly pulled away from Dylan, leaving my fingers lingering on the back of his neck.

"Luna, let him go!" Octavius' tentacle slid around my forehead, his tiny suction cups clamping onto my smooth, wet skin. Against my wishes, he yanked me away from Dylan.

I stole a glance at the wide-eyed man, who still had his arm wrapped around my waist. His heaving chest and rising flush were a perfect mirror of my own reaction to our brief embrace.

"Did you hear me?" Octavius' voice broke through my thoughts. I blinked again and turned to face him. "Luna? Barnacles and bubbles, girl. Where is your head at? Are you still suffering the effects of the ferrous poisoning?"

I had to squint to focus on my octopup. He was doing a lot of talking, but I had no idea what he had just said. Why was he frowning at me like that?

"Did you hear me?" Octavius squished his body between Dylan and me, forcing me to give him my undivided attention. "The sailors think you've died."

"Yes. I know. They think I've turned into sea foam."

"And did you hear what else they said, or were you too busy resuscitating this human for far longer than was necessary? Why were you both making those moaning sounds? Did saving his life somehow injure you?"

I was sure my face had turned a bright shade of pink. How long had I been *kissing* him? I couldn't remember when my attempts to save Dylan had changed from a life-saving requirement into an oh-so-pleasurable, passionate embrace. My heart had raced as he held me, our bodies pressed together, our lips locked in a deep, fervent kiss. A rush of heat had coursed through me as he pulled me close, pressing himself against me, igniting a fiery desire within my core that engulfed my mind and body.

"Focus!" Octavius said. "The first mate said you would be replaced with the other two merfolk Lord Vayne has captured."

Captured merfolk? Octavius' words cut through the haze that was clouding my mind. My heart sank at the news.

"If they've got Draven and Calypso, we've got to help them."

"We need to stay here," Dylan said. He released me and swam away, his eyes locked onto the floorboards. "You need to finish healing before we do anything."

"I'm well enough. My brother and my best friend are in trouble, and I refuse to wait here while Lord Vayne tortures them."

"They're going to be brought here," Dylan said, running his fingers through his hair. "Captain Roberts needs them, just like he needed you. Right now, Lachlan and the other hunters think you're dead and gone. That gives us the advantage. They have no way of knowing that we're down here in the bilge. When Calypso and Draven are locked in their cell, we'll free them, and then we can deal with Lord Vayne, Captain Roberts, and the rest of these merfolk-hunting monsters."

"What else did they say?" I asked, unsure if I liked Dylan's plan. I wasn't good at waiting.

"That was about it." Octavius swam over and curled around my arm. His body quaked as he nuzzled his head against my shoulder. "I'm frightened. I wish you had never come up here. We were safe and happy at home, and now look at this mess. This was even dumber than stealing shrimp from the sirens' garden."

How in the seas did he know that? I always made sure to give him the slip before I went on those particular adventures. Through his fear, he still managed to throw an accusatory glare at me.

"You know about that?"

The exaggerated way he rolled his enormous eyes nearly made me laugh out loud. "Of course, I know. I'm your watcher, and your chaperone, and I wasn't born yesterday. You have to wake up pretty early to pull the kelp over my eyes."

"How old are you?" Dylan asked, settling down beside me. He looked as agitated as I felt. "I thought you were just a pup."

"Old enough! My kind don't measure time the same way you humans do." Octavius threw as much bravado into his voice as he could muster, attempting to sound wiser and more worldly than he actually was.

"He'll turn five this winter," I said, drawing a look of ire from my companion. "But, as he said, his kind are not like us. He learns much faster than we can."

"And I can draw on the experiences of my parents as well." Octavius raised his chin in defiance to my speaking his true age. "That makes me wise beyond reckoning, and it's why I was entrusted with looking over the princess."

"The princess?" Dylan said, his eyebrows shooting to the top of his forehead.

"Yes," Octavius said, pointing one of his tentacles into Dylan's face. "The princess. She is the sister of Prince Draven and the daughter of King Triton."

Dylan slowly drifted away, putting some distance between himself and the octopup, his expression pensive.

"You're a god?" he asked. "If you're the daughter of Triton, and he's the god of the seas, doesn't that make you a god as well?"

My own eyebrows shot up so high I feared they might leave my head entirely. I had never considered that before. I knew my father was the king, and I knew he was often referred to as a god, but I wasn't like him.

"No. I'm not a god." I didn't completely believe what I had just said. "I might be the child of a god, if my father even is one, but I am also the child of a mermaid. My mother can be demanding and cold, but I still love and respect her. She's nothing more than a normal mermaid, and so am I."

I didn't know why this conversation was upsetting me so much, but it was. It bothered me that I couldn't find anything nice to say about my mother. Also, I didn't want to be special, and I certainly didn't want to be a god, or even a demigod. I only wanted to be me. I needed to change the topic of this discussion. It was making me far too uncomfortable.

"Tell me about your mother. Angelika? That's her name, right?"

A tapping on the hull of the ship sent my heart slamming into my throat.

"Did you say, Angelika?" The voice was Arion's, speaking from outside the hull. The fear I had felt instantly vanished at the realization he was nearby. The most powerful mage in the entire merkingdom was here to rescue us, and these humans were in for a world of hurt.

CHAPTER 27

DYLAN

The sound of Arion's voice substantially lifted Luna's spirits. I didn't really understand why knowing he was outside was making her so excited. He had been there since I arrived, and he had done nothing to help us with our situation.

"Oh, this is going to be fun," Luna said, her eyes sparkling with mischief. "Arion is the greatest mage in all the merkingdom. He will unleash his magics and these foolish humans will realize they cannot fight the power of the sea." She rapped on the hull, pressing her face against the salt-stained wood. "When will you start unleashing your fury upon them? I can't wait."

I wanted to say something, but I didn't want to disappoint her – especially if I was wrong and the giant red crab was going to do something amazing.

Silent moments ticked past like rain pattering against a window-pane. Either Arion had left, or he was choosing not to respond to the princess' question.

"Arion?" Luna said, tilting her head to the side. "Are you there?"

"I'm here," he replied. His voice was hesitant and subdued. My concern that he couldn't help us any more than he already had was immediately realized. "I can't help you. I'm sorry."

Luna's shoulders drooped, her brows furrowing with disappointment and worry. She hugged her tail tightly to her chest, her shoulders jouncing in silent sobs. I swam to her side and took her in my arms.

"Why?" she called out, her expression turning grim. "Why can't you help us? Is it because my brother banished you and Calypso? Is this payback?"

"No, princess. Never. It's not like that at all."

"Then why?"

Luna's words boomed throughout the bilge. I cringed, worried that the sailors on deck might hear her and find our hiding spot.

"Shhh." I pressed my finger to my lips, imploring Luna to keep her voice low. I turned my eyes toward the ship's floor directly above. "Not so loud," I whispered. Luna nodded and lowered her gaze.

"Under no circumstances whatsoever can I cast magic on humans. It is forbidden by Triton himself."

"I don't understand," Luna said, leaning her forehead against the hull.

"Dylan?" Arion said, a palpable worry in his voice. "Is your mother's name Angelika? Are there any other women in your town who have the same name?"

"Yes," I replied, suddenly filled with curiosity over his interest in my mother. "That's my mother's name, and no, there are no other women who share the same name."

"I feared as much." There was a long silence after Arion spoke.

"Why?" I asked, my pulse quickening, fearing that some ill had befallen the woman. "Is something wrong? Did something happen to her?" Again, there was another long silence.

"Not now," Arion replied. There was a tremor in his voice. What-ever it was, it was upsetting him deeply. "Your mother is the reason I am forbidden to cast magic on humans. I am the reason she is crippled, and she is the reason I'm a crab."

"What did you do to her?" I yelled, my rage getting the better of me, burning away my self-control.

"The story is too difficult to explain, but I promise I will tell you everything. For now, I can only offer you my apologies and a promise to do everything in my power to right the wrongs I have committed against your family."

"You'll tell me now!" I pounded my fist against the hull, sending a loud boom through the bilge. The realization that I may have just announced our location to every seaman aboard immediately diffused my anger. I held my breath, waiting for the sound of hunters pouring into the ship's hold, seeking out the source of the noise that had come from below deck.

There were no crewmen and there was no reply from Arion, either.

"I'm sure there's a good reason for Arion's behavior," Luna said. Her face was so close to mine; her sapphire blue eyes filled with con-cern.

"I can't wait to hear it."

Luna's head snapped back, distancing herself from my biting words. A lump rose in my throat. She didn't deserve that. She was offering me comfort and I... I was an idiot.

"I'm sorry. I just..." I just what? I was looking for a place to unleash my anger with Arion. I had no idea what his words meant, or how he was responsible for my mother's physical affliction, but the thought of anyone hurting that wonderfully kind woman... "I have no excuse."

"It's okay. If someone told me they had hurt my mother, I'd be upset, too." Luna flashed a quick smile. "Why don't we work on finding a way off this boat? It will take your mind off mister crabby. If they're bringing Draven and Calypso here, we need to be ready for them."

Heavy footsteps pounded down the stairs into the ship's hull. The echo of each step increased my heart rate. I instinctively wrapped my arm around Luna, protecting her from whoever was coming. The footfalls continued across the floor, stopping almost directly above us.

"Triton," a deep male voice called out. "Forgive my captain and my crew. Their hearts have been twisted by anger and fear. They are not the men I know them to be. I hate myself for the role I've played in the mermaid's death. I want to say that it wasn't my fault, but it was. I should have stood up for her. I should have stood up for that poor boy and his family. Instead, I took the coward's way out. If I can, oh merciful Triton, I will make amends. I will do everything in my power to right the wrongs I've committed."

A look of confusion spread across Luna's face. I was certain my own expression was no different. The voice sounded just like the first mate's, except for the fact that he seemed sorry for what was happening.

"I had not expected your daughter to die," Lachlan continued. "I swear it on my soul. I know there is nothing within my power to bring her back, but I promise, I will do what I can to ensure it never happens again to any of your children."

Luna's brow furrowed while her gaze was still locked on the floor above us. She had mouthed some words, but it wasn't clear what she was saying. If I were to guess, I'd have thought it to be, "What the fork?" It must be a mermaid expression. When we got out of this, I'd have to ask her about it.

"Is that the first mate?" Luna whispered into my ear. I nodded in soundless reply. "Do you think he's trying to trick us?" I shook my head. If the man thought she was anywhere below deck, he'd have ripped everything apart while searching for her. He sounded too sincere. If he was faking, he missed his calling as an actor.

"Should we trust him? Do we let him know we're here?"

I wanted to believe he wasn't the man he portrayed himself to be. If we had his assistance, it would make escaping from the ship a lot easier. He might even help us free Calypso and Luna's brother when Captain Roberts brought them here. But there was too much at stake. If we were wrong, if he fooled us with his words of contrition, it would likely be the death of all three of us.

All *three* of us. Where was Octavius?

I swiveled about, searching for the little black octopup. I hadn't seen him in a while.

The squeal of nails being pulled from timber resounded through the bilge water. My head snapped around to see the octopup pushing up one of the floorboards in Luna's cell. A moment later, he disappeared through the small opening, except for two tentacles he was using to anchor himself to the floor. I could only suppose it was to prevent Lachlan from scooping him up.

"An octopus?" The first mate's feet tromped across the deck, each one like a baton beating on a kettle drum. The grating noise of the cage door being swung open was followed by the splash of Octavius falling back into the water. A moment later, two more boards were pulled up, sending my heart into my throat.

"Octavius?" Luna called out. "What have you done?"

"I found us an ally," he said, looking exceptionally pleased with himself.

Lachlan's head suddenly appeared, having stuck it into the bilge water, searching for where the octopus had gone.

Luna darted in front of me, shielding me from the perceived threat. The way the first mate's eyes bugged out of his face, he was just as startled as we were.

CHAPTER 28

CALYPSO

The raucous cry of seagulls and the salty scent of the sea roused me from my slumber. My stomach knotted at the sight of the boat moored against the long dock. The fear gripping me offered a momentary distraction from the burning pain of the iron manacles digging into my wrists, sapping every ounce of strength from my body. By the time this human, a man referred to as Captain Roberts, had marched us down the hill from Lord Vayne's house, neither Draven nor I could walk any further. I had fallen not long after we'd cleared the manor's gates, unable to keep my legs under me. Someone had kicked me hard in the ribs, urging me to stand. While I was doubled over, face down in the dirt, hate-filled shouts filled my ears. Each word sent a shock of pain through my head like I was being stabbed with a shard of coral. From within the din, I could make out Draven's angry voice, but I couldn't identify any of the others. When it became clear that we could no longer walk on our own, the captain ordered one of his men to bring a wagon to carry us.

The sound of the cart's wheels bouncing over the dock's worn wooden slats grated in my head, with each clack sending another sharp pain stabbing into my brain. The skin on my forearms was turning black where the iron manacles bit into my wrists, while long, thin, inky tentacles snaked their way up to my elbows. My breath was becoming more labored, my vision blurred. These were all the classic signs of ferrous poisoning gripping me, an affliction I had spent a good deal of time studying under Arion's watchful eyes.

Judging by how quickly the poison was spreading, if these cuffs weren't removed soon, I'd be sea foam before Pele disappeared over the western horizon.

I glanced briefly at Draven, who was sitting bolt upright, his chin raised in defiance. Despite the brave face he was putting on, the cracks in his tough, impenetrable exterior were showing. His eyes no longer held their smoldering power, his wavy black hair now laid limp on his head, and a slight tremble coursed over his thick pink lips. He refused to show any signs of weakness to our captors, but they were there, his body betraying the façade he was desperately trying to project.

I gently leaned my body against his, trying not to add any additional burden to the man. His muscles tensed at my touch. Although his expression was stoic, fear rolled off him in waves. "We'll figure this out," I whispered in a pathetic attempt to offer him a morsel of hope, a beacon of light in the darkness. "With any luck, Luna is already free and plotting our escape. We just need to hold on a little longer. Do you hear me? Don't you dare give up and die on me!"

Draven sighed, his chin dipping down to his chest. We had come here to rescue Luna and had gotten ourselves captured in the process. I could only surmise that, in addition to his worry about his sister, he was not happy that he needed the help of others to get him out of this predicament. The prince was accustomed to being the unshakable master of his domain. His needing help lowered him, making him no different from the rest of us.

Then again, it could be the ferrous poisoning sucking the life out of him and he was simply too weak to hold his head high any longer. Seeing him like this hurt more than the accursed manacles searing my skin. A surge of fear rose in my throat when he collapsed against my shoulder.

"Play weak," he whispered into my ear, his breath warm and moist. I breathed out a sigh of relief at his words. "Bide your time until we're on the water."

The wheels of the cart hit a loose plank, jostling us about, sending Draven tumbling onto the dock. He landed hard on his side and let out a loud groan as he rolled onto his back, leaving him inches from the churning sea below. This must have been his plan all along, to play-act that he was beaten and defeated, and then, at the last possible moment, toss himself into the sea.

I waited for him to finish rolling off the dock, but it didn't happen. He laid there motionless, a hair's width from freedom.

"Get him back onto the cart and lash him to it if you must," the captain bellowed. "He almost escaped."

Two men grabbed my prince roughly by the hair and feet, yanking him from the edge of freedom. Even though Draven didn't resist, the man holding him by the hair felt the need to punch him in the face. Outside of the merman's head snapping to the side, he didn't react at all.

"He's dying," I yelled. "These damned cuffs are killing us. What good are we to you dead?"

"Until you die, I'll hang you both from the yard arm as a warning to merfolk," the captain replied, grabbing a hank of my hair, craning my neck backwards. "Your filthy people will learn that I, Captain Roberts, am the ruler of these waters and if they want to live here, they'll pay me for the privilege."

"You're the ruler of the Gaelinora?" I scoffed at the man. "I wonder what Lord Vayne would think of your egomaniacal ramblings. I'm also thinking Triton might have something to say about this. Do you think he'll just let you live after killing his only son?"

"Lord Vayne has much larger plans than ruling this oversized puddle of water," the captain said, mirroring my scoff. "As for Triton, he's nothing more than a myth perpetrated by your kind. If this vapid lump of seaweed truly is his son, then your supposed god is nothing more than a weakling. In the meantime, the prince will look terrific mounted to the prow of my ship. When he finally succumbs, he'll become sea foam just like the other mermaid we captured."

A lump grew in my throat at the man's words. Was Luna dead? Had they killed her? Sweet Triton, what had I done? I was the cause of all of this. I tried to help a human, and in doing so, I likely destroyed the entire royal family.

Darkness crept in at the corners of my consciousness, threatening to drag me into the abyss. It seemed as though my world was spinning out of control. How could I have been so foolish? Because of my childish crush on a human, I was about to bring ruin upon the entire merkingdom.

As I became engulfed by a swirling vortex of despair, agony suddenly ripped through me, as though I had been set ablaze and every bone in my body was being torn through my skin. The excruciating torment shook my soul, yanking me back from the brink, thrusting me into the harsh reality I didn't want to face. After a few unbearable seconds, the pain subsided, leaving me dizzy and breathless.

My eyes focused long enough to see I was being brought on board the ship. The only rational explanation for the agony I felt was because they had rolled me across an iron barrier, and judging by how badly it hurt, it was an extremely large one.

The pain had awakened me, saving me from drifting into the Beyond. I glanced down at the manacles binding my wrists. My hands were almost entirely black now and the once thin lines running up to my elbow were thicker, disappearing up under my sleeves. I peered over at Draven; a weak gasp escaped my lips. His skin was deathly pale. His eyes were wide open and utterly vacant. Like mine, his hands were blackened. His long sleeves hid any other effects his iron shackles were causing.

The sour taste of bile rose in my throat, the acrid flavor coating my tongue, making me gag. I shuddered uncontrollably as I tried to swallow down my fear. This day would be our last. Like a slap in the face, an unexpected thought cut through my hazy consciousness. I had finally learned why Draven had been such a hagfish to Arion and me, and I was opening my heart to possibilities I had thought had long since vanished, and yet, nothing good would ever come of it. At least I would die knowing he wasn't the horrible merman I believed him to be. A deep sadness gripped me as the weight of a missed opportunity for happiness slipped through my fingers. If only he had been able to tell me sooner. Perhaps our world would have been a very different place.

CHAPTER 29

LUNA

Barnacles and bubbles. What in the name of Gaia was my octopup thinking? We were safely hidden in this putrid tub of a boat, and he revealed our location to the man I feared most. I was suspended in the shallow water, frozen with indecision, while my mind raced with potential solutions, each one seeming more dangerous than the last. In that fraction of a moment, I weighed the risks and benefits and came up completely blank. I had no idea how best to proceed.

Dylan seemed to share my concern, echoing my behavior; his mouth agape, a thin stream of bubbles curling over his lips, floating to the surface. "What are we going to do?"

Lachlan was a disgusting merfolk hater. He was the one who had slapped those accursed iron manacles on me, laughing as he did. His face twisted in some perverted joy when he witnessed how much pain it was causing me. This man was a monster, and he was our enemy, and he had seen us. I was certain he had already called his henchmen to come and recapture us, to make sure that I never saw freedom again.

Like a thunderclap, the solution to our problem revealed itself to me. Lachlan had to die.

With a powerful thrust of my tail, I sped toward the opening, launching myself from the bilge onto the deck above. Dylan's cloak billowed out around me as I flew through the air. I imagined myself resembling a manta ray in flight, or perhaps something much scarier. The first mate's eyes widened in terror as he tried to back away from me, his boots slipping on the slick planks. His arms flailed at his sides as he stumbled backwards, falling hard on his butt, squealing like a guppy. I immediately shifted back into human form before my feet hit the ground. Much to my surprise, I was still wearing the dress that Dylan's mother had given me. I had no way of knowing that would happen, but I was thankful that it did. I shook off the thought and headed towards Lachlan.

Wrapping Dylan's cloak tight, I stepped through the open door of my cell. Fortunately, they hadn't bothered to put an iron threshold. Had they done so, I'd have been permanently corralled in my pen. My proximity to the iron stung badly, but it wouldn't have any lasting effects.

I stalked toward the prone man, my fists clenched in tight balls at my sides. As I neared, the first mate crab-walked away from me, desperate to evade my wrath.

"Please," he wailed, shaking his head violently. "I'm sorry. What I did was wrong."

I wasn't buying it, not a single word. I continued chasing him across the wooden floor, stopping when he slammed into a stack of crates, blocking off his exit.

"You're only sorry because you fear for your miserable life," I said, inching my way toward him. "You thought you killed Triton's only daughter, and you were hoping to escape his wrath through worthless prayers."

"You're the actual daughter of Triton?" the first mate said, quivering like a jellyfish caught in a swift current. But, like a jelly, Lachlan was dangerous, even if he appeared ready to ink himself. "I'm sorry for what I did. I swear on the bones of my ancestors. I had no choice but to follow Cap'n Roberts' orders. He's a madman, a tyrant. I obey his orders, or I suffer. The man is a menace."

There was a ring of truth to Lachlan's words. I wanted to believe him. I didn't want to take his life. But what choice did I have? While I paused, considering the man's fate, his eyes narrowed.

"You, boy. How did you get on this ship?"

I turned in time to see Dylan come hobbling towards me, a large piece of wood in his hand. His eyes were hard, his jaw set. He tightened his grip on the board, slowly drawing it back.

"I don't believe you, Lachlan. Not a single word." Dylan used the bars of the cages for support as he continued to draw near. "When I was a hand on this ship, you treated me like dirt, with or without prompting from Roberts. You enjoyed tormenting me at every turn. You are a mean-spirited waste of skin."

"I know what I've done in my past, but it's right now that matters. I could have screamed for help," Lachlan stammered, holding his hands out, shielding himself from his attackers. "But I didn't. I clamped my mouth shut, and I never said a word." He shook his head, his gaze darting back and forth between me and Dylan. "Even now, I could call for my crewmen and you'd be executed before you took another step. I'm not lying. I'm sorry for what happened to you, to both of you."

Dylan glanced down at me, perhaps waiting to hear my thoughts on how to proceed. When I didn't give him any guidance, he drew back the board in his hands, ready to deliver a blow to the man who had made his time aboard this ship a living nightmare.

"Wait," I said. Slowly, deliberately, I took a step toward Lachlan, still unsure of what I was going to do next. My pulse was thrumming in my ears as I reached out to him. "I believe you. I fear trusting you will be our undoing, but we need an ally if we are to escape this prison."

The man grasped my hand, his palm rough and calloused from hard labor. The muscles in his arm rippled as he tightened his grip. If he had played me for a fool, I had fallen for it, hook, line, and sinker. Without pulling me off balance, he lifted himself to his feet and lowered his gaze.

"Princess, I will do everything in my power to free you. My only request is that, if I am successful, you find a way to protect my family." When he raised his chin, his cheeks were wet. "They don't deserve to be punished for my acts of cruelty and cowardice. If either Captain Roberts or Lord Vayne discover my part in freeing you..." He let his words hang there, like I understood their implications.

"So long as nobody sees us, you are safe," I said, still holding the man's hand.

"Everyone expects Luna to be dead, and nobody knows I'm here," Dylan said, finishing my thought. "Is what we heard true? Are Prince Draven and Calypso being brought here?"

Lachlan slowly nodded and inclined his head. He gently released his grip on me and blew out a breath. "Lord Vayne has been planning his capture of Prince Draven for many moons. I don't know who this Calypso person is, but I'm assuming she is the other mermaid being held at the lord's manor. She has dark red hair, and if you aren't offended by my comment, she is the most attractive woman I've ever laid my sorry eyes on."

I knew in my heart that it was Calypso he was referring to. My friend was nothing short of stunning.

"Where do we go from here?" I asked, directing the question to Lachlan. "How do you plan on making this right?" The man's eyebrows shot up and a hint of a smile graced his lips.

"Me? A plan? Up until two minutes ago, I thought you were dead. I didn't know that *thing* was on the ship, and I believed octopuses were only found in the sea, not in my boat, ripping up floorboards."

"We need a way off this tub," Dylan said. "One that won't get us captured and executed." It was Dylan's turn to smile. It looked like an idea had crossed his mind. "And if we can sink this boat at the same time, all the better."

"You want to scuttle my fishing trawler?"

"It's not *your* ship," Dylan said. "And it's no longer a trawler. It's a prison designed to capture and torture mermaids. If you want to set things right, you might start with removing the weapons being used against Triton's children."

"Sinking this vessel will be no simple task," Lachlan said, scrubbing his hand down his face with a loud groan. "There's so much iron, it's practically a warship."

"We don't have to sink it," I said. "But we need to bring in more water so that it comes up through the floorboards. As soon as my manacles were removed and I was in the seawater below, the ferrous poisoning subsided and most of my strength returned. Even if there is enough to keep Draven's and Calypso's feet wet, it might keep them strong enough to fight back. As long as they don't get too close to the iron bars, they should be reasonably safe."

"The ship has two ballast pumps at the stern," Lachlan said. "They're not particularly effective, but it beats lowering buckets over the side of the boat and hauling them down here."

"Where's the *stern*?" I asked. I had never heard such a word before.

Both Dylan and Lachlan gave me a strange look, like I was a dim-witted child or something. I scowled and crossed my arms over my chest. "This is the first time I've ever been on land and you're going to mock me because I don't know the parts of a boat? Do you have any clue what a sea sapphire is? How about a nudibranch? No? Well, how about a Makara? Are you familiar with them? I could introduce you to one and I could tell it where to stick its giant, spiraled horn."

The smug expressions melted off their faces. In almost perfect unison, they both asked me the same question. "You can talk to sea dragons?"

Okay. I was confused again. "What's a sea dragon?"

"It's what we call Makara," Dylan said. "There are so many myths and legends about them, and how they sink ships by ramming them with their giant, spiral horns."

Heat rose in my cheeks. I didn't need to see them to know they were turning bright pink. I was angry at being belittled, and I had spoken too quickly. I hadn't expected them to know anything about Makara. They were reclusive creatures that rarely left the deeps.

"Yes," I said, trying to save face. "I can talk to them, but they rarely listen. About the only person they ever truly pay heed to is my father. Triton may rule the seas and oceans, but he doesn't rule the Makara. They are a kingdom unto themselves."

"Too bad," Dylan said with a smile. "It would have made scuttling this ship a lot easier."

"This way," Lachlan said. "I'll show you where the ballast pumps are. I'll explain how they work and then I'd better get topside. The crew might be wondering where I'm at."

"We need to fix the floorboards," I said. "We can't leave them pulled up like that." I turned toward where the floor had been dismantled. To my surprise, everything was already back in place and Octavius was giving me a look of supreme satisfaction. Ever since he had been assigned to watch over me, I had considered him to be nothing more than a barnacle on my scales, but he was really coming through when I needed him most.

"Get the prisoners secured and shove off," a commanding voice bellowed from above. "These two won't last much longer, and I want to use them to drag every single accursed mermaid from the seas before Pele rises on a new day."

My heart hammered against my chest. People were coming, and we were in the open.

"Hide," Lachlan said, pointing to a pile of crates near the ship's stern.

We were about to head out to sea to hunt my kin. If I couldn't find a solution, thousands of merfolk were going to die.

CHAPTER 30

DYLAN

I watched in horror as a man fell down the stairs into the ship's hold. His arms and legs were bent at unnatural angles as he lay on the floor unmoving. From above, the shrill cries of a woman filled my ears with dread. I glanced over at Luna, struggling to see her in the dim light of our hiding place. Judging by her wide blue eyes and the way she was clutching onto my arm, she was as terrified as I.

"What in the name of Triton are you doing?" Lachlan bellowed up the stairway. "Are you trying to kill him like you did the female? We don't have an endless supply of bait."

I breathed a silent sigh of relief at the first mate's words. He had a golden opportunity to sell us out, but instead, he was advocating for the man who had been tossed into the hold.

"He'll last long enough," a voice yelled down. "He only needs to survive the night."

"Well," Lachlan bellowed back up, "he's not even going to survive leaving port if we're not more careful."

"Are you questioning my ability to run my ship? If you are, I'll gladly appoint a new first mate and use you as bait for tonight's hunt."

"No Cap'n. Never Cap'n. I was just..." Lachlan stopped talking long enough to stare down at the lifeless body at his feet. "I'll get him locked in a cage right away and I'll do what I can to keep him alive until he's served his purpose. No sense letting him turn to sea foam before we arrive."

While the first mate dragged the man's body toward Luna's former cell, two more men were coming down the stairs, carrying Calypso. She was awake, but she appeared to be on death's door.

"They need our help," Luna whispered. "They can't wait."

"If we come out of hiding right now, they'll throw us in a cage, too." Luna tightened her grasp on my arm, digging her nails into my skin. She didn't like my answer, but I believed she saw the wisdom in it. "Lachlan will be true to his word. We just need to have a bit of faith."

As I said the words, my stomach tightened. The man was terrified of his bosses, and with good reason. Lachlan could turn coat at any moment. I needed to press the issue and remind him we were here and that he had promised to help free us. I stepped out from my hiding place, doing my best to keep to the shadows. Everyone who had come below deck would have trouble seeing until their eyes grew accustomed to the dim light in the hold.

"I'll adjust the ballast," I called out, making my voice gruff and confident. "I'll make sure we run true, just like you showed me."

"I already told you to start pumping," Lachlan yelled. "Why are you making me tell you a second time?" Even from this distance, I could see the concern etched into his face. He was trying to appear in charge, but the hate in his voice wasn't as biting as it had been when he first discovered Luna's origins.

"Bring that red-headed mermaid in here," he commanded to the sailors carrying Calypso. "Toss her in with this other sack of crap. There's enough of their friend's foam to remind them what will happen if they cross us. Get back topside when you're done. I'll finish up and join you shortly. No mistakes. Extra rations to the hunter who bags the most merfolk tonight."

The crewmen did exactly as Lachlan had instructed. They dropped Calypso onto the cell floor and quickly exited the hold. Before I could stop her, Luna bolted from her hiding place and raced across the room, dropping beside the unconscious man.

"Brother," she said, lightly tapping his face. "Draven, wake up. Don't you dare die on me. You're not leaving me to run our kingdom. That's your job and you know how father will feel if you shirk your responsibilities."

Draven's eyes fluttered open for a moment. He grunted out something unintelligible before falling back into unconsciousness.

"Get these cuffs off him," Luna said. "Right now. Remove them or he's going to die."

"I don't have the keys," Lachlan said, his gaze flashing to the stairs. "If I go get them, they'll know something's up."

We didn't need keys. Not when we had a clever octopup who could pop a lock as easily as he could open a clam shell. In moments, he had both Draven's and Calypso's manacles off.

"Get them into seawater," Luna said, removing my cloak, throwing it over her brother. "This will help a bit, but they both need to be fully submerged if they are to start healing."

Between Octavius and Lachlan, the floorboards were pulled up in seconds and the two merfolk were pushed into the water, while Luna knelt at the end of the hole with her face in her hands. Nobody seemed to care about the amount of water being sloshed over the cell floor, probably because I needed to get it submerged, anyway.

CHAPTER 31

CALYPSO

The groan of aged timbers and the gentle lapping of water against my body roused me from my slumber, dragging me from the nightmarish dreams that had plagued my mind. The insatiable hunger of iron manacles gnawing at my flesh still stung my skin, while the soul-crushing weight of ferrous poisoning coursing through my body continued to weigh on me, sapping me of my strength and my will to live.

I inhaled deeply, trying to cleanse the horrific visions gripping my mind. The scent of the briny water was off and its flavor was even worse, like I was bathing in a stagnant, tainted pond. My eyes snapped open to a murky world devoid of hope, and the brutal realization that it was no dream.

I reached up, finding the rough slats of a wooden ceiling inches above me. The foul humans had at least removed my bindings and placed me in a water-filled cage. Even though my head felt as though it had been slammed against a rock, and my mind was as porous a sea sponge, I no longer felt like I was one scale away from becoming sea foam.

My prison rocked heavily, slamming me hard against its wooden wall, sending a sharp pain through my shoulder. Each subsequent jolt sloshed me around in the fetid water, while a cloth-covered bag of flotsam bumped repeatedly against me. I recoiled from the grotesque refuse the humans had thrown into my prison cell, repulsed by the thought of touching whatever foul objects they were using to torture me with now. I pushed it away, my heart filled with revulsion and despair at the inhumane treatment I was being forced to endure.

As my fingers brushed against the bag's distinct texture, a memory surfaced; one that was as murky as the dark, turbid water in which I was submerged. I strained to hold on to it, but like silt slipping through my grasp, it eluded me. A sense of urgency swept through me, as if the recollection was the key to my freedom. With determination, I kicked my tail, propelled by the desperate need to remember, and to escape this prison of darkness and despair.

Cringing at the expected revulsion of touching the bag, I clutched onto its smooth silky fabric, running my free hand over its heavy, lumpy surface. My memory was shrouded, like searching for a ghost through a forest of kelp, but I refused to give up. I continued running my fingers across the bag, searching and probing, only stopping when the texture changed from smooth silky fabric to lightly textured, scale-covered skin. My heart sank when it became clear what I was holding onto. It crushed my spirit, sending my mind reeling, driving bile up into my throat.

"Draven!"

Terror gripped me as the realization of the situation crashed over me like a tidal wave. I had been captured while trying to find my prince. We had been locked in a strange cage together. We shared a moment, a wonderfully tender moment that rekindled a love that had long since been overshadowed by hatred and contempt. It was that same love that was now threatening to rip my still-beating heart from my chest.

My hands continued to seek the man's face. He was so cold, so lifeless. In desperation, I pressed my lips to his, trying to breathe life back into him, giving what I could of myself to save him. I could feel nothing of his presence, his spirit, and yet I maintained hope. He couldn't be gone, not fully. Had he passed to the Beyond, he'd be sea foam. With my hand over his still heart, I renewed my kiss, desperately hoping to revive him, to feel a single beat. Any sign that he would return to me would be enough, but I felt no sign of life. No heartbeat. No breath. No response whatsoever.

By all indications, my prince had passed, but for reasons unknown to me, his body was holding on, refusing to let go of the world he had so desperately tried to help.

I pressed my mouth against his again, willing him to return to me, to give us a chance at redemption, to heal the wounds we had inflicted upon each other. I had hoped that somehow, my kiss would be magical and I could... magic! I was a witch. Sure, I was still wet behind the ears, but Arion had trained me well and I would leverage what he taught me to drag my love back from the abyss. I would travel to the Beyond itself if I had to.

My body trembled at the thought of trying to use my magic. I didn't fear the power I held, but I was terrified it would not be enough and I would fail at the most important spell I had ever cast. Arion hadn't prepared me for this, not by a long shot. Outside of the one powerful invocation to break enchantments, he had only taught me simple spells and incantations that could cure minor scrapes and abrasions. My teacher helped me to find a cure for the effects of Luna's obsession with fire-shrimp. He was a mentor to me in so many ways, well beyond my desire to learn magic. I wished with all my heart he was beside me now. He'd know what to do, how to save Draven, how to return my love to me.

But he wasn't here. It was just me and Draven and my pitiful magic. I knew it was nothing more than wishful thinking that I could save him, but it was the only thread of hope I had left. Maybe Draven held a similar thread, and it was tethering him to this world, to me.

Just as Arion had taught me, I closed my eyes and reached out for the sea's power, drawing it around me. I breathed in the salty bilge water, allowing it to flow through me, to connect my magic to the vast power that surrounded us. The water felt different, diminished, like it lacked the deep resonance I typically felt whenever I tried to draw upon its magic.

It didn't matter. I would use what I had, and I would drag this merman out of oblivion's icy grip. I would not let him pass to the Beyond and leave me behind.

A dim light grew around me. It tickled my skin, traveling up my fingers, my arms, my chest until it rested upon my heart. Swirls of red and yellow came to life, engulfing me and Draven, illuminating his deathly pale face and his lifeless blue eyes. My heart wanted to shatter at the sight, but instead, my grief fueled my magic, filled me with resolve, and drove me to push forward. In that moment, the world stilled as if holding its breath, awaiting the spell I would cast to bring my love back to me.

I closed my eyes, letting my powers coalesce into a single pure thought, a simple incantation that would set my world to rights.

By the power of the sea, I give of myself to bring you back to me.

From the Beyond, I call your name, and bid you return, the way you came.

With every beat of my broken heart, with every breath that I impart, I call upon the winds and tides, to bring you back, where love abides.

With all my will and all my might, I summon you back to light my life.

The power of my incantation exploded out from my body, lighting the water in a dazzling display of colors, burning my eyes, stealing my breath. My heart was racing so fast I feared it would explode. I drew Draven to me, clutching him against my breast, desperately waiting for him to wrap his powerful arms around me, to draw me in to him, to bathe me in his warmth.

But it didn't happen. He remained as cold and lifeless as I found him. I opened my eyes, finding the sea water that surrounded us to be crystal clear. It was only now, in this moment of my deepest grief, that I saw the thin black lines that traced up from beneath his shirt and across his neck, covering his face in a lattice like a fisherman's net.

The man I had once cherished with all my being, then grew to hate with all my soul, had left this world just as I had rediscovered my love for him. Now, with his passing, a deep, gnawing emptiness gripped my chest, as if a part of me had been ripped away and left to wither in the sea's stiff embrace. The pain was overwhelming, and with each beat of my aching heart, I was reminded of what I had lost. The love that had burned within me reignited with fierce intensity, consuming me in a raging inferno of regret and sorrow. I yearned for his touch, his voice, his laughter, but they were forever out of reach, taken from me in a cruel twist of fate. All because of a childish fantasy of sharing my life with a human I didn't even know. I had accidentally unleashed a series of events that would ultimately gut me, rend me open, and leave a wound that could never fully heal.

Just as I was about to be forever dragged into the abyss of my sorrow, I caught the movement of a dark shadow. With a single pulse, it moved forward, a hazy, swirling blur of darkness. Through the tears that stung my eyes, I couldn't discern what it was, but as the shadow neared, an eight-legged form emerged, revealing the terror-struck eyes of Octavius.

"You need to save them," he said, his emotion-filled words barely comprehensible through his sobs. "Prince Draven is gone, but Luna and Dylan are not. They've been taken up on deck. The captain of this ship plans to use them as bait for the sirens. Hurry, before it's too late!"

LUNA

My body was stretched taut, lashed to the long, pointed protrusion at the front of the ship. The hard, rough wood of the bowsprit dug into my skin, and the ropes that bound me tightly threatened to cut off my circulation. The waters had been choppy ever since we left the harbor, but as the winds picked up, the sea had become an insatiable beast, sending wave after wave to crash against the hull. Each jarring motion of the trawler sent shockwaves of pain through my frame as the ship's bow bounced up and down, a relentless battering ram against my vulnerable flesh.

Why had I been so impulsive? I shouldn't have screamed when Dylan pushed my lifeless brother into the bilge. Even though Draven had not turned to sea foam, he showed no signs of life. His heart wasn't beating, and he drew no breath. I should have had hope. I should have remained quiet. Instead, I had wailed like a guppy as Dylan replaced the deck-boards, sealing the prince and my best friend in the ship's hull.

Both Dylan and Lachlan had tried to stop me. They pleaded with me to be silent, but my grief overwhelmed me. I had never lost anyone before, and from the looks of it, the two most important people in my life were going to die, and I was powerless to help them. If I was a demigod like Dylan suggested, I certainly didn't show it.

My incessant pleas to my father drew the attention of the ship's captain. Thankfully, Lachlan was able to explain the missing merfolk, saying they had died and turned to sea foam, but he couldn't explain why Dylan and I were on the ship. The first mate had taken a severe beating for his mistakes before being dragged out of the hold.

The men who took us were no less cruel. We had tried to resist, but we stood no chance against the sailors. We were quickly overpowered and subdued.

I don't know how long we were held bound and gagged, but each minute passed at a sea-snail's pace. I couldn't stop crying, mourning the loss of my brother. Even though a part of me knew that, since he hadn't turned to foam, he wasn't fully gone, but I had no way of knowing if he continued to linger in the bilge.

After an interminable length of time, sailors had come into the hold and had dragged Dylan and me up on deck and prepared us to be bait for my kin.

As we neared the Isle of Scree, the sirens' haunting melody wove itself through my mind, setting my heart pounding with a wild, inexplicable longing. Every note seemed to vibrate through my bones, drawing me irresistibly toward its source. It was as if the song had taken on a life of its own, a powerful spell ensnaring me in its grip. This was their magic, the same one that struck fear in the soul of any man who chose to sail across the sea's open expanse. Any time a ship ventured too close to the sirens' home, they would unleash this weapon upon its crew. I had always believed they lured ships into their treacherous waters to scuttle them as a warning to other sailors to steer clear of their isle. Now, I wasn't so sure. Where mermaids could lure fish from the deeps and command them to do our bidding, sirens appeared to be able to do the same thing to humans.

Normally, my cousins would leave merfolk alone, not wanting to draw the wrath of Triton or Prince Draven, but the winged mermaids knew me. I was the one who raided their fire-shrimp beds. Sure, I hardly took any, nowhere near enough for them to even notice had they not caught me, but it was the principle of the situation and, given an opportunity, they'd want to get some payback. They would make me regret the few mouthfuls of crustaceans I'd snatched. My life wasn't in peril, but they'd likely find a way to exact their revenge for my silly pranks.

My heart raced and my chest heaved as the sailors tightly bound Dylan with thick ropes and hoisted him up onto the yardarm, leaving him dangling at the end of a taut line. The mariners cackled with cruel delight as they swung the apparatus out over the side of the ship, suspending the young man high above the churning waves. Terror filled Dylan's eyes as he dangled helplessly, swaying back and forth with the movement of the vessel.

Lachlan, who had promised to help Dylan and me, was busy with the rest of the crew, preparing their iron-laced nets as we approached the island. The deckhands had filled their ears with candle wax in an attempt to protect themselves from the sirens' song. Even with the enchanting melody my cousins were weaving into the growing breeze, the mariners appeared unfazed as they carried on their duties, immune to their magical voices. Dylan, on the other hand, was glassy-eyed, completely entranced by the seductive sounds, but he never gave up his struggles to break free of his bonds, eager to answer the sirens' call.

I desperately wanted to get Lachlan's attention, but I was tied up and unable to signal him. I called out to the man, but my voice was lost amidst the haunting melody that hung heavy in the air. Lachlan, who had also stuffed his ears with candle wax, seemed oblivious to my plight as he continued to prepare the nets with the rest of the crew. A sinking feeling in my gut dragged on my spirit, realizing that I might not be able to free myself from the bowsprit in time to save Dylan.

Just as I was about to give up hope, Lachlan turned and glanced in my direction, his eyes locking onto mine. He seemed to understand the urgency of the situation and called out to me, his voice booming loud enough to cut through the enchanting melodies.

"As soon as my men are ready to cast their nets, I'll free you. I don't want to release Dylan, though. He has no protection from the song."

I yelled back to him that I understood, but he shook his head and tapped his ear, indicating he could neither hear my words nor understand what I was saying.

Our failed conversation came to an abrupt halt. Lachlan's eyes widened as he gazed towards the heavens. Several of his shipmates did the same, drawing my attention. I gasped at the sight of two sirens circling over Dylan, their scale-covered bodies reflecting Pele's dying light in a dazzling spectacle of colors. Despite having no actual power over me, I, too, was entranced by their sheer beauty. With each beat of their wings, they unleashed a mesmerizing kaleidoscope of reds, oranges, and blindingly bright yellows.

The crew's initial reaction to the sirens' arrival vanished. It seemed they were no longer affected by their beauty. With the sea tossing their ship about, threatening to slam its fragile hull against the sharp boulders protruding from the turbulent water, the men still moved with determined purpose. Years of running along the deck's slick wood surface in heavy weather had trained them for this. In silent pairs, they gathered up their iron-laced nets, making ready to cast them over their prey as they neared.

Four more sirens swooped in from the far side of the ship, their bodies transformed into creatures ripped from the pages of a horror story, their beautiful tails replaced with spindly, scaled legs and enormous taloned feet. Their faces were contorted by rage, exposing rows of wicked jagged teeth. Their fingers were elongated, tipped with deadly sharp claws.

The first of these monstrous sirens snatched a sailor by his shoulders, dragging his flailing, writhing body across the deck. The second and third threw themselves into the fray of crewmen who were gathering to rescue their shipmate.

The chaotic scene was unfolding too quickly for me to comprehend. The sailors who chose to fight hand-to-hand against their enemy were being ripped to shreds. Meanwhile, nets whirled through the air. Some successfully ensnared their targets, while others sailed harmlessly, missing their intended prey.

I tore my gaze from the horrors to search for Dylan. He was still dangling precariously over the hazardous waters, but he appeared otherwise unharmed. The sirens were completely ignoring both of us while they focused all their attention on the sailors.

"I'm coming," Lachlan yelled, his voice muffled by the dagger clenched between his teeth. He was scrambling up the bowsprit, the long pole I had been lashed to. In moments, he was slashing at my bindings, shredding the ropes with his wicked blade's sharp edge. As the last of the bindings fell away, he handed me the blade. "Help your friend. I need to get back into the fight."

I clutched onto Lachlan's heavily muscled arm, preventing him from leaving me behind. I shook my head violently. "Stay with me," I bellowed, desperate for him to hear my words. "If you're with me, they'll leave you alone."

My rescuer snapped around, his gaze raking over the bloody scene. "They're not all bad," he yelled. "I won't let my crewmates be slaughtered. I'm sorry. Save your friend and get out of here." A moment later, the first mate was racing across the deck, throwing himself into the fray. I feared for the man's life, but he had made his decision. I had other things to concern myself with, including freeing Dylan from his bonds and getting him clear of the carnage.

On unsteady feet, I made my way to the yard arm that held Dylan. I had no idea how to operate the device, to move it back over the ship. I stared up at the man, struggling to free himself, his body swinging in slow circles, dangling over the turbulent sea below. The entire apparatus looked too narrow for me to climb. I didn't have the man's nimble strength. I was a mermaid, and this was my first day on land. I was literally a fish out of water.

Barnacles and bubbles. I was a mermaid. I didn't need to climb to reach my human. I ran to the ship's railing, ready to throw myself over the side. I stopped short when I spied the iron band that ran along the rail's surface. I needed to get off this ship, but if they had wrapped it entirely in iron, I was trapped.

I stared up helplessly at Dylan, just like I had when they had hoisted him into the air. I had been tied to the long pointy thing at the front of the boat. I had climbed down from there. If I could climb down, I could climb back up. I had found my way off this prison. With Lachlan's dagger clenched between my teeth, I made my way to the front of the ship and dove into the sea's waiting arms.

CHAPTER 33

DYLAN

As I dangled precariously from the yardarm, I gazed in horror as the chaos unfolded below me. Considering all the challenges I had faced in my life so far, nothing had prepared me for the scale of mayhem I was witnessing.

Monstrous sirens, their sharp teeth bared, tore apart crew members with terrifying efficiency as the men tried to subdue them with their feeble attempts to net their prey. The air was thick with the sickly-sweet scent of the enchanting song that muddled my mind. The melody was inviting, alluring, promising a life filled with tantalizing sensations and hidden treasures that would satisfy the most secret yearning of any soul unfortunate enough to be ensnared by the seductive song.

Before the sirens had arrived, Captain Roberts had warned his crew of the dangers of the Isle of Scree. He had cautioned the men to be on guard against the mermaids' tactics, including their masterful use of misdirection to distract their victims from the threat that would come from behind. He had equipped himself and four of his crewmen, including Lachlan, with iron mail shirts designed to repel a siren's physical attack. It was these specially equipped mariners who would unleash the captain's secret weapon.

As yet another sailor succumbed to a siren's slashing talons and biting teeth, I wondered if the captain had underestimated his target's ferocity.

From the quarterdeck, the raised part of the ship at its stern which housed the senior sailors' quarters, Captain Roberts swung his twin sabers, fending off several advancing sirens. He had just called out an order, but it seemed to have fallen on deaf ears. None of his crew reacted to his words, all of them completely engrossed in their gruesome task.

Lachlan was the first to respond, but he didn't move to unleash the captain's secret weapon. Instead, he moved to free Luna from her bonds before scampering back into the fight. While she appeared intent on freeing me, the first mate swept across the deck, searching for the select few wearing chainmail armor, spurring them into action. Whatever it was they were going to do, it was about to happen.

My gaze turned towards Luna, and the confused expression she was casting at me. She seemed to be trying to puzzle out a problem, likely searching for a way to free me from my bonds. I tried yelling, to tell her how to operate the yardarm, but my words were carried off in the wind.

Her confusion suddenly melted away, hardening into resolve. My heart sank when she raced across the deck to the prow of the ship, clambered up the bowsprit, and threw herself into the sea. I refused to believe that she had just abandoned me in my hour of need and was thinking only of herself.

As the specter of fear enveloped me, I came to realize my death was imminent. The sirens would either be caught and the captain would execute me, or the flying monsters would prevail and I'd be eaten along with the rest of the crew aboard the *Abyssal.*

My short, meaningless life flashed before my eyes as I watched, in detached awe, the spectacle unfolding. Captain Roberts and his hand-picked selection of mail-clad men were moving about the ship, working to untie ropes in synchronized rhythm. While they performed their individual activities, the sailors kept a watchful eye on their captain, waiting for his signal to spring his trap.

Amidst the terror and chaos, a small black blob undulated over the deck, moving with a fluid grace that resembled a surreal dance. It zigzagged its way towards the stern, darting past flailing limbs and tumbling debris with effortless ease. As it approached the ship's wheel, I realized with a jolt that it was Octavius. He was surprising me, yet again, with his relentless dedication to Luna. When he reached the wheel, he clambered up its face, coming to rest with his tentacles stretched across its many spokes.

While I was distracted by the octopup, the captain must have signaled his men to spring the trap. I watched in amazement as an enormous boom swung around the main mast, dragging behind it a gauzy mesh that fluttered like a flag in a stiff breeze. The netting reflected Pele just as he dipped below the western horizon, catching my attention. From my vantage point, I was able to see its gossamer threads, but the captain's prey could not.

The trap scooped up every siren hovering above the ship before dropping down onto the deck. The creatures screamed in agony, their smoking bodies flailing, desperately trying to free themselves from the mesh. The disgusting scent of burning flesh filled the air, and a thick gray smoke rose, stinging my eyes, forcing me to turn away from the carnage.

As I averted my gaze, I caught sight of Luna, launching herself up from the waters below, a dagger held between clenched teeth, her arms outstretched, ready to grasp onto me.

"I've got you," she said as she clutched my waist. The impact of her slamming into me sent us swinging wildly, spinning and turning, the chaotic battle below now only coming in momentary flashes as we spun about.

As she took the knife from between her teeth, ready to slash at the ropes, I tried to warn her. If she cut the rope, we may well fall onto the ship's deck. The impact from this height would surely kill us both. But before I could speak, she pressed her lips to mine and breathed into my mouth, filling me with that now familiar sensation of a mermaid's kiss.

A moment later, I was completely weightless. Wind rushed past as we plummeted downward. If I was going to die, smashed upon the Abyssal's hard wooden deck, at least it would be in the arms of the woman I had grown close to, a mermaid I dared to believe felt the same way for me.

We met the icy sea with a thunderous splat, our intertwined bodies slamming into its frigid depths. My fear of breathing in the briny water had long since passed, and I sucked in a lungful of seawater, instantly refreshed and revived by its coolness.

A curtain of bubbles masked my view of Luna, after having been separated from her on impact. In moments, my vision cleared, and terror gripped me. She was being held by four sirens, their luminescent wings outstretched, their tooth-filled maws drawn back into macabre smiles.

I tried to swim towards the group, but before I could get near, they dragged her off, quickly outdistancing me. I swam with all my might, throwing every ounce of my strength into my arms, but it was a lost cause. With only one good leg to kick with, any attempt to keep up with the sirens was pure folly.

"She'll be okay." The unknown voice caused me to yelp. I spun around to find Arion suspended in the water only a few feet from me. "I believe they're trying to protect her, to take her away from the hunters."

"We need to help her," I said, straining to see through the rapidly darkening waters. Pele must have already sunk beneath the western horizon, reducing visibility to near zero. "I've seen what those monsters are like. They tore the Abyssal's sailors to shreds."

"They are reaping what they've sown," Arion said. There was no remorse in his words. He sounded almost pleased that the crewmen were being completely obliterated. "They've killed Prince Draven. They'll get what they deserve."

Quite frankly, I didn't care about Prince Draven. All I cared about was Luna at this point, and I wanted to help free her. But I also felt the need to tell Arion that he was wrong, and that the situation on the ship was not what he expected. "The sirens are losing. Captain Roberts has trapped most of them beneath some sort of special netting."

"That creates a problem," the giant red crab said. I could barely make him out in the blackness. "If the sirens are all killed, they may well blame the princess. With her brother's death, she's now the crown princess, heir to King Triton's throne. They might kill her in retribution for their kin being slaughtered."

"What are we going to do? We need to save Luna before it's too late and I can neither swim fast nor see in the dark."

A glow erupted from around Arion, engulfing him in a bright purple haze. "Do you wish to be a part of the kingdom of merfolk?" He asked the question like he was commenting on the weather. "I can only help you if it's what you truly desire and that it is of your own free will."

Confusion and fear gripped me as Arion's face contorted into a strange, maniacal expression. The swirling colors of purple and green illuminated the surrounding water, transforming the giant crab into a spectral apparition that only added to my unease.

"You must speak the words aloud if you want me to help you. You must say: 'I choose to accept your magic of my own free will.' It must not feel like I am, in any way whatsoever, coercing you into this."

I didn't know what to expect, but I couldn't have cared less. I would do anything for her, and I would agree to whatever Arion asked if it meant rescuing the mermaid.

"I accept your offer of my own free will, without hesitation or reservation. Do what you must. I need to save Luna."

No sooner had I spoken the last word, the swirls of purple and green engulfed me, bathing me in their ethereal light. A strange sensation cut through me, filling me with a sense of wonder, crushing my legs under the full weight of the ocean. My back arched in spasm, wracking my entire body with spiritual bliss.

Chapter 34

CALYPSO

"Now!" I bellowed, hoping Luna's octopup would heed my command. "Octavius, do it now!"

Over the din of the wailing sirens and the screaming sailors, I gave my order to Luna's tiny kraken. I couldn't be sure he heard me. My spirit was numb from the death of Draven, but it fueled me, driving me into action. Even though Arion warned me of the dangers of using my magic in anger, I didn't care. I would pay the price, regardless of the toll it took on me. I would have my revenge and these men would feel the true power of the sea witch. And when I was finished with these foul creatures, I would return to Dylan's fishing village and finish the job. The moon goddess, Medeina, would bear witness to my wrath. When I was done, she could exact her toll on me, if that's what she wanted.

The vessel lurched as Octavius spun the ship's wheel, steering its bulk towards a particularly vicious outcropping of jagged rocks. Humans and sirens alike skidded across the deck, their bodies slamming into side rails, sending more than a few overboard.

With their sisters trapped beneath the foul netting, several more sirens flew overhead, their bodies reflecting Medeina's light as she climbed into the night sky. The moon goddess wasn't in her full glory, but she reflected more than enough of Pele's brilliance to light the sea.

Captain Roberts continued to order his men to throw nets, ignoring the pleas from those already trapped. He fought like a man possessed, single-minded in thought, driven by rage. I understood that emotion, and I was going to show him exactly what unbridled fury was. Intimately.

My hair whipped about my face as the wind picked up, driving a series of waves against the hull of the ship, pushing it towards its doom. My access to the sea's power was limited while I wasn't wrapped in its chilly embrace. Nevertheless, I was close enough to harness some of its might and funnel it to create a small, localized storm. It wasn't much, but it would ruin this vessel upon the rocky crags. The boat would crack open, fill with water, and sink into the depths along with the entire crew.

Channeling the surrounding power, I spread my arms wide and inhaled the sea-spray deeply, its saltiness coating my lips and tongue. Swirls of red and yellow gathered around me, lighting me like a beacon. But for the men who stopped and stared at the phenomenon, there would be no hope. There would be no salvation.

Releasing all my anger, my frustration, and my sorrow for the death of my love, I cast my spell.

Fury of the sea, heed my call.

Crash and roar and shatter all.

Vicious storm, surge, lash, and rave.

Sink this ship beneath your wave.

My guts twisted as I unleashed my magic. With each new wave that washed over the ship's deck, a fresh bout of pain gripped me. The briny taste in my mouth turned metallic, acidic.

"Call it back," Arion bellowed at me as he skittered across the deck. I had no idea how he had managed to get on board, but here he was, interfering with my plans to destroy these wretched humans. "Calypso, you mustn't do this. Call back your magic before it's too late."

"They have to pay," I howled, consumed by an insatiable thirst for revenge. The driving rain stung my skin, each drop like the slash of a stingray's tail. "I don't care what happens to me, they must die."

Arion placed a firm grip on my wrists, pulling me towards himself. "Not all are wicked. You will destroy both good and evil. You are not delivering justice, you are exacting vengeance, and with that comes a price you cannot afford to pay."

I yanked my arms, hoping to break free, but Arion's pincers held tight. "I don't care!" I cried, my heart pounding, my tears mixing with the driving rains. "I want them dead! Do you hear me? I want to kill them all!"

The oversized crustacean hesitated, still holding firm, his expression softening. "I regret my actions every single day. I am who I am because..." his words cut off as an enormous wave swept across the ship's deck, sending us careening toward the sea.

"Please, Calypso. You must stop before it is too late. There is no salvation in revenge, only pain. Our magic comes at a price, and if you take the life of an innocent, you will forfeit your own."

"I don't care!" I jerked my arms, hoping to free myself, but my mentor's grip held firm.

"But I do," Arion said, loosening his hold on my wrists. "And so does Luna. She lost her brother today. Don't make her lose her best friend, too. She is going to need you more than ever. If you won't call off your magic for me, do it for her."

My teacher's words pierced through my hatred, shattering my already broken heart. My anger dissipated like a gust of wind, and with it, so did my fury-driven spell. The heavy winds instantly died away, but the ship continued to rock heavily, sending me sprawling across the deck, depositing me at the feet of Captain Roberts.

"Look what Triton has delivered to me," he said with a sinister laugh. The man's eyes were wild, filled with a crazed expression that was beyond my comprehension. He raised his curved blade, ready to thrust its keen edge into my chest, but the ship rocked again, sending us both to the side rails. With my body on the precipice of being tossed into the sea's waiting arms, I caught sight of an enormous blue-black body breaking the surface. Its dorsal fin, which measured at least twice my height, stood erect. Its rays stretched outward like spears, each supporting a thin, translucent membrane that seemed to glow in the darkness.

I rolled onto my side, fearful that the captain was preparing to end my life with his iron blade. The man stood over me, empty-handed, his crazed eyes now filled with terror, his mouth wide in a soundless scream.

The ship listed heavily, throwing the captain onto his back, sending him skidding across the deck to the far side of the boat. There, waiting for him with an open maw, its terrible spiral horn pointed skyward, was a Makara, a creature the humans had come to name *sea dragon*.

Its massive claws dug deeply into the ship's deck, shredding timber as easily as I might tear through seaweed. Rows of conical teeth filled its mouth, each one as long as my arm. Like hurricane-force winds whipping through a narrow cavern, it unleashed a blood-curdling screech as the terrified sailor slid towards it, towards certain death.

I watched with morbid fascination as the man slid into the Makara's gaping maw. With cries of dismay, he used his arms and legs in a futile attempt to prevent the creature from slamming its jaws shut, cutting him in two. The man's efforts were in vain and short-lived. A moment later, Captain Roberts disappeared from sight as the Makara receded back into the water.

I couldn't describe my emotions at that moment, torn between relief and pity. There was also the satisfaction of knowing that the sea had meted out justice to the man who had killed my prince, my love. The Makara were an island unto themselves, never dealing with the mermaids. We may not have lived in peace and harmony, but we had a healthy respect for one another, and we never interfered in each other's affairs. Why the Makara had come today was a mystery to me, but I didn't care. Some day, I would have to repay this kindness.

Even with Medeina's appearance in the night sky, the shrieking cries of a siren reminded me we were not done. We had dealt with the vile captain, but there was still a crew of men who were likely no better than he was.

As I tried to focus through the chaos, I could only assume that my eyes were deceiving me. While some mariners were actively fighting against the sirens in flight, others were busily freeing my cousins trapped within their terrible nets. Too many of the winged mermaids were beyond saving, but many flew away, throwing themselves into the sea to begin their healing.

Nothing made sense. The Makara and merfolk, who had never before worked together, now fought as a coordinated unit. And then there was the first mate, a man whose cruelty I had witnessed firsthand, working to free trapped sirens as if he were one of us. My mind raced, trying to make sense of it all.

"Call them off," Arion bellowed. "Tell the sirens and Makara to retreat. The foul human is dead, and the battle is over."

"I'll try," I yelled back. "But I doubt they'll listen."

CHAPTER 35

LUNA

"Release me," I yelled, thrashing with all my might, desperate to break the sirens' hold on me. Sweet Gaia, they were so strong. "I am Luna, the daughter of Triton, and I command you to free me."

"You are the last living child of our king, and we will not allow you to come to harm, princess," the siren replied.

Fear gripped me. What did she mean? Last living child? My brother had not yet passed into the Beyond. He had not turned to sea foam. Did they know something I did not? "What do you mean? Explain yourself!"

"I will explain everything as soon as we have you away from the madmen hunting us." The two sirens holding me by my arms dragged me deeper into an underwater cave. Luminescent lantern fish darted about, staying clear of the mermaids, lighting our way as we traveled through a narrow vent, barely wide enough to accommodate me and my captors.

With all my might, I twisted my body, breaking their grip. I gave a powerful kick of my tail fin, thrusting myself away from the sirens, and headed back to the open sea, to where Dylan, Calypso, and Draven needed my help. They had to be mistaken about my brother. He was unwell when we pushed him into the bilge water, but the ferrous poisoning had not yet reached fatal levels. Like it had done for me, the seawater should have already started curing him, flushing the toxins from his blood.

"Princess," a siren called out, racing to keep up with me. She was no longer showing her hideous, monstrous form, just her natural merfolk beauty. "Please, it's not safe in the open. The Makara have come."

That was enough to make me pause. The Makara never came to our aid. Not ever. We stayed clear of them, and they did the same for us. Why would they have come? What could have driven them to leave their deep-water gardens?

"You lie," I yelled, turning, swimming hard towards the *Abyssal* and my friends. "The Makara don't care what happens to the merfolk. They never have and they never will."

The siren swam up alongside of me, the muscles in her face and neck straining as she tried to maintain her speed. "Please. Slow down. I..." She stopped talking and fell behind. I stopped swimming, suspended at the mouth of the cavern. "They came at the passing of your brother. Even if they don't care about us, not like we care for each other, they respect your father. They've come to help retrieve Prince Draven's body, so that we can release him back to the sea."

The tightness in my chest worsened. They believed my brother had passed to the Beyond, and yet, he hadn't turned to foam and become one with the sea. I had never heard of such a thing before. I held out hope that Draven wasn't actually gone and that he might still be alive.

"If my brother has not become foam, then he is not dead and I'm going to return to him. He needs me and I don't care what I have to face. I'm going."

Without waiting for a response, or concern for my surroundings, I turned and kicked my tail fin, swimming with all my might. Suddenly, blinding pain erupted in my head and stars exploded in my vision. When I opened my eyes, Dylan was before me, wincing, holding his forehead. The collision must have muddled my brain because... he looked just like a merman, tail fin and all. I gaped, my mouth opening and closing involuntarily, unsure of how to react and with no idea of how to respond. My mind raced, trying to make sense of what I was seeing. My thoughts were already jumbled and incoherent at the news of my brother's supposed passing, but seeing Dylan as a merman nearly snapped my mind.

"I know," he said, rubbing his forehead, giving me an uneasy smile. "Arion did it, so I could save you." He looked past me to the two sirens who were swimming behind me. "I guess it wasn't necessary."

"They said Draven has passed." It was the only thing I could think of saying. I immediately burst into tears and clutched onto Dylan, bawling like a guppy. "He can't be dead, though. Draven didn't join with the sea. He has to be alive." The words came out in fits and starts, and all the while, Dylan held me close, remaining silent. I wanted to hear him say the words, that my brother was alive and well, and that he was taking me to see him. But he wasn't saying anything. He just kept holding me tighter and tighter until it felt like I couldn't catch my breath.

"We'll go back," Dylan said, a noticeable hitch in his voice. "We'll check in on him ourselves. They don't know the merman like you do. They're wrong, all of them."

I didn't believe him. His heart was hammering against my chest and I could feel the sorrow and fear in his words. His body was shaking uncontrollably. Although, that might have been me trembling, too terrified to face the reality of the situation. I nodded slowly, my cheek brushing against Dylan's shoulder.

"Let's go see him. If he is somehow stuck between worlds…" The sobs came fast and furious, my body wracking at the admission that my arrogant, self-serving, pompous brother might not ever speak to me again. I would give anything to hear his voice, to have him tell me I was wrong, or to offer me suggestions on how I should live my life. I didn't care how angry it would make me, I wanted to hear it. Over and over and over again.

At some point, I don't know when, Dylan had led me from the cave to the hull of the Abyssal. The ship had run aground on a shoal and was listed heavily to one side, partially submerged in the turbulent waters.

A Makara appeared from a cloud of silt, its body dwarfing my own. His mouth was big enough to swallow Dylan and me whole, but I harbored no fear of him. His eyes showed no malice, only solemnity for the situation, for the death of my brother.

"Princess," he said, lowering his gaze as he spoke. "I am Yanti, overseer of the northern seas. My people grieve with you this day. Your brother was a good man, deserving of your father's royal scepter. He treated me and mine with the same honor and respect as he did you and yours. Prince Draven was a merman above reproach."

I wanted to reply, but my throat had seized shut, making it impossible to utter a single syllable. When I heard the giant's words, I instantly understood why my brother had not joined with the sea. I knew why he stepped between worlds. Hope sprung, freeing my soul of the burden that threatened to crush me.

"Thank you!" I said, bowing my head to the Makara chieftain. "You have delivered good news. My soul is free, and for your kindness, I will forever be grateful."

I didn't care if I looked and sounded like an empty-headed child. The perplexed look on the Makara's face told me so. As much as he said he knew my brother, he really didn't know him. Nor did he know my father. Nor was he aware of the power of my father's royal scepter. It was what was holding Draven in this plane, preventing him from becoming one with the sea.

In that small golden stick was my brother's life and salvation.

"I need your help, Overseer of the Northern Seas. If you have love for my brother, I beg of you, grant me this boon."

CHAPTER 36

DYLAN

I watched in awe as the Makara stripped the iron bands off the outer hull of the Abyssal. Regardless of their intimidating size and tooth-filled maws, they were incredibly dexterous and meticulous in their work. The chief Makara, Yanti, didn't understand why Luna wanted the merfolk hunters to be spared, but he chose to not argue the point. All that mattered to him was that the princess needed the iron straps removed so that she could enter the ship and visit her brother.

While the sea dragons were working on the outside of the hull, Octavius was helping the crew clear out enough of the cages below deck that the mermaids could move comfortably without having to suffer the iron's effects.

And while all that was going on, I was with Luna, suspended in the water, lost in a world of our own. Once it was clear that it would be a while before we could get back on board the ship, we took the time to be together – under Arion's watchful eye. He didn't seem to understand or care that we wanted to be alone. Luna's fear and sadness at her brother's death seemed to wash away like the tides when she'd decided her father's scepter was keeping him safe. I couldn't believe things were as rosy as she was making them to be, but I knew nothing of the merfolk or their magic. So, who was I to argue?

"You make a beautiful merman," Luna whispered in my ear. "But you didn't need to do that for me. After we help Draven, will you ask Arion to turn you back into a human?"

I swallowed hard at the question. I hadn't even considered returning to being myself, my physically challenged, barely able to walk, self. Here, I was normal. I was free. I wasn't sure if this newfound freedom was enough to leave my home and my mother who needed me. I felt torn between two worlds, between land and sea.

"Ahem," Arion said, scratching the top of his shell with a claw. "We need to talk about that."

My back stiffened while my heart sank at the giant crab's words. No pleasant conversation ever began with 'We need to talk.' Luna moved between us, shielding me from Calypso's mentor. Using one of his claws, he gently pushed her aside. I could have sworn that he looked queasy, like this was a conversation that was going to hurt him more than it would me.

"I have a confession to make," Arion said, lowering his eyestalks. "I am the reason for your family's affliction. It's for the same reason I've been cursed to be a crab for the rest of my unnatural life."

A series of emotions swept over me, including confusion, anger, and worry. It was confusion that won out, mixed with an unhealthy dose of curiosity. I barely noticed Luna hooking her arm around mine, squeezing me tight.

"Your mother, Angelika, used to be a mermaid. It was why I was able to change you into one. You are half merman. I... I just coaxed that part of you to the surface." Arion's eyes swiveled about like he was making sure nobody was nearby. "Before you were born, I placed a curse on her. I was angry at her for choosing to wed a *man* and, in that moment of weakness, I cast a spell on her to permanently transform her into a human. If she was going to choose a life on land, I wanted to make it impossible for her to return to the sea."

Arion paused, perhaps waiting for my reaction to the news. Though I should have spoken up for my mother, who had been attacked by this giant crab, I found myself at a loss for words and simply stared in disbelief.

"I had forgotten the cardinal rule of magic," Arion said. "Casting a spell in anger takes a heavy toll, far more than an enchantment cast from a place of love or caring. Not only did my spell permanently turn your mother human, but it also had the unintended effect of leaving her disabled. It was as though a small part of her remained a mermaid. My actions also took away my own *merfolk-ness* and turned me into a giant red crab, to be forever shamed for my loss of self-control."

My curiosity instantly gave way to anger. I wanted to rip the claws off him, but his contrite expression gave me pause, allowing my curiosity to resurface.

"Do you know who my father was? He must have been someone special for my mother to leave this life behind to live on land." My stomach twisted, fearful of what Arion might say. I knew very little about my father, except that he was a good man who died protecting his family. I had always assumed that he was killed in the wars, and she was holding back the details to protect me.

"I knew your father," Arion said, his voice quiet, almost distant. It was as though he was recalling a painful memory. "Angelika insisted I meet him, to prove to me that he was worth the sacrifice of leaving my classes and the rest of the merkingdom. But your mother was a promising witch, and I was jealous of the human. I wanted her for myself. I refused to see the goodness in the lord's heart."

At Arion's last words, my mouth flopped open. "My mother is a witch and my father is Lord Vayne?"

The crab's eyes grew wide as he frantically waved his claws about. "No. Never. Your father was the lord of the town. When he wed your mother, his brother, Vayne, discovered Angelika was a mermaid and began a campaign of lies to sow discord within the townsfolk. Some people believed the lies and distanced themselves from your parents, but many more stayed loyal to their lord and his exceptionally kind-hearted wife.

"As time went on, Vayne continued to spread his toxic ideas, poisoning the minds of anyone willing to listen. He told the people that if your father died, as his eldest son, you would be the one to assume the lordship over the town. He argued that no merman could ever rule humans. He said it was unnatural and an affront to the gods.

"That was the key to Vayne's plan. Even though the townsfolk loved your father, the notion that you might someday take his place as their leader pushed them over the edge. It was at that moment that your uncle struck. He murdered your father and, for the *sake of the town*, took the title of lord for himself. He then set out to humiliate and belittle your family, ensuring you lived your entire life in pain and squalor."

I didn't know how to process that information. I never could have imagined that Lord Vayne was directly responsible for my family's misery, and yet it all made so much sense. I had always assumed we were ridiculed for being deformed and unable to walk normally, but it was more than that. They treated us that way because Lord Vayne told them to. Over time, people probably forgot why they started treating us like we were vermin and simply did it out of habit.

Overwhelmed by anger and determination, I pressed the matter. "Will I get my legs back when I am on land? Or have you permanently given me a tail fin? If I cannot walk again, I want you to undo this gift you've given me. I need to be able to face my father's killer and I'll wring the life out of him when I do. Lord Vayne needs to pay. You said casting magic carries a price. So does hurting my family."

Arion grabbed me by the wrists, his claws digging into my skin. "I beg of you, don't act on those impulses. Killing the man won't bring your father back, nor will it put you or your family in his lofty position. Destroying him is a path to damnation. When we get to your home, we will find Angelika, and I will try to undo the curse I cast upon her. If you wish, you and your mother can return to the sea or I can help you build a new life elsewhere. Please, leave revenge behind. Look at what you have. Don't throw it all away in anger."

Luna squeezed my arm tightly. I stole a quick glance at her. Without speaking a single word, she pleaded with me to heed the old crab's warnings, to not harden my heart, and to live my life with her, here in the sea.

"You didn't answer my question," I said, turning back to Arion. "If I return to land, will I have my legs again?"

The crab nodded slowly and closed his eyes. "Yes, but I suspect you'll still have the same affliction you have now. I cannot cure you of that."

The fury of a thousand hurricanes whipped through my thoughts. I understood Arion's warnings. There would be a price to pay for seeking revenge, and I didn't care. Lord Vayne had killed my father and left my mother to rot in the streets like yesterday's fish.

"I'm sorry," I said to Luna, pulling away from her. With Arion's words echoing in my head, I swam toward the Abyssal. Had I known the way, I could have swum home. I needed the ship to carry me back to my village. Once there, I planned to kiss my mother, tell her how sorry I was for what she went through, and then kill Lord Vayne, or die trying.

CHAPTER 37

CALYPSO

I entered the crystal clear bilgewater as soon as the iron bars had been cleared away. The water was warm, but it did nothing to ease the chill that had wrapped itself around me. Fear that Draven had already turned to foam and returned to the sea wracked my soul, but he was still there, just as lifeless as I had left him. My heart shattered into a million pieces as I held him in the darkness, knowing he'd never be able to hold me back.

"I don't know what is anchoring you to this plane," I whispered, my salty tears mixing with the briny bilgewater. "But if you are unable to return to me, you should let go and join the Beyond and swim forever with our ancestors. When I pass, I will seek you out and we can live and love together for all eternity."

I had been so focused on saying goodbye to Draven that I didn't hear Luna and Dylan slide into the bilge. Nor had I noticed that Octavius had curled up on my shoulders, gently stroking my hair.

"We need to get him into the sea," Luna said, her voice thick with urgency. "There is no time to waste."

I had no intention of letting go of my prince. I held onto Draven tightly, while Dylan kept me in place by swimming around me. It's not like there was anywhere to escape to. The ship's bilge wasn't very large. The shock of seeing the man's tail fin pulled me out of my morose feelings.

"You're a merman?" I asked, not bothering to hide the surprise and shock in my voice.

"For now," Dylan replied with a shrug. "Your teacher helped me discover my roots."

I had no idea what that meant, nor did I care. I gripped Draven tighter, refusing to relinquish him to his sister.

"Calypso," Luna said, pushing Octavius from my shoulder. "We can save him. He hasn't become one with the sea because he holds my father's scepter. It's keeping him alive. I'm sure of it."

Hope sprang in my chest, sending my pulse racing out of control. I brushed my fingers over Draven's cheek. I felt no life in him, but I needed to give the princess a chance to help. I had already said my goodbyes a hundred times. I nodded in agreement, but still refused to let anyone but me carry his body.

"Follow us," Luna said. "Half the hull is submerged. We can take him out through the porthole window that Octavius broke open, but we need to hurry. The tide is coming in and it will free the Abyssal of the rocks it's wrecked upon."

With Luna and Dylan at the lead, I followed them up through the hole in the floor. There was a fully submerged pathway leading to the porthole and the sea beyond. While my best friend swam easily through the opening, Dylan, who was once again wearing his oilskin cloak, struggled to pass through. I wondered why it hadn't disappeared when he switched into merman form, but there was no time to ponder such things. More pressing was how I would get the significantly larger Draven through the small exit. It was going to take some effort to get him out of the ship and into the open water.

Thankfully, it was easier than I expected, but I was forced to let him go and allow the others to pull him through. By the time I was out of the ship, Luna and Dylan were kneeling beside Draven's body as he rested on the ocean floor. The princess appeared to be searching him, her actions frantic and desperate.

"I can't find the scepter," she said as I approached. "I was certain. I was positive he was holding onto it and that it was keeping him from joining with the sea and passing to the Beyond."

"He's placed it within the ether," I said, trying to calm my friend. "You're going to need to retrieve it from there."

Luna shook her head, the panic in her eyes palpable. "I don't know how to do that. I've never…" Her words were cut off, turning to sobs. "Gaia, save us. He had tried to teach me, but I didn't care enough to listen."

"I'll teach you," Arion said, scuttling up next to the mermaid. "Be at peace, princess. I will show you the way. It is a gift from your father, an ability to connect directly with the nether realm."

"Connect with the Beyond?" Never before had my teacher mentioned magic like this. The ether was the realm of the dead, our final destination after becoming sea foam. It seemed to border on necromancy, a practice that had been outlawed since the creation of the merkingdom. Arion must have understood my expression. He shook his head lightly and offered me a wane smile.

"It's nothing like what you fear, I assure you. King Triton has the capacity to travel between realms." My teacher turned from me to address Luna. He spoke slowly and clearly, his calmness seeming to cut through her obvious anxiety. "A small piece of that trait was passed on to his children. Consider the idea of a bag or a shelf that exists in another realm beyond your sight, but not beyond your reach. You are able to place things in this bag, and retrieve them at your will, so long as you are in contact with the sea."

Regardless of the critical importance of the situation, the concept of reaching into the Beyond and retrieving an object was incredibly interesting. The inherent implications of what that could do, what doors it could literally open, boggled my mind. It was an incredibly powerful magic, far beyond anything I had ever imagined.

"Feel the water as it moves around you," Arion said to Luna. "The never-ending current that flows through the sea, the way the waves above interact with the sea, the way that Medeina pulls upon it."

I waited for the mermaid, holding my breath, allowing myself to be swept away in the moment. My friend closed her eyes and breathed deeply, and I followed in kind.

"Amidst the natural flow, you will sense something different. Something that doesn't quite fit, like a tremor that ripples across your senses."

No matter how hard I tried, I couldn't feel that tremor Arion was referring to. I was able to sense every other aspect of the sea he described, but nothing more. I turned my gaze to Luna, surprised to see her elbow-deep in the ethereal realm. A moment later, her eyes snapped open, and she yanked her hand back, revealing Draven's glowing red scepter.

"Quickly," Arion said, "Place it in his hand. Hurry, child."

In those precious seconds, between Luna retrieving the scepter and Arion's words, Draven shimmered. His black hair and dark skin turned translucent. My heart stopped, fearing he had passed to the Beyond, to become one with the sea, never to return to me again.

Anger pushed aside my fear. My friend, the mermaid I trusted more than anyone, was being too slow. Her eyes were transfixed on the relic, deliberately holding it back, preventing Draven from receiving its healing powers. My magic ignited, bursting forth in wild, unbridled chaos. The water immediately swirled around us, while streams of fiery reds and burnt oranges filled my vision. Fury exploded from within me just as a blindingly bright light slammed into me, sending me careening across the sea floor.

I shook my head, trying to regain my senses. My ears were ringing, my breathing ragged. A great weight pressed on my chest, making it difficult to draw breath. As my vision cleared, I found Arion standing on me, pinning me down, his claw at my throat.

"You would dare to use your magic against the princess?" Arion's words were sharp enough to slice me in two. "Has grief taken hold so deeply that you would commit treason against your kingdom?"

My first instinct was to lash out at my teacher, but reason managed to overcome it and win out. I closed my eyes and relaxed my body, ready to accept my punishment. I didn't care if I died. Life no longer held meaning for me. My best friend had just killed her brother, the merman I loved. I had no will to continue, no reason to live.

"I regret my actions," I whispered, never bothering to open my eyes. "But I accept my punishment, whatever it is you decide to mete out. I do not deserve to live in this world, nor do I want to. Condemn me to damnation and take my life, for that is the penalty for treason."

I waited, bracing myself for the inevitable. A ripple of fear rose in my belly. I might not want to live without Draven, but I didn't know what awaited me in the Beyond, especially after having committed treason against the royal family. Would I simply cease to exist, or would I be thrust into a world of perpetual torment, forced to endure pain and misery for all eternity? Neither option was appealing.

"Release her," a deep, resonant voice said, breaking through my morose thoughts. It was as though Draven was calling from the Beyond, asking Arion to send me on my way. Perhaps my death was going to send me to some happy place, reuniting me with my love, allowing me to share myself with him until the end of time.

Or maybe it was the abyss, preparing to receive my soul, setting the stage for my never-ending torment.

I waited for what I hoped would be a quick and painless death as fear of the afterlife took hold.

And still I waited.

Moments ticked by, but nothing happened. Or, at least, it seemed that nothing had happened.

The pain of Arion's claw across my throat vanished. Had he done it? Was I on my way to becoming one with the sea? It didn't seem any different. Nothing changed. Everything seemed to be just as it did a moment ago.

"Calypso," the deep voice said to me, gently shaking my shoulder, driving my fear to full-on panic. "Look at me. We need to leave."

My eyes snapped open and my heart exploded with joy. Draven was hovering over me, his wondrous blue eyes sparkling with joy and full of life. Something between a laugh and a scream escaped my mouth as I threw my arms around the merman's neck and dragged him towards me. I clutched him with all my might, not wanting to let him go. Never again would I let him go.

A bright-red glow suddenly illuminated the water, turning my entire world a deep shade of crimson.

"Release me, witch," Draven said, thrusting me away. He held his scepter out in front of himself. The prince's entire body glowed as a wave of foul magic poured out from the relic he held. "You are clearly too dangerous to be allowed to live."

CHAPTER 38

LUNA

Watching my brother teeter on the brink of existence, desperately clinging to life, was the hardest thing I'd ever endured. While he'd been floating lifeless in the bowels of the Abyssal, I feared my belief that he could still return to us was a childish dream and nothing more than wishful thinking.

But hope is a powerful thing. With enough of it, anything is possible. In the end, I believed it was Draven's hope that he would be reunited with Calypso that gave him the strength to anchor his soul in the Beyond, preventing his body from dissipating into nothingness.

All of my dreams were shattered when Draven's life returned to him. He clutched onto his scepter, his face immediately contorting with rage. With a hate-filled glare, he shoved me aside and raced to Calypso. When he turned the relic on her, I feared he was about to send her to the Beyond.

Without thinking, I thrust myself forward, ramming my head into the middle of his back. He bellowed something, but I was too badly shaken to make out what he said. My seaweed-filled brain cleared when he turned towards me, his scepter glowing a brilliant red.

In a flash, Dylan was on the much larger merman, his arm tucked up under by brother's chin, his face straining as he tried to contain the prince. Draven threw a punch over his shoulder, catching Dylan squarely in the face. Even with the jarring impact, and the blood pouring from his shattered nose, he never broke his grip.

Again and again, Draven punched, but never did Dylan let go.

Octavius quickly joined in, wrapping himself around my brother's head. While my octopup tried to subdue him, Arion grasped onto the merman's thick wrist with his huge pincer.

"Drop the scepter," Arion called out. "Let it go or I'll remove your hand."

A blinding flash of crimson illuminated my surroundings, leaving me momentarily stunned. As my eyes adjusted, I gasped at the spectacle unfolding before me. Arion, Octavius, and Dylan were all suspended in the water, ensnared in a mass of writhing sea snakes.

"Draven," Calypso called out. "Release them! Now!"

Sweet Gaia, save us all! There, in the midst of a spinning vortex of oranges and yellows, with her bright-red hair swirling around her head, was Calypso. Her face was one of pure serenity, a paradoxical contrast to the raging fury that surrounded her. My brother's mouth turned down in a distasteful sneer as he slowly leveled his scepter at her.

"Remember our conversation," Calypso said. "Think back to how you told me these were not your actions. You are being controlled by the scepter, but it is not your master. You are the Guardian of the Realm, the crown prince, the only son of Triton, God of the Seas. You cannot be controlled by some enchanted trinket."

"Silence, Sea Witch," Draven bellowed back. The muscles in his arm convulsed, as though straining against a tremendous force. My brother's jaw tightened while his eyes narrowed. The cords in his neck were standing out as he gritted his teeth together.

"Remember," Calypso said, her voice strong and commanding. "Remember our love for one another. The merkingdom needs you to be the leader I know you're capable of being. Free yourself from this burden. Return to me."

A blood-curdling scream issued forth, forcing me to cover my ears. Crackling jolts of energy sparked across Draven's body as he unclenched his fist, allowing the scepter to drop from his hand. As though it was fighting against the act of defiance, tentacles streamed out of the relic, reaching for my brother's arm. It seemed intent on not allowing him to let it go.

As the inky black appendages of darkness reached out to grasp my brother, a brilliant burst of shimmering light struck the relic. A deafening thunderclap exploded outward, sending an intense wave of force that drove me away, sending me head over fin.

By the time I had righted myself and regained my senses, Draven and Calypso were in each other's arms, locked in a tight embrace. My father's royal scepter lay on the sea floor, its ominous crimson glow now extinguished.

◈

As we swam from the Ilse of Scree to Dylan's village, Draven explained how he had managed to remain tethered to the mortal plane rather than becoming one with the sea.

"I knew my life was nearing its end," Draven said in a deep, overly theatrical voice. It was so nice to hear him being himself again. I hadn't seen this aspect of my brother in so long I had forgotten how silly and fun he could be. It was as though a great burden had been lifted from him and he could return to his old ways. "Thanks to my quick mind, I realized that my body could not join with the waves without my soul. In that moment, as I laid on the dock unable to move, I channeled the sea's might and tore my essence into two pieces."

It was at this point that Draven's overly dramatic theatrics swelled. He placed his fists against his chest, mimicking ripping himself in half. His face became contorted, his brow furrowed, and his eyes squeezed shut, as he mimicked being wracked with pain and unimaginable agony.

He claimed it was a novel idea, but I was certain he only came up with this plan because of the stories our mother had told us as children. She spoke of the dragon lord, Fury, whose soul had been ripped apart and scattered across the world to prevent him from ever returning and wreaking havoc on Orth.

Even so, even if he'd drawn upon mythical stories, the fact he made it happen was beyond amazing. Although I knew better than to compliment him and feed his over-inflated ego, I couldn't help but be impressed. After all, he was my big brother, and I had looked up to him my entire life. It took nearly losing him for me to realize just how important he was to me.

My heart swelled with joy when Draven said that it was his love for Calypso that made it all possible. As he told this part of the story, he took Calypso's hands in his and stared deeply into her eyes.

"I couldn't leave," he said, his voice thick with emotion. "Not while I had hope that we could be together. Placing my soul in the Beyond might have been what prevented me from dying, but it was my love for you that gave me the strength to try. I am bound to you. I swear, from the first time I laid eyes on you, I knew you were the only mermaid for me."

I gripped Dylan's fingers tightly as my brother declared his love for my best friend. I was thankful the sea water washed away the tears I had been shedding. As my brother finished his story, sealing it with an eager kiss from Calypso, I turned toward the young merman who was gripping my hand with equal enthusiasm.

Dylan's eyes were wide and glassy as he gazed at me. A warmth that caught me by surprise radiated through my chest as our gazes locked onto each other's. The corner of his mouth crept up as a blush kissed his cheeks, turning them a delightful shade of pink. A flush was creeping up my neck as well, making my face burn. I swallowed hard as a light current pushed me forward, leaving my body only inches from his. As I neared, the merman leaned closer; his eyes half closed.

"We're never going to make it to your village," Arion said, bursting the bubble of my precious moment.

Even though I had already kissed Dylan to pass the magic of water breathing on to him, this kiss, had we been allowed to share it, would have been different. I had been kissed before, but I had never experienced this strong a connection with anyone. Barely any time had passed since I'd met this young merman, but I already knew, all the way down to my tail fin, that I had fallen for him.

Dylan squeezed my hand again and shrugged. The half smile that had appeared grew until it nearly split his face. It was as though he was trying to hold back the excitement building up inside himself. As the anticipation mounted, another slight current whipped his hair about his head for a moment, leaving it draped across his eyes and cheek. I darted in close and brushed it aside, my fingers tingling as they brushed over the fine scales that covered his skin.

My tail fin curled in delight when Dylan quickly leaned forward and pressed his lips to mine. The kiss barely lasted a heartbeat, but in that brief instant in time, my fate was sealed. My brain instantly raced at the implications, bombarded by a million frightful questions. What if he didn't feel the same way? What if he wanted to stay with his mother, living out his life on the land? Could I join him? Would he want me to? What if everything I felt for him was nothing more than a fanciful moment brought on by the rush of adrenaline associated with the danger we faced together?

As we parted, Dylan's eyes remained locked onto mine, and my fears vanished. Whatever life held in store for us, I knew our connection was real, and I was certain he shared the same feelings for me.

By the time we reached the beach outside Dylan's village, Pele's first light was turning the eastern horizon a brilliant shade of orange. I chose to see the bright, clear sky as an omen, the perfect start to a perfect day.

While Draven, Calypso, and I all had no difficulty transitioning from our merfolk to human form, Dylan struggled. He tried to not let it show, but the panic in his eyes as his tail fin split into legs broke my heart. I wanted to help him through it, to ease his worry, but he waved me off, wanting to do it on his own.

The entire transition took place in less than a few seconds, but I expect it was an eternity for him.

Without the aid of a cane while he walked, Dylan was forced to lean on me, just like he had the night we met. I was thankful for his excuse to drape his body over my shoulder. That night, I had felt pity for his condition and how it affected him, but in this perfect moment of closeness, there was only joy. Dylan was strong of will and spirit, but his affliction was not enough to dull his love of life.

Calypso offered to ease his discomfort, but Dylan refused. Like me, he seemed to revel in the closeness we were sharing.

I chuckled at the sight of an octopus and a giant crab walking beside the group. With a bit of help from Arion's magic, Octavius was able to splay himself over the giant crab and use his natural camouflage ability to make Calypso's mentor nearly invisible.

Even though Draven and I wanted to go directly to Lord Vayne's manor, Dylan insisted we stop by his mother's house first. He wanted to tell her he was safe and that better days were coming.

As we walked, Arion seemed both agitated and excited at the prospect of visiting Angelika. He chattered non-stop, with most of it being nonsensical gibberish. I didn't understand why he was behaving this way, but it was fun seeing him so animated.

CHAPTER 39

DYLAN

"Absolutely not!" My mother slammed her fist on the table to drive the point home. "Under no circumstances, none whatsoever, will you confront Lord Vayne! Do you hear me? That goes for each and every one of you. What he did is in the past and nothing you can say or do will bring my husband back to me."

My mother's gaze raked across each one of us, daring anyone to object. Even Prince Draven shrank under the weight of her words. I knew my mother was a strong woman, but I'd never seen this side of her.

"Lady Angelika," Draven said, bending at the waist, using a very diplomatic tone. "As Triton's only son, and ruler of the Gaelinora Sea, it is my duty to protect our people. Lord Vayne's crimes against you are only the tip of the iceberg. The man has set plans in motion to wipe out the entire merfolk kingdom. I cannot allow his actions to go unpunished."

Regardless of the man's diplomatic approach and soft tone, his refusal to heed my mother's warnings was as dangerous as kicking a hornet's nest. If she'd had a cane in her hand, she'd have likely used it like a great sword and lopped off the prince's head. Even though she only had words, they were as keen and cutting as any blade. She would have likely eviscerated the prince had Arion not shown himself.

"Angelika," he said, his pincers clacking uncontrollably. He tried to hide them behind his bulk, but his shaking legs would still have given him away. "You must listen to reason. The kingdom's safety is in jeopardy. Lord Vayne is a blight that threatens to poison both land and sea."

"What are *you* doing here?" My mother's words were filled with venom. She hobbled forward, using chairs to support herself as she bore down on the giant crab. "Haven't you done enough to ruin my life? I'm guessing it was you who put all these ridiculous notions into my son's head, filling him with hope that he might destroy the man who killed his father, so that he can take his rightful place as leader of this village."

Arion didn't back down, even though his knees were buckling beneath him. He met my mother face on, willing to accept whatever words she would sling at him.

"What I did to you was unforgivable," Arion said, lowering his gaze. "I will spend eternity regretting my jealous reaction." The crab's eyes grew in size as they raised up to meet my mother's. "When you said you were leaving the sea to be with a human, something inside of me broke."

"Jealous?" my mother said, the word coming out like a bark. "Of what? That I had found happiness while you wallowed in self-pity, over a union that could never be? You were a coward then and you're a coward now. Why didn't you just tell the mermaid you were so desperately in love with, exactly how you felt? Why did you have to ruin my life just because you couldn't make yours work?"

"Because you were that mermaid."

My mother staggered backwards at Arion's revelation; her eyes bulged and her mouth gaped wide. A tiny squeak escaped her lips as she tried to blink away her confusion. Her unbridled anger snuffed out like a spent candle.

"You were my student. Even though you were nearly thirty, I was still far too old for you," Arion said, rushing to get the words out before my mother interrupted him. "I didn't intend to fall in love with you. I knew I could never act on those feelings, not for maybe a hundred years or more, when our age gap wasn't so... inappropriate. When you said you loved a human, I simply couldn't bear it. I didn't want you to ever return to the sea. I thought never seeing you again might bring me some comfort. But when I cast the spell, I was so filled with anger and jealousy, it became a curse. I disfigured you – and turned myself into this hideous monster standing before you. The price I paid for my folly wasn't enough, nor was the pain I've carried with me all these years. For what I did to you, my actions should have cost me my life."

"You should have told me," my mother said, staring down at her feet. "I might have been able to ease your pain. Even though you were my teacher, I also considered you my dearest friend. I never knew how you felt."

"I have been so ashamed," Arion said, cutting off my mother's words before she could say anything more. "I watched you over the years. I so desperately wanted to speak to you, to tell you how sorry I was, to try to fix what I had done to you, but I couldn't bring myself to do it."

"You can cure my mother?" I asked. Somehow, out of everything else he'd said, those were the words I clung to. "You can undo the curse?"

"I think so," Arion said, his gaze locked onto Angelika's. "If she gives me permission, like you did, I might be able to reverse the enchantment I placed upon her."

"What do you mean, like you did?" My mother's fury instantly reignited. This time she was directing it at me. "What did you do?"

"With my permission, he turned me into a merman," I said, my face burning. "It was the only way for me to save Luna. At least, that's what I thought. To my surprise, she didn't need my help after all."

At my words, Luna squeezed me tightly, a response that was not lost on my mother's hawklike, overprotective eyes.

"I see," she said. "If you were to remove my... challenges, would I be able to return to the sea, should the mood strike me?"

Arion shuffled his feet, his claws clacking uncontrollably again. "I hope so," he said. "Since curses are outlawed, I know very little about them. But I would willingly trade my life to try to undo what I did to you. Return with me to the sea and I'll do everything in my power to restore your mermaid self."

"Return to the sea? I have no plans to return to the sea with you. Not now, not ever." Arion's eyes bulged at the end of their stalks while a bizarre, strangled sound escaped his mouth.

"I need us both to be standing in the water for me to break my spell," he stammered. "That's all I meant. What you do with your life after I undo what I did, that's entirely up to you."

"Then I accept," she said, her eyes narrowing slightly in response. "Even if you can return my mermaid self to me, I am not coming back to the merkingdom. I have business to deal with here. I'm only agreeing to your request because having full use of my legs will help me do what needs doing."

"And what exactly is it that needs doing?" Draven asked, crossing his arms over his sizeable chest muscles. "Might it have something to do with the man who murdered your husband?"

"It has everything to do with Lord Vayne, and nothing to do with you, my prince. Respectfully, I'll ask you to keep your fins out of my business."

"This is all our business, mother." A surge of anger welled up inside my chest. Never before had I spoken up against her, but right now, she was talking like a crazy woman. "I grew up without a father because of my uncle. I watched you suffer through the years trying to provide for me. I saw how the townsfolk treated our family. They despised us because of Vayne. He launched an attack against the merkingdom, killing dozens of merfolk. He held Luna, Calypso, and Draven hostage."

"We all have a stake in this," Luna said, supporting my words. "Surely, you can see this is not something you can do on your own. At the very least, leave it to my father to deal with."

"And who is your father and why would he care about what happens to me?" my mother said, with far too much spite in her voice for my liking. I wanted to lash out at her, but a gentle squeeze from Luna stilled my tongue.

"I am the daughter of Triton. If I tell my father of your troubles, I am certain he will take action." My mother deflated at Luna's announcement.

"Princess," Angelika said, lowering her eyes. "Aside from being a friend to my son, I had no idea who you were. I beg of you, forgive my harsh words."

"There is no forgiveness necessary," Luna said. "I only want what's best for you and Dylan. Arion has already shown what happens when we act out of anger. It only leads to darkness. So, I beg of you, don't let hatred be your guide. You have allies who care about you. Don't turn your back on us."

"What do you suggest we do? How do we deal with the man who killed my husband and left my son without a father?"

"We have a plan," Draven said, giving Calypso a nod as he spoke. "We've been working on it since we left the Isle of Scree. We can be in and out before Pele has reached his zenith. But first, we need this giant crab to work his magic and return you to your proper self."

CHAPTER 40

CALYPSO

I shivered as I watched my teacher and his former student standing in the shallow water near to shore. The sound of waves lapping on the beach and the lonely cry of seagulls overhead did nothing to calm my jangled nerves. Arion's declaration of love for this woman, his inability to act on it because of their age difference, and his all-consuming remorse over the affliction with which he had cursed her, had shaken me to my core.

I feared, deep in my gut, that my friend and mentor meant to undo the curse he'd placed on the woman at any cost. Even if it meant pushing his own life force into the spell. I understood why, but the thought of losing him was more than I could bear. I clutched Draven's hand, searching his eyes for support.

"Be at peace," the prince whispered. "Arion is the most powerful, most resourceful mage of our time. He will lift the curse. Have faith in him."

I wanted to trust that everything would turn out for the best, but life had a nasty habit of biting you in the tail fin when you least expected it.

"After my inexcusable behavior," Arion said, swirling his claw in the water. "King Triton has forbidden me to cast spells on humans. I am willing to accept his wrath for breaking my word to him, but I need you to tell me this is what you want. You must ask me to remove the curse I placed on you."

I glanced over at Dylan and Luna, both of whom were standing just a few feet from the water's edge. He was leaning on Luna, who appeared more than happy to offer her help. What had I started by helping this handsome human to catch mooneyes to provide for his family? My own childish fascination with the man had kicked off a series of events that could have ruined my entire kingdom. Somehow, things turned out well for both him and me, despite following my foolish whims. In the midst of the insanity going on around us, we both found someone we cared for deeply.

I allowed myself a moment of joy before turning my attention back to my teacher, watching in terror, fearful of what might happen to him.

Angelika wrapped her arms around her skinny, shaking body, while her thin, water-soaked dress clung to her slight frame. She had been trembling uncontrollably since we arrived and standing waist deep in the frigid sea wasn't helping. The woman took a cleansing breath and calmed herself. In moments, her tremors ceased, and she raised her chin confidently. "I ask you, without doubt or reservation, to remove the curse you cast upon me. Free me of this burden I've carried for too many years."

Arion nodded and held his claws out to his side. He closed his eyes and drew in a deep breath, summoning the power of the sea. As swirls of purple and green appeared around the crab, casting him in an unearthly glow, Angelika called out.

"Wait," she said, moving beside the crab, placing her hand on his shell. "There is one more thing I wish to say to you before you try to undo what happened nineteen years ago." Arion's claws clacked several times while he waited for Angelika to continue. "Whatever happens here, I'm sorry for whatever part I played in hurting you. If only I had known your true feelings, I might have been able to spare you the grief you suffered. For what you did to me... I forgive you."

Barnacles and bubbles. Never in a million years could I have anticipated this. A lump grew in my throat as tears spilled down my cheeks. I clutched onto Draven, using him as a lifeline before I drowned in the joy that was overwhelming me, shattering my heart, and slowly piecing it back together.

"You forgive me?" Arion choked out, his legs wobbling beneath his bulk. "After what I've put you through, you would willingly push your anger aside so that I might be free of my guilt? I don't deserve this, but I thank you for your kindness. This gift you have given me... it... you have lifted a burden that has weighed on my soul for so long. Many nights, as I laid in quiet solitude thinking of this moment when I would undo what I had done, I never dared to hope for such a thing."

The purple and green swirls that had surrounded Arion dissipated until they were barely more than threads of pale colors. Tears gathered in the giant crab's eyes. They gathered like an incoming tide, growing until they burst like a dam, spilling into the sea. As the first tear struck the salty sea water, the tiny filaments of purple and green that surrounded Arion ignited into a mesmerizing array of colors. Blinded by the brilliance, I stumbled backwards and gasped in awe.

As I was bathed in the radiance, joy leapt in my heart. The purest, most unabashed feeling of love washed over me, carrying me away to a place of utter and absolute bliss.

As quickly as the light show had started, it fell away, leaving me shaken and breathless. When I pulled back my hands, Angelika was laying in the water, with a spectacular purple and green tail swishing lazily beside her. The woman's hair, which flowed over her shoulders in soft, loose curls, was the color of a sunset, and her eyes were the most exquisite emerald I had ever seen. If this was how she looked when she was Arion's student, I understood his infatuation with her. She was stunning beyond words, breathtaking in every possible way.

It was only then that I noticed she was alone in the shallow waters. Arion was no longer beside her. I looked around frantically, scanning the sea for any sign of my teacher. The wonder I had experienced just moments earlier turned to ash, leaving a bitter taste on my tongue and a heavy weight in the pit of my stomach.

"Arion?" I whispered, barely able to get the word out. As confusion and worry overwhelmed my senses, I wrapped my arms around Draven's waist, clutching onto him for emotional support. My chest seized, making it impossible to draw breath. "Where are you?"

"I'm sorry," Draven said, wrapping me in a powerful embrace. "I'm so sorry."

I couldn't breathe. My worst fear had suddenly been realized. My teacher, my mentor, my friend – he was gone. He sacrificed himself to undo the effects of a spell cast in anger; a curse, an unforgivable sin.

Tears stung my eyes and blurred my vision. Grief grasped my heart and twisted my mind. In my desperation, I hallucinated that a merman had now appeared beside Angelika. My desire for the old crab to be alive was so acute, I saw my teacher as I had imagined him to be, with long blue-black hair, a thick beard, and eyes like the bluest sapphires ever beheld.

Luna's shrill squeal shattered my trance. She was racing into the water with Dylan right behind her. The pair left a wake behind them as they sped toward Angelika and the stunning merman standing beside her. While Luna tackled the stranger, Dylan swept his mother up and carried her towards shore. Each step he took was strong and sure, his twisted leg now healthy and whole.

"Do you not want to give your teacher a hug?" Draven said, motioning with his head to where my two favorite merfolk were rolling around together in the shallows. "If you don't hurry, Luna may squeeze him to death."

"Arion?" I blurted the word out, my head swiveling back and forth between Draven and the merman that Luna was still smothering in the water. I turned towards my love, my heart exploding with joy, my spirit soaring beyond the seagulls above.

With my pulse racing, a Makara-sized lump in my throat, and my face wet with tears, I burst into the sea, not stopping until I threw myself onto my teacher and my best friend. I had no idea what words I was saying. I doubted anybody else understood me either, as my emotions came spilling out of me in a series of incomprehensible babbles.

Life had a way of surprising you. Sometimes in ways that could crush your soul. Other times, it lifted your spirit to the stars and granted you your wildest wishes. This was not the time to rejoice in my happiness; we had a lot of dangerous work ahead of us. We needed to remove Vayne, the vile human at the head of this problem. Human-merfolk relations would never heal if we couldn't remove him from his seat of power. To do that, we'd need to face him in his lair, the place where he was strongest. The place that was filled with anti-merfolk devices, each of which was capable of subduing us or killing us outright.

"Are you ready to finish this?" Draven asked after I rejoined him on the beach. It was as though he was reading my mind. I shivered at the thought, giving him a curt nod, ignoring the eels writhing in my belly.

Chapter 41

Luna

Following Calypso's and Draven's plan, we swam up the freshwater river that flowed under Lord Vayne's manor. The sparkling, clear water was so rich in oxygen that I was becoming increasingly lightheaded with each passing moment. The narrowness of the stream forced us to swim in single file.

"What are we going to do with Lord Vayne when we catch him?" Octavius said, clinging onto me like he was a knapsack, his tentacles wrapped around my shoulders and waist. "Maybe we can feed him to the sharks. Oh, wait, I have a better idea. You should call the Makara and let them deal with him."

"We're not killing him," I growled at my octopup, giving him an incredulous expression. "We are going to capture him, expose him for the man he is, and lock him in prison until he's too old and feeble to cause any more problems."

"That seems cruel," Octavius said.

"In what way is that cruel?" My brow furrowed as I considered my octopup's words. "It's a normal punishment for humans to be locked away for the crimes they've committed.

"Because it's too slow of a punishment. I want him to pay now!"

"Trust me," I said, giggling uncontrollably. "He's going to pay."

"Hush," Calypso scolded from in front of me. "We're nearly there."

The water was intoxicating, and it was making me giddy. This wasn't good. All I could hope for was that the effects would quickly wear off and that nobody else was being affected the same way I was.

Calypso stopped short, and I slammed into her, my face smooshing into her scaly butt, which made me giggle even harder. My friend reached back and yanked my hair, sending a sharp pain into my scalp. I was about to screech out when I realized my giggles had stopped. I didn't approve of her methods, even if they were effective.

"Draven's checking to see if the coast is clear," Calypso whispered. "We're close to where Vayne held us prisoner. There is a lot of iron in the area, so we'll need to be extremely careful."

"My oilskin cloak had helped to protect Luna when she was ill," Dylan said over my shoulder. A tingle ran down my belly at his closeness, making my tail fin curl uncontrollably. A giggle wanted to surface, but Calypso's stern face kept it at bay.

"I'll talk to Draven about that," my best friend said, her eyes wide and her brow furrowed. She was glaring at me like I had done something wrong. I hadn't giggled, and I never said a word. Why was she behaving that way? Her head suddenly tilted to the side and her gaze became more intense.

"What's wrong?" I asked, anger flaring up, joining the school of little fish swimming circles in my belly. "Why are you staring at me?"

Calypso slapped my hand. I hadn't realized I was caressing Dylan's cheek this whole time. I needed to focus and get out of this river. Fast!

"Let's go," Draven called out. "The coast is clear. There's nobody down here in Lord Vayne's cellars."

Relief washed over me as we climbed out over the banks. Never had I been so happy to not be underwater. As we exited the stream,

I noticed everyone was wobbly on their legs. Fortunately, the strange feeling of euphoria quickly passed.

I hissed at the musky aroma that filled the room. It reminded me of the stagnant scent of my prison in the ship's hull. Panic was creeping up my spine, making me want to dive back into the river and beat my tail with everything I had to get myself out of here. The memories of my incarceration, the pain of the manacles biting into my skin, the feeling of death gripping my soul as the ferrous poisoning made its way through me, they all haunted me and it was more than I could cope with.

Dylan slipped his cloak over my shaking shoulders and wrapped his arms around me. The familiar scent, Dylan's scent, enveloped me, driving away my fears, bolstering my confidence. I gazed up at him, into his soft, caring eyes. "I promise," he said. "I will protect you with my life."

His voice was so earnest, so full of truth, that it stole my breath. I swallowed the lump growing in my throat. "I appreciate that, but that isn't a promise you can keep. I may come to harm while I'm protecting you. If I do, then that will be my choice to make."

He squeezed me tighter, resting his chin on my head. "Let's hope it doesn't come to that, then."

"Come along, you two," Octavius said, after clambering up onto my shoulder. "No more cuddling and lip puckering. You need to steel yourselves for what's coming."

I chuckled at my octopup's words, despite the seriousness of the situation. The little guy's behavior was enough to diffuse the growing tension between Dylan and me, and it helped chase away the fear that was still churning uncontrollably in my belly.

With Arion and Angelika at our rear prodding us to move along, Dylan and I followed Calypso and Draven as they wove their way through the maze of hallways, stopping at a narrow flight of stone stairs that lead to an iron-bound door.

"How are we going to get past that?" I asked, knowing none of us could touch the barrier that was blocking our progress. Dylan, who had previously been unaffected by iron, now suffered the same limitations as the rest of us. The only member of our group impervious to the metal's burning effects was...

"Allow me," Octavius said as he slid down from my shoulder. He closed one of his bulbous eyes in what I thought might have been a wink, before slithering his way up the stairs. I couldn't tell if it was the lingering effects of the river water, but I found watching my octopup undulating over to the door to be captivating.

Using his suction cupped legs, he scaled the wall, drew back one of his tentacles, and slammed it into the keyhole in a dramatic fashion. He worked his body in a strange dance as he performed his task. After several long moments, he grabbed hold of the iron handle and swung the door open. The tiny kraken beamed with pride, having completed his mission. He dropped down to the floor and pushed the door wide until we had a clear path through the iron-banded barrier.

"Thank you," I whispered, giving the octopup a proper wink. "You're a lifesaver." The little guy bowed with a flourish before scampering up my leg and onto my shoulder.

"Anything for you, princess."

Draven was the first to approach, pausing as he neared.

"We can't get through," he said, looking down at the door's threshold. "There is an iron band spanning the floor of the entrance."

I looked down at the still saturated cloak that hung over my shoulders. I didn't know if it would work, but it was worth the try. "Octavius? Can you lay this across the threshold? Fold it as many times as you can to make it as thick as possible. Perhaps it will be enough to allow us to pass over."

The little guy nodded and slid down my back, taking the cloak with him. He undulated his way to the door and laid it on the ground, folding it as many times as he could. After a short while, he motioned for me to try it out. I was about to step forward, but my big brother shook his head and took the lead.

Slowly, cautiously, he extended his foot towards the threshold, his face twisting in pain as he did. "It's not enough, but I think it's close. If I can conjure up some more of these cloaks, we may be able to safely cross over."

After stepping back, he carefully grasped the leather coat and yanked it towards him. Just like the first time I smelled the garment's musky aroma, he winced at its fragrance. "Whale oil? Where did this cloak come from?"

"It was my husband's," Angelika said, stepping up to the prince. "After he passed, I saved it for my son. The tale of how he came by it is too long to share. The leather is sealskin if my memory serves me."

"Creatures of the North Sea," Draven said, blowing out a small whistle. "I fear this is not regular seal hide. I believe it is the skin of a selkie. Somewhere on land, I suspect there is a fae who abandoned life at sea in favor of living among the humans. It would be the only explanation for this magical garment."

"My cloak is magical?" Dylan asked. "In what way?"

"I don't know for certain," Draven said, scratching his head. "It's possible that the selkie's magic has long since leached out. I cannot fully replicate this material, but I will do my best."

The big man ran his hands over the stiff leather as he moved past the group, back to where the river was. We all followed closely behind, curious as to what he was planning.

CALYPSO

I watched with rapt curiosity as Draven jumped into the river. He reached into the ether and pulled his scepter from the Beyond. After having cast my enchantment breaking spell on the relic, it no longer held any power over him, but it still seemed to be imbued with never before seen levels of magic. Whoever had put the curse on the artifact had to have been an incredibly powerful mage. I had asked Arion if he had the ability to wield that level of magic, but he couldn't, or wouldn't, tell me. All he had said was that it was magic of the darkest kind and, under no circumstances, should such enchantments ever be used. He would sooner see the merkingdom destroyed than cast that sort of spell.

As much as I understood and appreciated what he said, I wasn't sure I felt the same way. Sometimes, you had to fight dirty to have any chance of winning against evil. I hoped I never had to find out just how far I was willing to go to protect the people I loved.

Without saying a word, Draven slipped beneath the surface, fully immersing his body in the fresh water. I held my breath as lights swirled around the man. For whatever reason, he had chosen to remain in his human form while casting the spell. Perhaps he felt it would give him a better connection with the clothing he was trying to replicate. I didn't know why I noticed, or why I even cared. I guess I just found it interesting.

A moment later, Draven came stepping out of the river with a pile of cloaks in his wonderfully thick arms. I spent far too much time watching how his muscles rippled as he emerged, his wet shirt clinging to his back.

The wet slap of a bright-red cloak hitting me in the head roused me from my musings. I pushed my face into the soft leather fabric and inhaled deeply. I immediately pulled away and coughed uncontrollably.

"Sorry," Draven said with a shrug. "It was extremely difficult to duplicate. Hopefully, it is still effective. Since I couldn't recreate the selkie hide, I infused it with extra whale oil."

I slipped my arms into the cloak and shrugged it up over my shoulders. The fit was absolutely perfect, fitting snuggly in all the right places without being confining or restrictive. He shot me a shy smile, and I blew him a kiss.

After running my fingers over the fabric several times, I looked around at the others. They all had similar looking coverings, but each one was uniquely cut and colored to match the wearer. I smiled when I saw Arion's. Like mine, it was red, but it was much darker; an almost perfect match to the crab shell he used to have.

"No time like the present," I said. "Let's put these wonderful new cloaks to the test." After giving the prince another warm smile, I added to my comment. "And thank you for this. If you ever get tired of running the kingdom, there is a future for you as a tailor."

Once again, we made our way up the stairs to the doorway with the impassible threshold, and once again, Octavius placed Dylan's cloak over the iron strip. Draven offered his own coat to be added, and as soon as it was set in place, he tried to cross the barrier.

As his foot neared, his eyes narrowed and his jaw tensed. A moment later, he was across. "Octavius. Add another one. Two is sufficient, but it still stings like a jellyfish to cross over." In seconds, there were three overcoats sailing through the air, drowning the octopup in smelly leather. As he unfurled the pile of clothing, he glared at those who were without overcoats, and got to work.

"Is there enough water in the cloak to access your magic?" Luna asked me, keeping her voice low. "We would be so much more effective if you three could cast your spells."

"Us four," Angelika said. "It's been a long time since I used magic, but I felt its surge fill my body as soon as I had been turned into a mermaid again."

I had completely forgotten that Angelica had been Arion's apprentice. I didn't know how long she had trained or how powerful she was, but at this point, any help would be better than nothing. I tried to push aside those thoughts and concentrate on Luna's question.

My skin was moist from the waterlogged cloak, but I couldn't tell if it was enough from which to draw power. I centered myself, reaching into the small amount of water that surrounded me. Like a tiny spark of hope, there was power infused in the garment, but was so little, I didn't think I could make use of it.

"No," I said, shaking my head. "There isn't nearly enough to make anything even remotely powerful. We're going to have to rely on our original plan."

"Which is?" Arion asked, moving in beside Angelika. "You and the prince have yet to share what you intend on us doing."

I shrugged my shoulders, heat rising in my face. Truth was, the plan was exceptionally weak, but it was the only one that Draven and I could come up with.

"We're going to threaten him," I said. "Draven is going to say he'll use his scepter and destroy him if he doesn't step down from his seat of power and leave the lands." My skin heated further as I spoke the words. In my head, the plan sounded weak, but uttering the words aloud made it exceptionally clear to me that the idea was nothing short of pathetic.

"Good," Arion said, nodding his head appreciatively. "Very good."

"Really?" I asked, my face burning even hotter when I heard my teacher's praise.

"Yes, really. I was afraid I had nothing left to teach you." The man's eyes suddenly went very wide. "But I see now that you still have much to learn. That is the lamest, most useless plan I've ever heard."

"Do you have something better, old crab?" Draven growled, using his considerably larger, and significantly more heavily muscled body to intimidate my mentor. "Do you truly believe that I am incapable of intimidating a human?"

"I could ask a dozen of my students to come up with a plan to get us out of this situation, and I guarantee I'd get at least three that would put yours to shame." Arion raised his eyebrows to the prince, daring him to continue using his size to intimidate him. "But if you want to give me a moment or two, I'll see if I can't come up with a more viable solution."

Angelika stepped forward, her chin high. "I have an idea, but it's going to be risky. And I'm going to need Prince Draven to give Arion his royal scepter."

"To what end?" Draven asked, gripping his scepter, pulling it close to his body like a possessive child. "Without being in contact with the sea, it has no power."

"She knows that," Arion said, his gaze fixed on Angelika. "I'm guessing it's a prop for a ruse of some sort?"

"In a way," Angelika replied, giving my teacher a crooked smile. "It's going to be a part of a bribe. My dead husband's brother may hate us merfolk, but his greed and lust for power knows no bounds."

"What more could he want?" Dylan asked. "He's already wealthy beyond imagination, and he rules the town without contest."

"You're not thinking on a large enough scale, my son. Lord Vayne is a large fish in a small pond. I suspect he'd give just about anything to be a big fish in a big pond. The northern realm is rich in resources, and there are several enormous cities on the shores of the Gaelinora. These cities grew in power because of their ability to trade their resources with the southern nations. They do this by sailing their wares to their destination. Control of the seas might be something the new ruler of the merkingdom could offer him."

"New ruler?" I asked. The words had barely escaped my lips when I realized what she was saying. "Ah – Arion is the new ruler. This is why he needs the scepter."

"Quite right," Angelika said. "After Prince Draven and Princess Luna perished aboard the Abyssal, our high mage took advantage of the situation and seized power for himself. He has always loved me and has offered to make me queen if I accept his hand in marriage." Angelika gave my teacher a wink and shook her leg like she was doing some strange dance. "He even cured me of my ailments. The high mage's magic is strong, and he would be a much better ally than enemy. After all, with the royal scepter, he can even control the Makara."

"And what if you're wrong?" Draven said, still possessively clutching the relic. "Then what?"

"Then you can show up and threaten him," Arion said, bowing low to the prince.

"Fine," Draven said. "I don't like it, but the idea has merit."

"Fear not, my prince," Arion said, holding his hand out, his eyebrows raised expectantly. "I will return this to you as soon as we are finished here."

"This is all well and good," I said. "But how is this going to solve our problems? If you can convince Vayne to agree to your plan, what happens next?"

"We take him for a boat ride," Dylan said in a very cheery way. "We will offer to show him firsthand the power he wields. When we get him on the water, we show him the true beauty of the sea, and just how deep the Gaelinora is."

"No, we're not murdering him!" Angelika said, looking at her son like she had never met the man before. "We're going to have him address the people of the town, to admit his errors and explain his new relationship with the merkingdom. He will stand shoulder to shoulder with Arion and together, they will set human-merfolk relations to rights." The woman paused for dramatic effect, taking time to look at each person gathered around her. "And then we take him for a one-way trip to the bottom of the sea where he will be tried by our courts, be found guilty of his crime, and will spend the rest of his life learning about the kingdom he has grown to hate."

"I liked Dylan's plan better," I said with a shrug. "But that works, too, I guess."

"We need to return to the river first," Angelika said with dramatic flair. "Arion, Dylan, and I each require appropriate attire for our respective roles. Arion should exude the presence of a powerful ruler, while Dylan must look every inch a prince. As for myself, I shall require clothing befitting a woman of my elevated station."

CHAPTER 43

DYLAN

My heart thundered in my chest as I walked through the halls towards the loud, angry voices echoing through the manor. I eyed a grand staircase that led to the second floor of the home. Worry crept into me, concerned that guards may be posted up those stairs, ready to attack as soon as we made our presence know.

My mother's plan sounded so good when she shared it with us, but as we neared Lord Vayne's sitting room, the source of the boisterous debate, doubt crept in and settled into the pit of my stomach. Most likely, it would fail, and I would die, as would my mother and Arion, who were walking on either side of me.

"Be at ease, my son. The plan is sound. We will make it work." My mother had a way of calming me down, even when I was at my worst. "Just remember to look proud and powerful. You need to exude confidence and, through your body language, tell Vayne that we are in control. Show no fear, no matter what happens."

"It seems there is an argument going on," I replied. My ears were ringing, like the peel of warning bells. I was not a hero. I was a survivor. Survivors didn't waltz into the dragon's den, which is exactly what I imagined we were doing.

"If they're busy fighting amongst themselves, they'll not be looking for infiltrators," Arion said. "This is good news for us. When we enter the room, be silent and let us do the talking."

I swallowed hard, or at least I tried to. My mouth was so dry it was nearly impossible. I wiped my hands on my pants, trying to rid myself of the sweat collecting on my palms. I stole a glance at my mother. Dressed in her shimmering, body-hugging gown, with her golden hair flowing down her back, she was absolutely stunning. Her bearing and mannerisms screamed power and poise. On my other side, Arion was dressed in green and purple robes that swished about his feet with every step. His long black hair was pulled into a tight braid that hung over his shoulder. It made his face look severe, commanding, and utterly terrifying. His arms swayed easily by his side, Prince Draven's scepter in hand. There was a quiet confidence in him, like he was a hero capable of walking into a monster's lair without the smallest hint of fear. Their demeanor and self-assuredness boosted me, lifted me up, filled me with hope that this was going to go exactly as we had planned.

We stood for a moment outside the grand archway that led to the room with the raised voices.

"Remember what I told you," my mother said as she strode forward, like a knight ready for battle. "We are in control." Following her lead, we stepped through the archway.

There were four men seated in enormous plush chairs. Two of them I recognized to be Lord Vayne and his manservant, who was impossible to miss because the man's nose was the size of a melon. The third man appeared to be a soldier, a general of some sort, based on his elaborate, highly polished armor. The fourth, a tall and slender man, sat silently as the other three bickered wildly at each other.

"Lord Vayne," she called out with a powerful, commanding voice. "We need to talk."

Their heated conversation came to an immediate halt, and they all turned to face the interlopers who dared to invade their space. The quiet man appeared amused at our presence, his gaze locked directly on Arion. His thin, lipless mouth pulled back into a bizarre smile. Like a predator about to consume its prey, he stared. His black tongue raked slowly across his lips.

"Screaming starfish," Arion muttered. "This is not good. Not good at all." At his words, my confidence shattered.

"What is the meaning of this?" Lord Vayne said, leaping from his chair. "Guards! Guards! Get in here." The man servant and the general both leapt to their feet, with the soldier drawing his sword.

My first instinct was to run. However, I found enough courage to keep my feet firmly rooted in place, paying no heed to the ringing in my ears, and the hammering in my chest. I was tired of living under the man's thumb, and I wasn't going to squander this opportunity to remedy that problem.

"Sit, Vayne," the thin man said, sounding quite bored, or perhaps irritated by our presence. "They are of no consequence." Surprisingly, all three heeded the slender man's words and slowly lowered themselves into their seats, even if none of them appeared to be at ease.

"Why are you here, Beithir?" Arion asked, stepping forward. He still managed to have that air of superiority, as though these *dragons* were nothing more than common rodents.

"Headmaster Arion?" the tall man said, giving a nod of approval. "I see that you've managed to remove your unfortunate... curse." As he spoke the last word, a wicked smile pulled at the corners of his mouth. "Kind of you to come to me. It will save me the trouble of hunting you down."

"Who is that?" I whispered to my mother.

"That is Beithir," Arion replied, his back straightening, his voice loud and strong. "He is the royal advisor to Queen Morwynneth. But seeing him here, cavorting with this bottom-feeding human, it all makes so much sense to me now. He's been playing the long game, doing his dirty work behind the scenes, whispering into the ears of the weak-minded, bending them to his will. But why he would do this remains a mystery to me."

The man Arion referred to as Beithir inclined his head, as though Arion's words were a compliment.

"Who are you suggesting is weak-minded?" Lord Vayne said, once again leaping from his place, barely able to contain his obvious rage at the insult. "Who are you, and what are you doing with this street trash?"

"I said, sit!" Beithir motioned briefly with his hand. The way Lord Vayne fell into his chair, the shock on his face, suggested to me that he had been forced into his chair through the use of magic. The slim man calmly rose to his feet and smoothed out the wrinkles in his deep green tunic. "Thank you for bringing the scepter to me. So much easier than having to search for it. I do hope the prince died a horrible death before you took it from him."

"Strange that you can cast magic this far away from the sea," Arion said, striding forward, meeting the enemy head on. "It might even make me think you're not a mermaid at all."

Beithir raised his hands, palm up, while his shoulders crept up to his ears. "It's taken many years for my plans to come to fruition. It would have been so much easier if I could have been given the headmaster role of the Arcane Academy. With so many talented merfolk spell-casters, I could have created an army strong enough to overthrow the northern merkingdom, but alas, it was not to be. Instead, I have taken control of the queen and killed all her children. She will denounce Triton and take me as her husband, and I will rule the north."

"You're insane," my mother said, stepping up beside Arion. I hurried forward, not wanting to be left behind. "Triton will vaporize you with nothing more than a thought. How can you possibly hope to survive his return?"

"He will not," Beithir said, his smile becoming even more menacing. "I am forever bound to the queen. If I die, she will die. Regardless of Triton's many strengths, it is his love for the mermaid that will be his undoing."

Arion was right. This was not good, not good at all.

"I will have no such compunctions," Arion said. He lifted the scepter, holding it lightly in his hand like it was nothing more than a child's plaything. "I have no love for the queen. She has proven herself to be a weak-minded fool. Any mermaid who could fall to your charms is not worthy to lead."

"You would kill an innocent?" Beithir said, gliding across the floor until he was no more than two strides away from Arion. "Her actions are not her own, just like Prince Draven's actions were beyond his control. My kind, we can poison any minds, bend them to our will, force them into doing things they would rather die than do."

"Sea serpent!" Arion hissed the word out, taking a half step back. "A remnant of bygone wars. Your kind were eradicated, but somehow, you survived."

"The fates are truly fickle," Beithir said with a wry chuckle. "When my kind were all but wiped out by the merfolk and the accursed Makara, they didn't finish the job. Somehow, the fates decided I should live, and my existence went unnoticed. I only needed to lie low and bide my time. Like you, we are exceptionally long lived. In the depths, where no one ever dares to venture, I waited. I am the last of my kind, but I will rebuild my race and we will rule the world, as the gods intended."

Beithir held out his hand, tilting his head slightly to the side. "Now, be a good merman and give me the scepter. If you do, I'll even give you a place in my court as the royal jester."

"This piece of junk?" Arion said with a chuckle. "Sure. You can have it."

And with that, he passed the relic into Beithir's eager hands.

"You old fool!" Beithir called out, cackling like a madman. "You have given me that which I desire most. With this scepter, I can destroy Triton himself. I don't need any of you sniveling bits of flotsam."

The man pointed the scepter at Arion, his eyes wide and wild.

CHAPTER 44

LUNA

"Now!" Octavius bellowed out from the doorway. He had been using his natural camouflage abilities to spy on the proceedings, while Calypso and I waited for his signal.

"Draven, now!" I echoed. "We need you now!"

I had wanted to call him as soon as Octavius reported Beithir's presence, but Arion insisted that, regardless of the circumstances, we wait until the last possible moment. Even though nothing had changed, their lives in no more peril now than they were a few minutes ago, Octavius had decided we couldn't hold on any longer.

A great roar filled my ears, the harbinger of my brother's approach. Calypso motioned for me to move forward, to be in position when Draven arrived. As I took my place near the great archway, Octavius clambered up my leg and onto my shoulders.

"Hold tight, my friend," I yelled, hoping he could hear me over the now deafening sound of my brother's approach. Calypso moved in beside me, taking my hand in hers. She gave me a wide-eyed smile, as though we were about to embark on the adventure of a lifetime.

"I love you," she said. I couldn't actually hear her, but I could read her lips well enough. I squeezed her hand tightly in response.

A wall of water came surging down the hallway towards us. Riding on the crest of the wave was Draven, in all his merman glory, his scepter glowing white in his hand. Dylan had suggested that, rather than Arion carrying the real scepter into Lord Vayne's meeting room, that a replica be made and the real scepter be left with my brother. And, when the time was right, Draven would bring the water with him.

My heart swelled when he shared his amazing plan, heightening my already out-of-control infatuation with the merman.

As the wall of water neared, Calypso and I dove into the wave, immediately changing into our mermaid form. As good a swimmer as I was, I was no match for the unbridled fury of the raging rapids. Head over fin, I tumbled, barely able to maintain a sense of where I was.

When the torrent finally eased, I switched back into my human form, standing waist deep in a shimmering pool that filled the entire room. Even though the wave had subsided, the depth continued to rise at a steady pace.

"Insignificant fools," Lord Vayne bellowed. "None can stand before the might or magic of Beithir. You may feel you have the upper hand, Prince Draven, but in bringing water into my home, you have amplified his power tenfold."

It seemed evident that neither the gold-armored general nor the manservant were convinced of Beithir's superiority. The pair were busy clambering up onto a large table, desperate to stay out of the rising tide.

"Except he's not the one you need to be worrying about," Angelika said, while swirls of blue and gold gathered around her. The water glowed with an ethereal incandescence, igniting the sinister expression on her face.

"Remember what I told you, Angelika," Arion warned as swirls of purple and green flowed around his body. "We will deliver him to justice. We are not here to seek vengeance."

Thankfully, since I was not a spell caster, I was not bound by such rules. Lord Vayne had killed dozens of my kind. He had killed Dylan's father, and he had systematically oppressed his family until they were forced to live in shame and squalor. I dove beneath the water, immediately switching back into my mermaid form.

I brushed my long hair out of my face and sucked in a breath at the sight of a sea serpent, whose length easily exceeded thirty feet. It was deep green, with small milky eyes, and a tall fin that ran from its head down the full length of its body. Fear gripped me as I saw my brother swimming hard towards the creature and the wall of pointed teeth that filled its maw.

The serpent's black forked tongue flicked from its mouth as though tasting the surrounding water. Its gaze immediately spun towards Draven before surging forward, opening its jaws wide enough to swallow my brother whole. With amazing grace and agility, the merman darted past the danger just as the creature's jaws snapped shut.

My brother's scepter flashed white as a beam of light shot out from its jewel-encrusted top, raking across the leviathan's side, eliciting an ear-piercing scream from it as he did. The behemoth's head twisted in the direction it had been struck, its tongue once again flicking from its mouth, pausing for a moment, before flicking out again and again. Its milky eyes widened slightly before its massive head rotated off to its left, directly to where Draven was located.

Screaming starfish. "I think the serpent is blind," I yelled as loud as I could. "It's tasting the water. That's how it sees!" The reptile's gaze turned my way, drawn by my voice. "And it hears well, too!"

No sooner had the words left my mouth than the behemoth lunged at me, its black mouth wide. It looked like I was about to be swallowed by the abyss itself.

From somewhere to my side, Calypso streaked past, her blue and green tail flashing bright. She was bathed in a luminous aura as she sped forward, swimming head-first into the creature's gills, slamming into them in the same way that porpoises head-butt sharks. She struck with enough impact to push the behemoth off course, its mouth slamming shut inches from my body.

I might not have had magic like the others, but I wasn't a helpless guppy either. Following my friend's lead, I propelled myself forward, ramming into the leviathan's scaley side. On impact, bright lights exploded across my vision.

From the force of my attack, the sea serpent recoiled, its massive bulk twisting to come around at me. Barely able to see amidst the stars dancing before my eyes, I somehow managed to avoid the creature's bite, its jaws clamping shut, missing me by mere inches. I gave a quick kick with my tail to move away before the serpent's aim improved.

The bright lights that obscured my vision subsided. I regained my bearings, determined to continue the assault. I swam around the serpent, using my agility to avoid its fearsome, snapping jaws. With each swift movement, I continued to aim my attacks at what I perceived to be its vulnerable spots – striking directly behind its gills.

Draven darted past, once again raking the enemy with his brilliant white light. Calypso, too, continued her assault, ramming her glowing form into its gill plates.

The serpent thrashed in response, its long body twisting and turning.

We were winning. With our synchronized attacks and swift maneuvers, we kept the creature off balance, wearing it down bit by bit. The water churned with our battle, as waves and currents surged around us.

As we continued to strike with relentless force, the serpent's movements became sluggish. Its fearsome presence began to waver, and I sensed victory drawing near. Yet, I remained cautious, aware that even in its weakened state, the creature could still swallow me whole if it managed to catch me in its snapping maw.

With each passing second, my confidence grew, fueled with the knowledge that I was not alone, that I was working with a team. My heart leapt with joy as my brother swam at the enormous reptile, a steady beam from his scepter focused on the serpent's head. Just when it appeared victory was ours, the leviathan's eyes glowed red and Draven immediately ceased his attack. A moment later, my brother's gaze snapped towards me.

The beam of white light, the same one with which he had been targeting the serpent, was suddenly focused on me. With incredible force, it struck me directly in the chest, sending me hurtling away from the battle.

CHAPTER 45

CALYPSO

My heart exploded in my chest at the sight of the merman I loved attacking his younger sister, my best friend. Luna's body floated lifelessly, her green hair hovering around her head in a sea-foam cloud.

I glared over at Draven. His scepter still glowed white, but the merman's eyes were glowing red. Beithir had taken control of his mind, using my prince as his own personal guard. I had read about these creatures of the deep in Arion's private library. Their magic appeared to be a thing of legend. Their ability to control the minds of others was a power unlike anything I'd ever seen before.

In the stories I had read, the sea serpents had used their power to take over the minds of Makara, forcing them to fight at their side. Once the creature had taken hold of its prey, breaking the bond was nearly impossible. Together, the leviathans were a nearly unstoppable force. It was only through the heroic acts of a school of merfolk that they were able to win the day. After many of my kind had been killed, it was discovered that blinding the serpent weakened their psychic grip on their prey. It didn't break the connection, but if the merman had sufficient will, they could sever the magical ties.

"Go for his eyes!" I yelled out. "Blind Beithir. I'll deal with Draven."

From out of the frothing water, Arion shot forward, his body gliding through the turbulence on a wave of purple and green. He was saying something, likely casting a spell of some sort, but his words were lost in the chaos.

A beam of brilliant white light shot through the water, barely missing my teacher. Undaunted, the merman continued forward, his arms outstretched before himself, like he was planning on strangling the enormous serpent. A great stream of purple light flew from his fingers, missing Beithir by a good distance. Disappointment crushed my spirit, sucking the life from me.

Draven pointed his scepter and launched another attack, forcing me to dodge out of the way. As I turned to avoid the beam, I saw the true target of Arion's magic – Octavius!

The tiny octopup, engulfed in a violet aura, expanded in size before my eyes. His form stretched and elongated, limbs extending and body swelling with each passing moment. What was once a cute, diminutive creature had now grown to an astonishing scale. He was nowhere near the size of the sea serpent, but he was a truly formidable force. I had often joked about how much he resembled a kraken, but now he was one.

Another bolt of white light shot out. This time, I was not the target of Draven's attack, it was Octavius. Even after taking a direct hit, Luna's chaperone appeared unfazed. His enormous eyes narrowed, and he shot forward, looking ready to rip Draven to shreds.

"Octavius," I bellowed out, infusing my voice with magic, magnifying its volume. "Use your ink. Flood the area with it and then concentrate everything you have on blinding the sea serpent."

As a cloud of inky blackness spread out from the kraken, I launched myself at Draven, intent on subduing the merman. My teacher had the same thought, leaving the behemoth for the kraken to deal with. He sped forward, slamming himself into the prince, wrapping his arms around the much larger merman.

Arion's grip didn't last long before Draven broke his hold. With his eyes blazing, he turned the scepter towards my mentor, sending out a stream of writhing sea-vines. Like the tentacles of a great squid, they shot forward, enveloping Arion, binding him in a thick tangle of sharp, thorny tendrils.

From within the ever-growing obsidian cloud, the serpent screeched out. I could only hope that Octavius had successfully struck the creature's eyes. If he had, this was my chance to free Draven from his psychic bond.

With every ounce of strength in my being, I surged forward, throwing myself into my prince, wrapping my arms around him. I pressed my forehead against his, our gaze locking onto each other.

"Come back to me, my love," I sang, pushing as much magic into my words as I could manage. I continued swimming, pushing Draven away from the others, desperate to separate him from Beithir.

"Release me, sea witch," the merman spat. It was not his voice. They were not his words.

"Break your bond, Beithir," I hissed. "Free the prince and I might let you survive the day. Continue with this course and you will be sent to the Beyond."

Draven laughed. It was a high-pitched, maniacal laugh that sent a shiver down my spine.

"Release him, or I will snap his mind, condemning him to spend eternity in a world of fear and shadows." Once again, these were not Draven's words. His face contorted in agony as he tried to fight the magic. His head snapped back, and he stiffened in my arms. "He is powerless against me. Let him go, or he dies."

As I felt my love's body twisting in pain, fury consumed me and my self-control shattered. My entire world turned to shades of crimson. Hatred and loathing coursed through me. Under no circumstances would I allow this oversized eel to hurt the merman I loved. I didn't care if casting spells in anger was a path to my own destruction. I was going to destroy Beithir. I was going to obliterate him for what he did to me, and Draven, and the entire merkingdom.

While my love continued to contort under the pain Beithir was inflicting, I held tight. I would not let Draven go. Never again would I be apart from the merman I loved. If my plan failed, we'd likely both die and we could spend eternity together in the Beyond.

I pressed my face to Draven's chest, the sound of his heart beating in my ears. Pouring every ounce of myself, my magic, and my love, I cast my spell.

In depths profound, where my love lies,
I cast a spell through tear-filled eyes.
My mermaid heart, in torn despair,
I seek to break the serpent's snare.
With a whispered word, I'll break the bond.
And let my hatred fiercely respond.
With this final chant, the ties I sever,
The merman is free, now and forever.

My magic exploded out of me, as though every bone in my body had been simultaneously shattered. My crimson vision turned into a brilliant red before becoming a blinding white. The intensity of the searing pain ripping through my body was too much, forcing me to give way to the darkness of oblivion.

CHAPTER 46

DYLAN

While my cohorts dealt with the sea creature that had suddenly appeared in the room, I had made my way towards Lord Vayne. With the water rising as fast as it was, he would have little chance of surviving for more than a few minutes. Not to mention the general, dressed in his golden armor, would never be able to swim. He might as well have had an anchor tied to his neck.

Despite being at home beneath the waves, something I had never expected to experience, I struggled to find Lord Vayne or his allies. The water was murky, making visibility near zero. I swam up to the surface, hoping I would see them swimming, but, again, I found nobody.

Not that they didn't deserve death, but I didn't want them to drown, or worse, be eaten by the giant sea serpent that took up a large part of the space. I tried to recall the room, the details I'd seen when I had entered with my mother and Arion. At the time, everything was happening so fast. My heart had been racing and, if I was being honest with myself, my belly had felt like it had turned to liquid. But when Arion and the tall, slim man started going at each other, my fear turned to raw excitement.

There was a table surrounded by fine wooden chairs, I recalled, along with several much larger, plush chairs near the back of the room. That's where Lord Vayne and his guests had all been seated. Behind them was a huge fireplace, and along the wall opposite the door we came in, there was a series of tall, narrow windows.

Nowhere did I see a place for the three men to escape. Unless they were in the hearth. Could they have climbed up the chimney flue?

Unsure of where I was in the room, I swam until I found a wall, or in this case, a window. From there, I followed the perimeter until I came to the large stones that surrounded the hearth. The water was a little less murky here, allowing me a few feet of visibility. With a kick of my tail, I shot into the oversized fireplace and looked up into the flue.

Sure enough, some ten paces above me, was the general, his golden armor shining brightly through the darkness. I couldn't tell if the others were above him, but his body was mostly submerged, and the way his hands were clamped onto the stonework, I guessed he had no place else to go. If the water rose any higher, he'd drown in minutes.

I didn't know the man. I had never heard of him or seen him. I had no way of knowing if he was good or evil, but, based on his association with Lord Vayne, it was a safe bet to assume he was rotten to the core.

Still, I couldn't let him drown. I remembered the panic I felt when Arion held me under, waiting for me to suck in a breath, a breath he knew would save me. In those moments, terror gripped me. Nobody, no matter how cruel, deserved to suffer like that.

I swam up the flue until my head came out of the water next to the general. There was no one else with him. The chimney narrowed just above us, no more than a foot across. This was the end for the man in gold.

"Save me," he cried out. His face was bright red, in stark contrast to his bright blue lips. His teeth were chattering uncontrollably. "Please, for the love of the gods, don't let me drown. Use your mermaid magic. Make the water go away."

I could do nothing to help with the rising tide, but I might have been able to offer him the ability to breathe underwater, doing the same thing that Luna and Calypso had done for me. I had no idea how to make that happen. They had kissed me. Breathed into me.

I didn't relish the thought of pressing my lips to this man's mouth, but it was a small price to pay to save a life. Whether the man was good or evil, he would survive, and he'd be tried. His guilt or innocence could be determined by someone else. The general squealed and slipped beneath the surface, plummeting to the bottom of the hearth like a stone. I was out of options.

I darted down to where the golden man was once again trying to clamber up the chimney. I grabbed him roughly by the neck of his armor to spin him around. His hands flailed about, clutching onto my shoulders, yanking my hair. He was beyond thinking rationally, and he was going to fight me to the bitter end.

Grabbing him by the ears, I drew his face to mine, pressed my lips against his, and blew.

Fists struck me repeatedly about the head and shoulders, but I refused to let go. I kept holding him, breathing into him. After what felt like an eternity, he finally stopped thrashing. Either my efforts were successful, or the man had drowned and was on his way to the Beyond.

When I pulled back, the bewildered look on the man's face told me he would be okay.

"Follow me. I'm going to get you out of here." The general nodded in agreement, his expression still a mask of confusion. "Stick close to the walls. My friends are dealing with the sea serpent."

My friends. What about my mother? I hadn't seen her since the mayhem started. Worry gripped me, urging me to hurry.

"Sea serpent?" the general yelled. His eyes went wide and his hands shot over his mouth. A moment later, he pulled them back. "I can talk underwater."

I didn't have time for this. I grabbed him roughly by the wrist and dragged him along the wall.

Flashes of white and red told me the battle with the leviathan was raging on. I needed to get this man out of here and return to help in the fight. I had no idea what use I could be, but I wasn't going to abandon my friends in their moment of need.

We finally made it to the grand archway. I had seen a staircase not far from here. I dragged the general forward, ignoring the incessant questions that were pouring from his mouth.

Relief washed over me as I found the staircase. The second floor of the home should be free of water. I had no idea how long it would be before this ordeal was complete, and if my merman magic wore off, the general would be safe. With nothing more than a thought, my tail fin changed into legs and I was walking up the stairs.

As my head broke the surface, my heart leapt into my throat. My mother was standing ankle-deep in water, with Lord Vayne and his lickspittle manservant at his side. In each of my mother's hands were rolling balls of fire.

"They must die," she said to me as I climbed the last step. The general was only a few steps behind me, looking as though he was ready to turn around and head back into the water.

"Not like this," I said. The words Luna had spoken to my mother flooded into my mind. "Don't let hatred be your guide. Don't become what you despise most. Do this properly. Remember Arion, and what happened to him for casting magic in anger?"

"I don't care," she said, the orbs of flame in her hand suddenly growing larger, illuminating her face in a crimson glow. "He must pay, even if it costs me my life."

"You'd leave me behind because of your anger?" I said, holding my hands out to her. "You would rather have your revenge than stay with me? What of this town and its people? They need you. Who else can explain to them what happened here? Who else can lead them from the darkness?"

An intense white light exploded out from the grand archway, so brilliant that I was forced to shield my eyes. The entire house shook, knocking me off my feet. The water that had covered the floor rushed down the stairs, as though someone had pulled the drain plug in a bathtub. Unearthly shrieks echoed off the walls, sending chills up my spine. A second flash of brilliance, this time a red so deep it bordered on black, forced me to turn away again. A blood-curdling scream accompanied the light, followed by complete silence.

"I should have killed you both when I murdered my miserable brother," Vayne said. I looked up to find him standing over my mother, a dagger poised at her throat. "You and your kind are abominations. I will see you exterminated. Even in my death, my hatred for the merkingdom will live on. I will..."

"You will lower your weapon, or I will kill you myself," the general said, his sword drawn and ready to strike. "Your reign of prejudice stops here and now."

With a deft swing of her fist, my mother knocked the blade from Vayne's hand while her foot shot up between the man's legs, landing with a resounding thump. The lord blew out a groaning breath before buckling to his knees and falling to his side.

"I'll take it from here," the general said with a bow. "He will stand trial in Cormorant before Lord Karter."

"He will stand trial before the merkingdom court, Captain Wind-speak," Prince Draven said from the bottom of the staircase. Beside him stood Arion, Calypso, and Luna. My heart sang at the sight of the trio. Joy turned to terror as an enormous octopus came undulating through the archway. When he sidled up to Luna, placing an enormous tentacle on her shoulder, I realized my fear was misplaced. It seemed Octavius had grown somewhat while I wasn't looking.

"As you wish, Prince Draven," the captain said, hoisting Vayne up by the collar of his cloak. He motioned to me with his chin. "I owe my life to this man. While others may have thought only of themselves, he saved me without knowing if I was friend or foe."

"He's like that," Luna said, blushing hard. Oh, sweet Gaia, she was beautiful – even sopping wet.

"What of this one?" Captain Windspeak asked, pointing his sword at Vayne's manservant. "Do you wish to try him as well?"

"Do with him as you will," Draven said. "There will be a good number of humans that will need to be dealt with. Can I count on you to look after that?"

I watched the interactions between Draven and the captain, unclear as to who the man was. Clearly, he and the prince were allies, but I didn't know why or how they came to be. Truth was, I didn't care. I just wanted the ordeal to be over with.

"What of the dead serpent?" Octavius asked. "Can I have him?"

"I'm guessing the Makara will want the body," Arion said. "He was the last of his kind and they'll likely hold a celebration at his death. The sea serpents were a blight, and we can finally say with certainty, their threat is no more."

"We can parade him through the streets," Draven said with a hint of a smile. "We can let the people know what we merfolk have saved them from. It might be a good way to start repairing the damage Vayne has caused."

"Then let's get that started," my mother said, "before the wretched creature stinks up the whole house. I can't live here with that indomitable stench."

"You're going to live here?" I asked. "You will take father's place as lady of the town?"

"Only until you're ready to accept your heritage," she replied. "That is, if you choose to stay here on land."

I looked down at Luna, trying to gauge her reaction to my mother's words. She only smiled and shrugged in response. I raised my eyebrows, wordlessly asking her to speak her mind.

"I'd be willing to help you," she said, her face reddening. "If you want."

My heart practically exploded with joy.

"Before any of that happens," Calypso said, wrapping her arm around Draven's waist, squeezing him tightly. "We have an overdue ceremony to conduct." Her eyebrows shot up as she turned her gaze to the prince, a coy smile pulling at the corners of her lips. "You no longer have a cursed scepter to get you out of proposing to me."

Prince Draven's throat bobbed and his cheeks reddened.

CHAPTER 47

EPILOGUE: CALYPSO

"And then you got married, right mother? Tell me again about how father proposed and how you accepted, and tell me again how many people came to your wedding." I smiled warmly down at my wide-eyed daughter. She ran her fingers through her long red curls, waiting impatiently for me to continue my story.

"Oh please, no!" her twin brother said, rolling his overly large blue eyes at me. "Leave that part out. I don't want to hear about you and dad kissing. Never again!" He brandished his wooden sword, performing a series of complex maneuvers. "Tell us about the merfolk hunters and how you defeated them. That was the best part of the story."

I blew out a stream of bubbles as I tried to subdue a laugh. My son only cared for adventure while my daughter was desperate for romance. They were a perfect replica of Draven and me. I wasn't pleased that Uncle Dylan had given Morgan that sword, but as the only son of the Guardian of the Realm, Luna insisted he needed to be adept with a blade.

"No, mom. No!" Ursula said, grabbing me by the cheeks, thrusting her face directly in front of my own. "Tell me about how dad took you to the grotto in the western shallows!"

I pushed my daughter back, appalled by her suggestion. "Where did you hear that?" I asked, magic flashing in my eyes. My poor daughter pulled away, clutching her breast.

"Aunt Luna told me that's where father proposed to you," she said, her bottom lip quivering, her deep blue eyes suddenly becoming glassy. "She said it was the most romantic story she had ever heard. Oh, mother, please tell me how he held you and told you that he will love you for all eternity."

Morgan groaned. "Gods above, no. No more kissy stories. If you're going to talk about anything like that, I want to hear how grandfather came to the wedding with an entire squadron of Makara at his back and how he made father the supreme ruler of the northern seas."

"He did no such thing," I said, my tone far more scolding than I had intended. "He came with three Makara, including their chief, Yanti. Grandfather wanted the sea dragons to know who ruled the northern realm and who they would have to deal with on all matters of diplomacy."

"And now father is in charge of them, right?" Morgan thrust his toy sword at some unseen enemy. "The sea dragons have to listen to him, right?"

"No, my son," I said. "The Makara are a kingdom of their own, but they are grateful to your father for having destroyed the last of the sea serpents. We are... allies of sorts."

"Mother?" Ursula said, her voice barely more than a squeak. "What of grandmother? When you told the story, you said that if father killed Beithir, that grandmother would die, too."

"The serpent lied," I said, drawing my daughter close. "You know full well that grandmother is safe and happy, living in the southern seas with your grandfather. It's time for you two to get to bed now. Aunt Luna and Uncle Dylan are coming tomorrow."

"I hope they bring Octavius," Morgan said. "He's the best."

"Does that mean you have to go back to that silly school?" Ursula said, her lower lip sticking out past her button nose. "Why can't Uncle Arion run it without you? I liked it better when you stayed home with us all the time."

"The Academy of Arcana is not a *silly school*," I said with a laugh. "And now that I am headmaster, I have a lot of new responsibilities. I want to make sure that everything is just right for when you and your brother enroll next semester."

Ursula gasped and Morgan groaned at my news. "I get to go to school with you?" Ursula practically screamed out the words, wrapping her arms so tightly around my neck that I couldn't breathe.

"Why do I have to go?" Morgan said with way more whine in his voice than I'd have liked. "You know I have no magical abilities. I'm a *dweeb*."

"Don't use that word," I said, appalled by my son's colorful vocabulary. "The proper word is *mundane,* which I can guarantee you are not. You are the grandson of Triton, god of the seas. You just haven't come into your own, yet."

"Because girls mature faster than boys, right mother? That's why I have magic and Morgan doesn't?"

"Don't count your brother out," I said, shaking my head. Even though what she said was true, I knew my son had unlimited potential. "Remember what Uncle Arion said. 'A merman's power comes from his heart.' And your brother has more heart than anyone I've ever known."

Morgan flashed a quick smile before tucking himself into his thick bed of kelp. He was clutching his sword tight to his body. He yawned widely and pulled the kelp up over his shoulders.

"Mom?" Ursula said, through a yawn of her own. "Will Grandma Angelika be coming tomorrow, too? We haven't seen her in a very long time."

"Maybe," I said, carrying my daughter to her kelp bed. "She's very busy looking after her humans."

Truth was, I didn't expect her to come, but I couldn't tell my daughter that her grandmother didn't want to return to the palace. She was extremely busy trying to repair all the damage Vayne had caused. Even with the help of Lachlan, her newly assigned fleet commander, many people could not be convinced that merfolk were not the enemy. Draven visited the town often, and even with General Karter's visits from Cormorant, people were slow to change.

Just as I had finished tucking her in, my husband came swimming into the room. "I hope I'm not too late to kiss them goodnight."

Ursula held her arms out for her father, puckering her lips in hopeful anticipation of her goodnight kiss. Morgan, on the other hand, feigned snoring for several seconds before bursting out laughing.

"Father?" Morgan called out from his little nest. "Do I really have to go to the academy tomorrow?"

"I'm afraid so. Don't worry, the forty or fifty years it will take to train you will pass by quickly."

"Fifty years? That's almost your age."

"Many stay much longer," I said. "There is no end to learning. The senior students help with research and organizing field trips. It's not just a school. It's a community."

"Oh no!" Draven said, his eyes wide. "I'm turning into a sea serpent!" He scooped a squealing Ursula up into his arms and raced over to Morgan. The little scampi tried to evade his father's grasp, darting through the kelp, but his escape attempt was futile. The big merman blew bubbles into their bellies, making the twins scream out in laughter.

I couldn't help but smile as I watched my massive husband cuddling with his two tiny children. To the outside world, he was the guardian of the realm, a symbol of power and leadership. But when we were alone, in the privacy of our home, he transformed into the sweetest, most caring merman I had ever known. The way he interacted with our children, his gentle touch and warm embrace, filled my heart with pure joy. I considered myself the luckiest mermaid to have ever swum the seas, blessed to share such tender moments with him. As I looked into his sapphire blue eyes, I knew that our story was far from over. Our love would continue to grow, and I eagerly awaited the adventures that lay ahead of us in the vast depths of the sea, the place we called home.

The End

THE STORY CONTINUES...

If you want to read more stories from the Veil of Entropy universe, visit my website for a complete list of all my novels.

https://paulmouchet.ca

AFTERWORD

Thank you for reading my novel. Reviews are critical to the success of every indie author. I would ask that you leave a review on Amazon, GoodReads, and BookBub. If you have any thoughts or comments that you'd like to share directly with me, I would love to hear from you. You can email me at paul@paulmouchet.ca.

Do you want more stories? You find links to all my novels on my website. You can also sign up for my newsletter, Marvelous Mondays, which I send out every other week. They're full of fun pics, snippets of what's going on in my life, and book news.

Also, if you'd like to discuss my stories with me and other fans, in a safe, friendly environment, please connect with me on my Facebook group ~ Paul Mouchet's Reader's Group.

You'll find the link to all my social media accounts on my website. I look forward to chatting with you.

Happy Reading!